Praise for

Do I Know You?

"Sarah Strohmeyer made an impression on me two decades ago with the first of her Bubbles Yablonsky mystery novels, full of humor, verve, and a slightly manic air. . . . It's welcome to see that early spirit revived in *Do I Know You?* . . . Kept me reading, near breathless, until all assumptions were gloriously upended."

—Sarah Weinman, *New York Times Book Review*

"A fabulous read packed with suspense, unexpected twists, glamour, and humor. Prepare to be gripped from the first to the last page!"

—Liane Moriarty, #1 *New York Times* bestselling author of *Big Little Lies*

"Gripping and emotionally resonant, Sarah Strohmeyer's thrilling new novel introduces readers to a relentless heroine who's driven by the power of sisterly love."

—Alafair Burke, author of *The Better Sister* and *Find Me*

"This riveting story of class warfare, ambition, and family loyalty—with the highest of stakes—will have you reading as fast as you can. *Do I Know You?* is everything a suspense novel should be."

—Hank Phillippi Ryan, *USA Today* bestselling author of *Her Perfect Life*

"Incredible! A hard-to-put-down read full of twists and turns. Just when I thought I had it all figured out, everything changed! An absolute must read!"

—Heidi McLaughlin, *New York Times* bestselling author of *Forever My Girl*

"Tense and suspenseful . . . a shocking yet satisfying ending."

—*Booklist*

"An entertaining suspense novel. . . . Strohmeyer knows how to keep the pages turning."

—*Publishers Weekly*

WE LOVE TO ENTERTAIN

ALSO BY SARAH STROHMEYER

FICTION

The Secret Lives of Fortunate Wives
The Cinderella Pact
The Sleeping Beauty Proposal
Sweet Love
The Penny Pinchers Club
Kindred Spirits
Do I Know You?

NONFICTION

Barbie Unbound

BUBBLES YABLONSKY MYSTERIES

Bubbles Unbound
Bubbles in Trouble
Bubbles Ablaze
Bubbles a Broad
Bubbles Betrothed
Bubbles All the Way
Bubbles Reboots

YOUNG ADULT FICTION

Smart Girls Get What They Want
How Zoe Made Her Dreams (Mostly) Come True
The Secrets of Lily Graves
This Is My Brain on Boys

WE
LOVE
TO
ENTERTAIN

A Novel

SARAH STROHMEYER

HARPER

NEW YORK · LONDON · TORONTO · SYDNEY

HARPER

WE LOVE TO ENTERTAIN. Copyright © 2023 by Sarah Strohmeyer. All rights reserved. Printed in the United States of America. No part of this book may be used or reproduced in any manner whatsoever without written permission except in the case of brief quotations embodied in critical articles and reviews. For information, address HarperCollins Publishers, 195 Broadway, New York, NY 10007.

HarperCollins books may be purchased for educational, business, or sales promotional use. For information, please email the Special Markets Department at SPsales@harpercollins.com.

FIRST EDITION

Designed by Jamie Lynn Kerner

Library of Congress Cataloging-in-Publication Data has been applied for.

ISBN 978-0-06-322438-4 (pbk.)

23 24 25 26 27 LBC 5 4 3 2 1

For David & Dorinda Crowell, who were there at the beginning.

All houses wherein men have lived and died
Are haunted houses.

From "Haunted Houses," by Henry Wadsworth Longfellow
(1807–1882)

PROLOGUE

I'M SO SORRY, MOM.

The apology is spoken in a whisper, somewhere between a prayer and a sob uttered into a dark, cold void. She is alone. Forgotten. Left to die. Her most feared childhood nightmare of being buried alive actually happening.

There's no point in shouting. She's already tried that, of course. She yelled and begged when he walked away, when he climbed the makeshift ladder and dragged the rough piece of plywood over the hole. She screamed as he laid the heavy rocks one after the other—*thunk, thunk, thunk*—in rhythm to her panicked heartbeat. She'd screamed and screamed until, already exhausted, she collapsed, her throat dry as the dust beneath her feet.

He would not return. That was clear.

Was that yesterday? This morning? Three days ago? Impossible to tell here in this windowless cave. In the dimming light of the lamp, she can make out desiccated potatoes, rotted, dried, and darkened to black lumps scattered here and there on the dirt floor. The air is dank and thick. Oxygen is running low. It smells of urine and vomit. Hers.

No one will look for her here—if they even realize she's

been abducted, which is doubtful. Her captor will have fooled them with artful lies: She went on the lam to save her own hide, she is not who she appears to be. She's cunning, ambitious, greedy—and now look what she's done, what misery she's caused! Good riddance to bad rubbish, they'll all say.

Except her mother. She will keep on searching, never giving up until her daughter is found.

Though by then, it will likely be too late.

IT'S ON . . . TMB!

BEHIND THE SCENES OF *TO THE MANOR BUILD* WITH CONTESTANTS ROBERT BARRON AND HOLLY SIMMONS

Lights! Cameras! *Reveal!*

We can't believe the big day is almost here! After weeks of sweating contractor delays, faulty electrical wiring, disgusting black mold, emergency asbestos remediation, and—gulp!—a snake infestation, the three couples facing off in an epic competition on *To the Manor Build* are about to show the world their fabulous rehabs.

And the stakes couldn't be higher.

From design consulting to the last penny nail, *TMB* will cover 100 percent of the costs incurred by the lucky winning couple, who, in a twist, won't be chosen by our experts but by . . . *you!* So log on to ToTheManorBuild.com and get ready to cast your vote. The polls open online after the Big Reveal in just two weeks.

While you're waiting in tense anticipation, we caught up with one of our star couples, Robert Barron and Holly Simmons, for a

Q&A on some behind-the-scenes details—and, oh my, are those wedding bells we hear???

TMB: Thank you so much for taking a break from your super-busy schedule this week as we get down to the wire. How're you handling the final crush?

ROBERT: Thanks for having us. You know, the truth is, Holly's borne the brunt of this rehab, starting with the original vision, lining up the contractors, and making decisions every five minutes. I just stand around looking pretty.

HOLLY: That's not true. I saw you swing a hammer—once.

ROBERT: Must have been your secret lover. You know how I hate to ruin my manicure.

HOLLY: That's actually kinda true. (*Laughs*)

TMB: See? This is why you guys are fast becoming the fan favorites. Everyone loves your banter and obvious genuine mutual affection. Why don't you tell those new to *TMB* how you met.

ROBERT: Not much to tell. Holly saw my bodacious bod on Tinder and swiped right.

HOLLY: (*Sighing*) Don't believe a word out of this man's mouth. He is a congenital liar. The truth is, in my other existence I run a real estate vlog and I'd been following Robert's alternate persona as The Robber Barron for years. I was really impressed by his creative approach to real estate investing, but I told him he needed a better platform to showcase his properties other than a subscription newsletter. In that way, he's kind of an unfrozen caveman.

ROBERT: Grunt.

HOLLY: Then, out of the blue, he called me last winter and asked if I

wanted to go skiing in Vermont and check out this kooky property he'd recently acquired for a song at a tax sale. Thought
maybe I might be interested in making a video of it.

ROBERT: Yeah, that was BS. I didn't care about the video. I only
wanted the girl.

HOLLY: I'll admit, I had my doubts. All I knew about Vermont was it
was cold and snowy and short on retail. Not exactly this southern girl's dream destination. But, as soon as I saw the potential
house site and the apple orchard and mountain views on eighty
fabulous acres, I was in love.

ROBERT: To be clear, not with me. The property.

HOLLY: Then Robert told me about his plans for a net-zero spec
house. I knew immediately this was the perfect project for *To
the Manor Build.*

TMB: Who had the idea to submit a test tape to *TMB*? I bet it was
you, Holly.

HOLLY: Guilty as charged. Robert was on the fence, but I was determined.

ROBERT: Technically, it wasn't just the fence I was on . . .

HOLLY: (*Slapping him playfully*) While we were filming, Robert and I
discovered we share a commitment to saving the environment
and thwarting climate change. I do everything in my ability to
reduce my carbon footprint whenever I can, grocery shopping
at local farm stands—

ROBERT: My personal sacrifice is driving a Tesla . . .

HOLLY: (*Rolling her eyes*) Anyway, there's so much exciting, cutting-
edge stuff happening now in environmental construction.
We're so glad *TMB* was on board with that, too, and chose our
rebuild to help bring our passion to light.

TMB: Actually, we were floored by your sizzle [note: that's reality-show lingo for the infamous test tape]. We absolutely loved your design concept and your on-air chemistry, and, judging from the chatter on Reddit's r/ToTheManorBuild, so do your fans. The question is, how do you think you'll fare against the competition? They've both got pretty moving backstories.

HOLLY: And we couldn't love them more, honestly. We are Joel and Sean's biggest cheerleaders.

TMB: They're the couple building a therapeutic ranch in New Mexico for LGBTQ2+ teens who've been bullied at school or cast out by their families.

HOLLY: Besides championing a noble cause that's near and dear to my heart, from what we've been allowed to see of their design, I am floored. All those bright southwestern colors and the horses and the bridal path! I mean, where do I sign up?

ROBERT: We're gonna lose, aren't we? Ah, it's okay. Good run while it lasted.

TMB: And then, on the other side of the country in South Carolina, you have Drs. Sam Chidubem and Concita Jimenez, who are establishing a seaside retreat for healthcare professionals and their families, who sacrificed so much during the pandemic. Extremely inspiring.

ROBERT: Yup. We definitely are gonna lose.

HOLLY: First of all, hats off to anyone who worked in the medical field during the pandemic. I cannot even imagine the trials they endured. Secondly, I've been following Doctor Concita's blogs online and she and her husband embrace such a soothing aesthetic, lots of tranquil pastels and sand tones. I am dying to swing in one of their rope hammocks overlooking the beach and watch my troubles disappear.

ROBERT: I agree with everything Holly just said.

HOLLY: For once . . .

ROBERT: All kidding aside, while both of these are incredibly worthy projects, they represent the present, while, in my humble opinion, I like to think we represent the future.

TMB: Interesting. How so?

ROBERT: Our rebuild reflects a whole new way of approaching home construction in the era of climate change. We've employed the most advanced environmental technology. Thick concrete walls. Heat pumps that rely on geothermal energy. A peaked rubber roof that insulates and doesn't need to be replaced nearly as often and yet is sturdy enough for a solar array. We're going to generate so much power from the sun, even in chilly Vermont, the local power company will have to buy the excess from us. Think about that!

HOLLY: He's right. Fingers crossed that viewers will be amazed at the reveal to learn they can live in a spectacular, energy-efficient house that's also stylish and able to be heated by a candle. Even, like Robert just said, in frigid Vermont.

ROBERT: Upfront costs are made up by massive energy savings down the road. There's your future, folks.

TMB: Speaking of future, as if you two don't have enough to do, you're squeezing in a spontaneous wedding soon.

HOLLY: (*Clearly blushing*) You know, Robert and I didn't want to make a big deal of it, but instead of spending the final week stressing over the *TMB* contest, on the spur of the moment we decided what the heck! Autumn's a magnificent season for an outdoor ceremony here in Vermont. The trees are absolutely on fire.

ROBERT: We're thinking of doing a flash wedding, so keep checking the website for the pop-up live stream, just in case anyone's interested in seeing me in a skirt—I mean "kilt." I do have extremely attractive knees, if I do say so myself. Show them the ring, darling.

HOLLY: (*Displaying a halo engagement ring of blue and ice-white diamonds in a platinum setting*) Robert designed this himself. It's ethically sourced, by the way. The platinum is recycled.

ROBERT: The center diamond is lab-grown, which means it's only slightly less expensive than a normal two carat would be if it were mined by oppressed children in a Third World country. And yet I've been assured by the jeweler it'll retain its value long after death do us part.

HOLLY: Oh, baby. Don't even say that!

ROBERT: (*Leaning down for a kiss*) I swear nothing can part us, sweetheart. Not even death.

TMB: Awww. Who doesn't love lovers in love? We at *TMB* wish you all the very best. And to all of you on Team H&R, do keep checking this site for your personal digital invites to Holly and Robert's flash wedding that could happen any day now. You don't want to miss a moment of romance.

ROBERT: Not to mention my knees.

ONE

ERIKA

On the morning of the wedding, Erika Turnbull plugs an Air-Pod into her right ear, syncs it with her iPhone, and grabs her pink metal travel mug of coffee with three splashes of half-and-half. The day's schedule printed and secured in a plastic page protector, she exits her tiny studio apartment at the top of her mother's garage, locks her door, and jiggles the handle twice to make sure it's secure.

Call her superstitious, but with so much on the line, she's not taking any chances. Nothing can go wrong today. Absolutely nothing. And if anything does—if Robert's Cuban cigars aren't delivered or the caterers forget to swirl the figs in chevre with the small-batch balsamic vinaigrette she specifically ordered from a farm in Modena; if the blue skies cloud and rain falls right as the couple are exchanging vows—then, yes, fingers will point toward her.

All part and parcel of being an assistant. None of the credit and all of the blame. No problem, she thinks, trying to summon more confidence than she actually feels. If only she had more experience being in front of the cameras . . .

She's been working for Holly and Robert less than a year and always behind the scenes doing what assistants do on these home-remodeling shows—nagging vendors, checking orders, updating calendars, running to the hardware store for paint and extension cords or to the general store for sandwiches and coffee to sustain the crew. In other words, executing the many mundane tasks that keep the boat afloat.

This wedding will be the polar opposite. She will be Holly's only bridesmaid, the first one to walk down the grassy aisle and the center of attention for three excruciating minutes. Thousands of fans are predicted to tune in, perhaps hundreds of thousands, and the ceremony will be recorded, which means any faux pas will be instantly uploaded online, where it will permanently reside to humiliate her forever. The prospect makes her almost physically ill, since, unlike her photogenic employers, Erika isn't one for basking in the limelight. In fact, she's gone out of her way to avoid being in the public gaze. She has her reasons. Valid ones. Not that they're of any importance today.

Hey, at least the weather's nice, she thinks. Clear and warm for mid-October. Say what you will about climate change, but so far it's been a boon to this part of Vermont. The new Napa Valley, they're calling the Green Mountain State. Lush and fertile. Ranked number two right behind Michigan as the place to live if you're trying to avoid future floods and drought, blistering summers and wildfires. Holly and Robert were ahead of the curve choosing a rebuild here. But that's their combined superpower, isn't it? Always two steps ahead of everyone else, like chess players.

A wispy autumn fog rises from the creek running through the ravine behind the woods surrounding the home where she grew up. Since her breakup with Colton, she's been living in the little apartment above her mother's garage, what she likes to call a "carriage house," even if it never housed horses or carriages.

Erika prefers the term for the optics, though she didn't use the term *optics* until she started working for *To the Manor Build* and was introduced to the power of verbal tweaking. There are bathrooms. And then there are spa retreats. Basements versus man caves. Patios versus outdoor-entertainment areas. Bedrooms versus suites.

When she told the LA producers of *To the Manor Build* she lived above a garage, they were appalled. When she told them she lived in a carriage house, they were intrigued, envisioning Victorian gables and trellised roses instead of what it really is—a second-floor, eight-hundred-square-foot studio above a one-car bay infused with the metallic smell of engine grease.

This is the magic of property rehab. With fresh paint, new flooring, a kitchen reno, and flowery descriptions, anything can be reborn, better than ever. God willing, the same will be true for her. She just needs to work her ass off so Robert and Holly win the contest and the producers realize she was the ticket to their success and want to hire her. Then maybe she'll finally have a chance of blowing this quaint and claustrophobic town.

She starts up her new apple-red Kia and pulls off the gravel driveway, taking a left on the dirt road. First order of business: picking up the mail before the post office closes at noon. Second assignment: those damned cigars.

Cuban Cohiba Robusto Reserva at $100 a pop, and that's before the expensive shipping requiring the illegal smokes to be routed via Switzerland to Bert's general store in a crate of fancy Swiss chocolate. Erika can't imagine the total cost, which must be outrageous, but Robert was determined. He insisted that surprising his groomsmen with the treasured contraband would be worth risking a $250,000 fine and ten years in prison.

Us Weekly lied. The stars, in fact, are not like us. Not one little bit.

Erika's phone pings when she hits a rare pocket of cell reception.

HOLLY: At the spa and going in for a facial. Last chance!!!

She smiles at Holly's text, how her boss never uses fewer than three exclamation points. If she had any idea Erika was in the process of helping her soon-to-be husband commit an international felony, she might not be so enthusiastic with her punctuation. Holly was dead-set against his breaking the law to blow close to $3,000 on Cohiba Robusto Reservas, so the cigars are one more of Robert and Erika's little secrets.

She replies in her Bluetooth:

ERIKA: Have fun. I'll hold down the fort. Going to get everything ready for the BIG EVENT.

HOLLY: You are the BEST!!! No worries when Erika T's in
charge!!!

That makes her feel so good. It's nice to be of value . . .
again.

Replacing the phone in its charger, Erika lowers her window and lets in the breeze, her cream lace dress hanging in its
garment bag fluttering in the wind. Holly chose and paid for the
outfit online. Then, on a whim, she made an appointment for
Erika with her hairdresser in Burlington for a balayage. *Soooo*
generous. The three-hour session cost way too much—Erika
was mortified—but Holly insisted.

"Please, let me," she pressed in her lilting southern accent.
"Nothing makes me happier than a good old-fashioned make-
over. A bridesmaid can't say no to a bride."

Bride. What a wonderful word. Erika grips the wheel as
she negotiates the serpentine dirt roads. Driving still makes her
nervous even when the conditions are dry and sunny. She's trying to stay focused, but then she sees herself walking down the
aisle where Robert is waiting in his kilt, hands clasped behind
his back, his muscular legs spread, his smoldering dark gaze
regarding her with raw desire. The setting sun illuminates her
newly golden hair, transforming her into a princess.

Suddenly, the unspoken, forbidden attraction between
them, the pulsating connection they've both tried so nobly to
suppress, becomes too much to bear. To hell with the thousands
of viewers and the show's producers, Robert decides. True love

is true love even if declaring his undeniable feelings hurts, for now, the woman he thought he loved, the one he was *supposed* to love, simply for hits and ratings.

He doesn't wait for his bride. In two long strides, he goes to Erika, grasping her by her bare shoulders (oh, how he's longed to caress her bare skin, to claim her as his own), and bending down before all the world to see he gently brings his lips to hers and . . .

Shit!

A brown blur leaps into the edges of her peripheral vision, causing her to swerve the car wildly. In any other situation, she would have quickly gained control. But the deer lopes past the dreaded wooden cross, knocking her off kilter. The homemade memorial's fading blue plastic flowers and fluttering ribbons trigger horrific memories of another October day long ago at this very spot.

Thankfully, the antilock brakes activate and Erika comes to a full stop before hitting the cross, her heart pounding, lungs squeezing. In the rearview, she watches the panicked deer disappear into the thick foliage. A spikehorn. No doubt crazed by the surging hormones of early mating season. Not his fault.

Not anyone's fault.

Erika's damp palms slide down the steering wheel as she wrestles for composure. "It's all over. No harm, no foul," she mutters, gradually pressing her foot on the gas and resisting the urge to give up, to ditch the car and walk the four miles back to home. Lord knows she's done it before.

Body shaking, she resumes driving slowly until she reaches the covered bridge leading to Snowden's picturesque village.

The maples ringing the town green under the bright blue sky are ablaze in a riot of red, orange, and yellow leaves, a few of which are falling gently over the white-painted rail fencing. They remind her that, no matter what, the earth continues to rotate, seasons change, and life goes on. Nothing lasts forever. Taking a cleansing breath, she continues.

Circling the village square, she passes the white clapboard Snowden town hall, its black slate roof and matching shutters imposing and yet reassuring in their historic stability, and the Snowden general store. To the general store's left is the brick Snowden Volunteer Fire Department with its one bay for its one truck, and to the right of the store is the Snowden post office.

The post office foyer is about the size of Holly and Robert's mudroom, except more cramped. It's infused with the scent of ink and paper, like the stacks in the village library. Brass mailboxes line one wall over an old wooden desk into which holes have been drilled for holding certified mail receipts and forms, along with a pen tied to a dirty string. Across from that is the larger window with a bell and a sign that reads RING FOR SERVICE.

Erika taps the brass bell and Dylan emerges from the back room, flicking a lock of hair that tends to fall over his left eye. She and Dylan graduated from their regional high school the same year. He's one of the few from their class who doesn't blame her for what happened. Or, if he does, he's kind enough not to let on.

"You look different," he says.

"Do I?" She makes the effort to strike a pose. "Good or bad?"

He frowns, actually taking the question seriously. "You kind of look like your boss, no offense."

"Is that bad?"

"No. Just different. Like I said." He hands her a letter with a green certified return receipt attached. "You can sign as your boss's agent, I guess. It's addressed to her."

Erika doesn't have to check the address. She cringes at the lacey purple penmanship with the star instead of the *o* in *Holly* and the faint whiff of coconut suntan oil that managed to survive the long trip from Homosassa, Florida.

What to do? Whether or not to accept is Holly's decision, not hers. But she doesn't want to upset her boss by asking, not when she's lying on a massage table, her face slathered with a chamomile mask.

Screw it. Erika takes the pen and dashes off her name. Better to be safe than sorry. Dylan hands her the certified letter on top of a hefty stack. Erika removes the fliers for flooring and junk mail from furniture stores and mortgage companies, Realtors and florists, tossing them in the recycling on her way out.

"Thanks, Dylan," she calls over her shoulder as she exits. But he's already disappeared.

She dumps the mail in the back seat of the Kia and crosses the green to the general store, feeling slightly anxious. She's unclear if Bert's aware the chocolate delivery contains a $2,500 worth of contraband cigars, and she's not about to inquire. The story Robert told the store owner was that the Swiss chocolatier would not deliver the handmade confections to a residence, only to a retail establishment. The truth is neither the smuggler nor the recipient wanted the permanent documentation of an address.

Her assignment is to ask for the box and go, but as soon as she opens the door to the tinny chime of the overhead bell, she senses hostility. Doc, the retired veterinarian who had to put down their basset, Nell, years ago, and his wife, Judy Ann, Erika's third-grade teacher, end their chat with Bert midsentence and set their jaws in matching scowls. Neither makes eye contact nor makes the effort to offer a begrudging "Good morning." With curt nods to Bert, they exit quickly, brushing past her, eyes averted.

Nothing new there. She steps back and lets them pass, adding with false cheer, "Nice to see you, guys. Enjoy the lovely day."

The screen door shuts with a slam.

"Don't give them a second thought," says Bert, otherwise known as Mayor Bert to the locals and even tourists, who find it adorable that the shop owner of sizable girth and no shortage of opinions has proclaimed himself the town's unelected leader, since Snowden, like most Vermont communities, has no official one. For Erika, he's been a bedrock of public support, though she harbors no illusion that once her back is turned, he's no better than the rest when it comes to rehashing her crimes.

"Whatever. I can't change other people, only myself."

"You get that off the *Oprah Winfrey Show*?" Bert's cultural references are often a decade or two behind.

"Actually, I believe it was . . . *Barney*?"

He hasn't a clue about the purple dinosaur of her child-hood, which means she's in danger of becoming as much of a relic as he is. "You here for the, uhm, wedding chocolate?" He gives her a skeptical grin.

"Yup. I hope it came in. Robert is *reeeeeeally* excited about serving it at the reception."

Bert goes to the back and reemerges with an elaborately packaged black box decorated with gold writing in French. "Could've bought from Lake Champlain. Didn't have to order from Zurich. Or Mary Kay Bellows at Kay Confections in Pomfret does a bang-up job. Local first!"

The local-first scolding is a veiled dig at Robert and Holly, who chose a high-end vegetarian chef from out of town to cater the reception instead of him. She can't say this was a mis-take. Erika's attended Bert's events, and while roasted corn, hot dogs, hamburgers, and pasta salads might fit the bill for fam-ily reunions or end-of-season softball games, they definitely would not rise to Holly and Robert's epicurean standards.

At the very least, however, they should have ordered the wine, beer, and soft drinks through the general store. That would have softened the blow. Now they'll have to deal with his orneriness, his occasional jabs, and his bad-mouthing them to his other customers. Holly and Robert are city folk, unac-customed to the delicate nuances of small-town diplomacy.

"An innocent oversight, I'm sure," she says, taking the pre-cious box, "what with this wedding being so last minute and hush-hush."

"Buying local is to their benefit in the end. You never

know when you're gonna have to rely on your neighbors. I don't have to tell you that."

No, he does not. Erika thanks him and quicksteps across the green to her car, checking over her shoulder as if the FBI agents were waiting. She gets in and, even though she knows she's being silly, she locks the doors before slicing open the package with the edge of her house key. Sure enough, wedged amid shiny blue boxes of Swiss truffles is a nondescript wooden case marked in Spanish.

She opens the notes app on her phone and checks CIGARS off her to-do list. Then she calls Robert, per his instructions.

He answers on the third ring. An explosion of boisterous laughter in the background and glasses clinking indicate the wedding festivities have started early. She pictures hungover groomsmen lounging about Robert's suite in the Snowden Inn attempting to restart their engines with a round of bloodies.

"Turnbull!" he bellows. "Tell me the eagle has landed."

"The eagle has landed," she confirms. They're talking in code because Robert's eager for the cigars to be a surprise treat for his attendants. "You want me to bring them to the inn?"

"No, no. You can leave them in the bottom drawer of my filing cabinet. You still have the key, right?"

"Right." Robert entrusted her with the small silver key only the day before. Erika fingers it, feeling a strange sense of honor since not even Holly has this, which is the whole point. The cigars must be stored in a secure location out of his bride's suspicious snooping. "You want me to leave the mail there, too?"

Robert is strangely preoccupied with snail mail. He's like a little boy when it comes to demanding he be the first to sort through the daily pile. Fortunately, Holly couldn't care less. Fans don't pen letters; they email or post on Instagram. Contracts are digitally sent and signed. Payments are automatically deposited; bills automatically paid.

Robert, on the other hand, is obsessed, snatching the pile and taking it to another room, most often Holly's office, whereupon he closes the door for ultimate privacy until he's finished sorting and opening. Erika can usually predict his mood for the rest of the day depending on what the USPS delivered that morning. A letter from the IRS, for example, can send him into an endless funk.

"The Internal Revenue Service doesn't text," he once quipped after he received a terse notice about a discrepancy in his most recently filed 1040. "That's why you check the mail, Turnbull."

More disturbing, she's noticed, are the occasional handwritten envelopes addressed to "The So-Called Robber Barron," in angry quotes. Those can really pitch him into the void, turning him dark and mercurial and generally unpleasant to be around. Erika hasn't had the nerve to ask him what those are about, for fear he'd snap her head off.

"I don't care about the mail, unless there's something crucial," he says.

"Nothing that popped out at me."

"Great. Then, yeah, leave it on the desk. I'll go through the stuff on Monday. Holly has made me swear not to do a lick of work from now until then."

"Believe it when I see it." She highly doubts either of those workaholics will be able to resist sneaking into the office on Sunday, not with the reveal a week away.

After they hang up, Erika's about to put away her phone when she receives a text from an unfamiliar contact. That's not unusual. Her number is on the RFPs they send out to contractors and all her email correspondence for *TMB*. But the image slowly loading has nothing to do with the project.

It's of the flowered wedding arch set up in the field behind the house. Considering the arch wasn't completed yesterday, it must have been taken this morning. That would be creepy enough without the added effect of a dark-red blood spatter dotting the screen.

"Shit," Erika whispers, gripping the underside of her car seat, tamping down a frisson of alarm.

You'd think that after months of dealing with trolls on Reddit and the occasional perv who's managed to get past *TMB*'s site filters, she'd know better than to get ramped up about an image threatening bloody violence. Humans are a weird breed, she's discovered in her brief stint as Holly and Robert's assistant. Lonely, disturbed, jealous, or simply bored people can be stunningly vicious online—provided they can remain anonymous. Chances are, this is simply the work of some disgruntled teenager tooling around with Photoshop in the basement of his parents' house hundreds of miles away.

Except, no one aside from invited guests, approved vendors, and authorized *TMB* personnel are allowed on Holly and Robert's property today. The foliage in its periphery means it wasn't taken overhead by a drone. It appears to have been shot with a long lens from the hillside opposite, indicating the photographer was there—*might even still be there*—waiting. The idea of a disturbed fan lurking in the woods planning to do God knows what when Holly and Robert say their vows is more than chilling.

It's sick.

And then Erika remembers they won't be the only ones standing at that spot. The wedding is being officiated by the Snowden town clerk—who just happens to be her own mother.

TWO

KIM

I was deeply honored when Holly asked me to officiate at her wedding—and slightly taken aback. We've barely spoken, aside from when I registered her Range Rover and her occasional calls to the office inquiring about building permits—though she never fails to compliment my daughter.

"Erika is so sweet and super efficient," Holly said when she came to town hall yesterday to apply for a marriage license.

She was dressed to the nines, exquisite in her fine Italian coat, the diamond on her engagement ring glittering under the fluorescents. Most people don't make the effort when they come to the office. Most come in sweats.

Her blond hair was pulled into a neat ponytail at the base of her neck, her makeup tasteful with a light gloss of pink on her lips. She was even more chic than she is on TV, where she normally appears in clear plastic safety goggles and paint-stained tees powdered with drywall dust. She's an itty-bitty thing, Erika's size. You could sweep them both away with a feather.

"You and Erika are so lucky to have a close relationship." Holly opened her leather binder and handed me the app, to which had been affixed a check made out in neat handwriting. "My Mama and I. . . . we're more like oil and vinegar."

Obviously, she intended to say oil and water, not salad dressing, but I got it. I reviewed the application and noticed she'd left line 9 blank, the info about her father.

Her legal last name is that of her mother, Beauregard, instead of Simmons, which is what she uses on the show. And, it turns out, her legal first name isn't Holly but Haylee. Haylee Dawn Beauregard versus Holly Simmons, as she's known to her hundreds of thousands of Instagram followers. That was a little odd.

Reading my mind, she reddened slightly and said, "It's complicated. When we first met, Robert kept accidentally calling me Holly and it stuck."

"Your secret's safe with me," I said with a wink, though it wouldn't be once the license was recorded and became a public record. Nothing you could do about that.

"Robert's father's going to walk me down the aisle," she said as I went to my computer to process the license. "But we haven't found someone to officiate. Is that something you can do? I mean, if you're okay with being live-streamed online. We're calling it a flash wedding and there'll be thousands, tens of thousands, watching."

The prospect of being on camera before an audience of that magnitude was absolutely petrifying. I mentally inventoried my closet: jeans and button-down shirts, practical skirts and easy-care blouses, the black dress I keep for funerals, the navy shift for church. I had nothing to wear and the wedding was in twenty-four hours. Kohl's was not going to cut it.

I was about to beg off when tears pooled in the corners of Holly's clear blue eyes. "I'd be so grateful. My own mama won't be there, so you'll be kinda like a stand-in. A girl needs a mother figure when she gets married, wouldn't you say?"

That cut me to the quick. "I'm so sorry to hear that about your mom."

Holly's gaze drifted to the ceiling and she sighed the most pitiful sigh. "Yeah. It's been rough."

Obviously, I couldn't turn down a motherless daughter who wasn't much older than my own. Which, when I thought of it, was another valid reason to accept her offer. It would be to Erika's benefit if her mother was around to keep her in line.

Not that I'd expect her to overdo the Dom Pérignon and dance on the tables. That's not her style. For the most part, Erika has a practical head on her shoulders. She's good with money, with taking care of her health, and she's got a hell of a work ethic. She's as sensible as my LifeStride wedges.

With men, not so much, especially when they're tall, dark, and ambitious like her boss—and Holly's betrothed—Robert Barron.

Robert's an unusual character, unlike most men you find around here. Whip smart and charming with flashing brown eyes, silky black curls, and a killer half grin, he could talk you into signing over your life savings, if you're not careful. I get that he came from privilege—his own father is a controversial real estate developer back in Boston—but I can see why he's been successful in his own right.

Others might have been scared off by the potential pitfalls of the property he snapped up at deep discount in the tax sale, but not Robert. He had a wildly creative vision for the land, and, luckily for my daughter, he was smart enough to realize she could be an asset in making it real.

Erika was a hurting bird when she ran into him last January. At the time, she was sequestered on my couch nursing a heartbreak and suffering from a mid-twentysomething ennui exacerbated by maturing student loans and dawning awareness that a double major in psychology and art history, while intellectually stimulating, had been a complete waste in the marketplace. Unable to find meaningful employment, broke, and smarting from her ex's decision to choose smoking pot over her, my poor, wounded daughter desperately needed a boost in self-esteem.

And then along came Robert Barron. He happened to be in the office when she stopped by with a cup of coffee. Luckily, she was showered—a rarity back then—with clean hair and makeup and wearing the lovely black wool swing coat I'd given her for Christmas. On the surface, my daughter came across as perfectly normal.

"Well, hello," he said.

That was it! Erika took one glance at Robert's electric smile and blossomed like Snow White kissed by a prince. Color rose in her cheeks and her lips turned pink. Her lovely hazel eyes, so dull of late, sparkled.

She was instantly besotted, dammit. Falling for an older guy who tooled around in $100,000 cars and called himself "The Robber Barron" while jetting off to Whistler for winter weekends and hunted for bargain-basement properties wasn't what I wished for her. But he had something else in mind.

"You know, if our rehab on the hill is chosen for *To the Manor Build*, we'll need an assistant." The enticing line was directed at me, though it was meant for Erika. "Preferably someone who knows the area and can hit the ground running and is willing to give one hundred and ten percent."

"I love *To the Manor Build*," Erika piped up. "HGTV is my favorite channel, next to Investigation Discovery. That's all I watch these days. Murder and real-estate porn."

"And you are?"

"Erika Turnbull." She pointed to me. "Daughter of the town clerk."

His mouth slid into a devastating smile. "Awesome."

Erika was hired that afternoon with decent pay and a barely acceptable health insurance plan. The following week, she moved into the apartment over the garage I'd been renting as an occasional Airbnb and the following month leased a new car.

Ever since then, she's been glued to her phone, texting Robert constantly. Eating dinner, watching Netflix, going out for ice cream, there's my daughter, head bent, her thumbs flying. She once confessed she bookends the day by texting him first thing in the morning and last thing at night.

When she's not communicating with him directly, she's talking about him obliquely. She's like a starstruck teenager the way she finds any excuse to insert Robert's mundane observations into any conversation.

Robert doesn't pay tolls, he uses E-ZPass. Maybe I should sign up for E-ZPass. It saves a bundle.

Robert says linoleum is actually a natural material. Did you know that? Might want to think about using linoleum if you ever redo the kitchen, Mom. Far more affordable.

Robert makes the best sandwich with bacon, tomatoes, and avocado. He calls it a California BLT. We should make a California BLT in the summer when the tomatoes are good. The trick, he says, is to not overcook the bacon.

I'm slightly worried. Yes, Erika's an adult and free to make her own mistakes, but it's hard for me to resist my maternal instincts to spare her more heartbreak, especially considering she's only recently recovered from Colton's rejection. And heartbreak there will be!

Soon, *To the Manor Build* will wind to a close, and with Holly and Robert saying their vows, cementing themselves publicly as a married couple, Erika's going to find herself suddenly very much unemployed, again, and, worse, alone. I'm petrified the combination of losing her job and the man she secretly adores will steer her toward a big, messy, personal crash. And who will be left picking up the pieces?

Her mother, of course.

Which is why I finally accepted Holly's offer. "I'd love to officiate," I told her. "Erika will be thrilled."

Though, I suspected, nothing could be further from the truth.

◇ ◇ ◇

The weather for the wedding could not be more ideal if it had been scripted by the *To The Manor Build* producers themselves. The leaves are at the peak of autumn foliage—orange, yellow, and red against a backdrop of dark green pines in the mountains. The sky is a brilliant blue dotted with fluffy white clouds. No bugs. No blazing sun or oppressive humidity. Merely a gentle warm breeze carrying a tinge of woodsmoke.

The ceremony is to take place in the backyard of Holly and Robert's house, commonly referred to around Snowden as the "Stricklands' place" after the former owners, Zeke and Gretchen Strickland. I haven't been here since the tax sale and am itching to see what improvements *To the Manor Build* has made to the property, having been treated only to glimpses online.

An electronic gate decorated with redwood pots of blue and pink hydrangea stands guard at the end of the driveway. A sign reads WELCOME TO HOLLY HILL. Cute.

"Here for the wedding?" Steve Winette, looking uncomfortable in an ill-fitting seersucker suit and pink bowtie, leans into my lowered car window. Holly and Robert likely haven't a clue whom they've hired here; namely, a guy ordered to perform community service for stealing a user's manual from his neighbor's truck. The most shocking part of that story, everyone agreed when he was arrested, was the discovery that Steve could read.

"Hey, Steve," I say. "I'm here to perform the ceremony."

"Oh, hi, Kim. Yeah, I saw you were added to the list." He ticks off my name near the bottom of the page. Last-minute additions. "Um, so, when you go through the gate, head to the right. You'll see the signs where to park. It's all happening down at the lower field. No one's allowed at the house."

"No one's allowed at the house?" My rearview's been darkened by grate of a hulking Land Rover. "Why?"

"Show rules."

Naturally. Even my own offspring is forbidden from divulging so much as the color of a paint chip. It's right there in the nondisclosure agreement she signed. I sometimes forget this is more than your average property rehab show; it's a competition with hundreds of thousands of dollars and lucrative endorsement deals in the balance. The other contestants are likely just as secretive as Holly and Robert, guarding the juicy details of their rehabs so as not to lose a single valuable viewer—and voter.

I thank him and continue up the gravel drive until the structure comes into view. To my disappointment, most of it is hidden behind a fresh plywood fence. These guys aren't messing around.

As I pull into the makeshift lot, I spy Erika's red Kia, which sticks out like a circus clown at a funeral among the luxury cars. Judging from where she's parked, she must have arrived bright and early. As I said, she's a hard worker.

I apply nude lipstick and layer my eyelashes with another coat of mascara. My hairdresser, God love her, was able to fit me in for a few auburn highlights and trim up my shoulder-length bob to prevent me from being a total frump. Even so, in my muted rose shift, patterned silk scarf, and reading glasses, I'll be just another middle-aged woman fading into the background. Fine by me.

Signs direct us away from the house toward a pair of striped tents for the reception and the area where the wedding will be held. White wooden chairs have been lined in neat rows on the freshly mowed grass. A lush arch bursting with greenery interwoven with dahlias, goldenrod, ranunculus, and garden roses in muted orange, yellow, purple, and dusty pink marks the finish line at the end of a makeshift aisle. Behind the arch, a flowing field of uncut golden hay extends to a hillside of virgin pines.

A glorious setting. Picture perfect.

Interspersed among the milling guests are men in suit jackets over kilts laughing and jostling one another boisterously. Groomsmen, I assume. Robert's friends and family flying high. There is no sign of Erika, but I imagine she's hanging back before she precedes Holly down the aisle.

"I bet you're Kim," declares a woman in a crisp black pantsuit marching across the lawn, iPad tucked under her arm. "I'm Janelle, the wedding planner."

She directs me where to stand, and we do a quick runthrough of the ceremony, which I calculate from her description to be no more than ten minutes long, bagpiper to bagpiper. "Keep it by the book," Janelle says. "Do you take him? Do you take her? By the power vested in me I now pronounce you . . . Done and done."

This was not what Holly wanted yesterday, and I'm concerned Janelle's being hasty. "It's my understanding from the bride that they wrote their own vows. Also, she said something about a poem—"

"Change of plans," Janelle interrupts brusquely. "An hour ago Robert took me aside and expressly insisted we keep it super quick. Don't ask me why." She raises a hand in surrender. "I do what the client wants."

Four beefy men in dark suits and sunglasses fan out along the edge of the area. Behind us, two others are walking into the field, pressing their earpieces and conversing. If I didn't know better, I'd peg them as a professional security detail, which seems slightly over the top for a couple of mere internet stars.

But then I wonder . . . are *they* the reason for the abbreviated ceremony?

Following my gaze, Janelle says quietly, "Also, last-minute additions."

"Is something going on?"

"Supposedly, there's a VIP guest who needs extra protection." She clears her throat. "That's all I've been told."

Well, if that's true, that's kind of exciting. As I scan the scene trying to spot the celeb, my gaze lands on a strange interaction taking place under one of the tents. Robert, in his kilt and tailored Braemar jacket, is in a heated conversation with Holly in her beautiful lace gown. *Tsk, tsk.* I'm old-fashioned enough to hold that the bride and groom seeing each other before the wedding is bad luck. Their argument being a case in point.

Except, on closer inspection, I see, to my deep consternation, that it's not the bride he's sparring with; it's my daughter, who happens to be *dressed* like the bride. She even looks like the bride now that she's . . . blond!

When did that happen? Just the other day, Erika had my brunette coloring; though mine, admittedly, is aided by monthly application of Nice'n Easy.

"We're starting." Janelle waves me to my spot.

I hesitate, torn between my duty as officiant and my maternal curiosity to find out what's up with the hair and the dress. There's no time, however. The groomsmen have managed to clear their heads enough to form a semistraight line by the arch.

Robert extends his hand, which is surprisingly sweaty. "Thank you so much for doing this at the last minute, Kim," he says, palming his kilt. "I'm afraid I'm a little nervous."

I tell him not to worry, that saying "I do" is the easiest part of marriage. It's later on, when you have to say "I don't," where it gets dicey.

He grins out of politeness but doesn't laugh at my standard line, and I can tell he didn't hear a word. He's too preoccupied with whatever's on the opposite hillside, not taking his eyes off the woods.

The bagpiper starts up with the romantic "Skye Boat Song," which I know only from the *Outlander* TV series, and my daughter in her cream lace dress, clutching a small bouquet of dusty pink roses and dried ferns walks up the aisle. Everyone assuming, as I did minutes earlier, that Erika is the bride— especially since she can't take her eyes off Robert.

And vice versa.

I'm embarrassed for both of them, though mainly for Erika. I don't know who had the bright idea to set her up as a decoy. Certainly not Janelle, who's sucking her cheeks in disapproval.

The moment passes when Holly appears on the arm of her groom's father, Robert Barron Jr., the hard-nosed real estate developer from Boston. He's bald and tan from a summer on the links, I'm guessing. His mouth is set into a stern scowl, as if the honor of escorting his future daughter-in-law is a legal transaction deserving of scrutiny.

The bagpiper takes it up a notch, launching into an ear-splitting, nasal rendition of Wagner's bridal chorus. The song might be overplayed, but it's a welcome cue to the assembled that this woman is the actual bride, as they hold up their phones and murmur in awe.

Holly is elegant in her deceptively simple gown, tea roses in her hair, a huge smile on her face. Robert gives her an approving nod and then he's back to squinting at the hillside again. The muscle in his jaw spasms. This boy's strung tighter than piano wire.

The abbreviated ceremony is over in a flash and I'm relieved to see him visibly relax when the bagpiper begins "All You Need Is Love." The newlyweds dash joyfully down the aisle under a shower of rose petals and straight into a waiting circle of men in suits who whisk them away. Perhaps Robert was suffering from nothing more than a case of the wedding jitters.

"Mom?" Suddenly, Erika's by my side. She grabs my arm and jerks me behind the wedding arch. "You did a great job. Couldn't have been more perfect."

"Thanks." It's rare for my daughter to give me a gratuitous compliment. Even rarer for her to be clutching me like an anxious child. I'm tempted to ask what's up with the blond hair and the dress and decide to pick my battles. Besides, Erika seems pretty on edge, too. "Is everything okay?"

"Fine. Absolutely fine. I just want to get you out of the . . . cameras." Though she's not looking at the cameras, which are trained on Holly and Robert, who are being interviewed against a backdrop of peonies. She's looking at that same hillside.

"Why does everyone keep staring at the hill?"

She snaps her head around, pupils dilated. Oh, man, she's just as brittle as Robert was, sweat beading her heavily made-up face. Unless that's not sweat, it's tears. "Who's looking at what hill?"

"Robert. You. Those security guards."

"You could tell they were security guards?" As soon as the words leave her mouth, she dismisses them with a wave. "Of course you could tell. Everyone's been talking."

"Who's the VIP?" I ask, trying to get a bead on the guests, who are leaving their chairs and filing toward the tents.

"Not allowed to say. Listen, don't take this the wrong way, but I'm thinking it might be better if you skip the reception. I'll bring you home a doggie bag, a piece of wedding cake to tuck under your pillow."

Insulted, I break free of her grasp. "Why? My off-the-rack Kohl's not good enough for the LA types in their Versace couture?"

Erika shakes her head. "Nothing like that."

"Then what?"

"I wish I could tell you but I can't. No one knows, not even Holly. Only Robert and I. Kind of our secret."

And then it dawns on me why she wants her mother out of the picture. She's going to find a moment to bare her heart to Robert and she doesn't want me running interference. "Erika, don't."

"Don't what?"

"Whatever you're planning to say to Robert. It's not going to make a difference. I hate to be blunt, but . . . it's over. He's married now. He belongs to another woman. Leave him alone."

Erika recoils, crimson blotches spreading across her neck and chest. Clearly, I must have hit the nail on the head because she's mortified.

"Thanks, mom," she hisses. "Thanks for giving me the benefit of the doubt, for trusting that I'm mature enough not to proposition my boss. Geesh." With that, she marches down the aisle to the tent.

I detect eyes on me and turn to see a waitress in the standard white blouse and black pants, her salt-and-pepper hair twisted in a tight updo. She's holding a silver tray of champagne flutes, but makes no move to offer me a glass, and I wonder if I'm being judged for taking my adult daughter in hand.

"Can I help you?" I say testily.

"You don't know who I am, do you?" she says.

I meet a lot of people as town clerk. They often expect you to remember their names and can be quite prickly when you come up short. "I'm sorry," I reply, my thoughts still swirling around my daughter. "I don't."

"Shame on you." With that she follows Erika down the aisle toward the tent and I can't help thinking that despite trying my best, in the end, mostly I disappoint.

PROPERTY IS THEFT–OWN IT!

DISPATCHES FROM THE ROBBER BARRON

Hark, fellow thieves!

Those of you who are regular subscribers to my newsletter may know I did a thing today. Yup, I took the plunge and got hitched. The ceremony was held on the eighty-acre Vermont estate I bought last year at tax sale (newsletter #183) for a steal at $8,500 and was later streamed on *To the Manor Build*'s YouTube channel. (Check it out.)

To recap for you neophytes, twenty-two months ago, I was the only bidder at a municipal auction because other investors were too chicken to take a risk. They were afraid of evicting the prior owner, who'd made the one mistake real-estate investors must never, ever make: falling behind on property taxes. That gave the right for the Town of Snowden to immediately put his property up for sale, which it did. Like I said, I was the only bidder, because I was the only one with balls. When the prior owner failed to redeem by paying me back for the overdue taxes I paid + 1%/month in interest after a year, I was deeded the whole shebang.

Repeat: eighty Vermont acres, 360-degree mountain views, apple orchards, streams, already developed, for 9 percent of its listed value. Hell yeah.

What followed was tough work, I ain't gonna lie. I had to tear down (most of) the existing log cabin with a goal of building a mountain retreat that's not only architecturally superior, but also energy efficient. *To the Manor Build* liked our concept so much, they chose our project to be in their contest for best rebuild. If we win—and in my not-humble opinion that's a given—*TMB* will eat all the costs, not including what I paid for the property, which, in comparison to the design, construction, finishing, and decorating expenses, is a drop in the bucket.

Now, I don't usually mix personal with business, but in this case, my personal life *is* my business life. You see, I never would have met the goddess Holly if it hadn't been for *The Robber Barron* newsletter and my updates about the Vermont tax-sale house, which brought me to her attention.

I never would have had a project featured in *To the Manor Build*.

I never would have found the happiness that'd eluded me for forty years.

I never would have been on the verge of making millions.

There's a lesson here you can all learn from my experience, one that I'm eager to impress on you, my fellow robber barons, and it's this: The only way to achieve any level of success is to take a huge risk.

I'll say that again: The only way to achieve success is to take a huge risk. Period.

Let me be clear: I don't mean to suggest you should take ill-informed risks. No one's proposing that you jump off the clichéd bridge. Quite the opposite. But if after doing the research and the homework, after burning the late-night oil reading the prospectus, you find out that to get from A to B requires a courageous leap of faith then . . .

Do it!

Most of all, don't let anyone stand in your way. Remember, the only one who's going to look out for you is you. Every robber baron for himself, is my motto. That's not greed. That's called survival. And in the dog-eat-dog world of real-estate investing, it's not just helpful—it's essential.

Okay, that free advice is my wedding gift to you. Meanwhile, don't forget to tune in a week from Monday night and, most importantly, VOTE for us at ToTheManorBuild.com.

You know what the kind of cool thing is? Now that I've got Holly by my side until death do us part, I don't even need a house. Because wherever Holly is, that's my home.

Guess what they say is true. Marriage makes you a softie. (Not THAT way, dudes!)

In the meantime, never forget: PROPERTY *IS* THEFT—OWN IT!

—Robert Barron, a.k.a. The Robber Barron

r/ToTheManorBuild: Talk about the episodes and your favorite rehab teams

Posted by BarronFangirl22–1 hour ago

r/TMB: Whaddya all think of H&R's wedding? Robert was TO DIE FOR, but for a woman who supposedly has style, what was with Holly's dress? Capped sleeves? Did she buy it from Target?

(12 comments)

Cutiepatootie117–55 min. ago

Not even close to my beloved Tar-jay. Googled designer. That dress cost $$$$$ and H probably got it comped. I've said it before and I'll say it again. These 2 are in it for the $ only. That energy-efficiency stuff is bullsh!t. They don't hold a candle to those doctors in SC. Samita are GOOD people. They literally care. These guys are posers. They need to lose!

Cherishthelove88–25 min. ago

Harsh but true. So much wasteful spending. Makes me kinda ill, TBH. #TeamSamita

teambarron4thewin–20 min. ago

The ceremony was tasteful. H was elegant. R was sexy as hell. Stop stirring up trouble, BarronFangirl22, like you always do.

BarronFangirl22–17 min. ago

Who, me? *Bats eyes*

lawyersgunsandmoney66–15 min. ago

Did not watch. Don't care. These rehab shows are scripted fakes.

teambarron4thewin–13 min. ago

> And that's why you hang out at a TMB subreddit. Riiiiight.

Beachhousedreamer976–10 min. ago

> Check out the (only) bridesmaid at 1:46 . . . Watch out, Holly. That girl after yer man

Cutiepatootie117–8 min. ago

> Hahahahahaha! Agreed! She thot SHE was the bride????

Cherishthelove88–6 min. ago

> ^^^^ THIS! I luv me some drama. Wanted a bridesmaid-from-hell moment. At least a little hair pulling. R ditching H at the altar. Didn't happen . . . :(

lawyersgunsandmoney66–5 min. ago

> Writers off there game . . .

[Deleted]–4 min. ago

> [Deleted]

Beachhousedreamer976–2 min. ago

> I don't know who this ^^^^^^ is, but I bet he's vengeanceismine92 who got blocked on the TMB Q&A thread, too. What does he have against these guys? One seriously f'd up dude *shudders*. Reporting him for breaking the rules with that shit.

BarronFangirl22–1 min. ago

> Even if his comment was deleted, I can't unsee that. Sick MOFO. Stay safe H&R 'cause he's out there, somewhere. Prayers for their safety.

THREE

ERIKA

Back home after leaving the wedding reception, albeit earlier than she'd planned, Erika stretches out on the couch in her apartment, finally able to unwind with a glass of chilled pinot grigio. She should be thrilled the day went off without a hitch, or at least without a major hitch. There were two uncomfortable moments when her mother acted inappropriately, which isn't unheard of when it comes to Kim and her tendency to hover.

Though, to be fair, maybe that's why Erika's feeling slightly blue. Because her mother's intuition, goddammit, was on target. So annoying how often that happens.

Yes, there is—or was—a powerful, unspoken attraction between Robert and her. He didn't have to say in actual words that he felt it, too. The message came across loud and clear in the way he sometimes laid a reassuring hand on her shoulder when she was at the computer or pulled up a chair next to her so their knees brushed together under the table. You could feel the charge between them, her positive drawn to his negative. Pulsating, yet forbidden.

Robert tells her personal stuff he would never dare share with Holly. Like how when he was sixteen and announced his intention to spend the summer hiking a portion of the Appalachian Trail, the elder Robert Barron nixed his plans and made him work construction on one of his gentrification projects that was the focus of daily protests. If he wasn't getting picked on by the tough crew, he was being mocked and taunted by the protesters who gleefully pelted the loathed developer's son with half-empty cups of Dunkin' and bags of dog poop.

Robert didn't want Holly to see him as weak, didn't want her to view him as anything less than perfect and strong, so he kept those stories from her. But Erika he trusts. Erika knows he's worried they might not win the contest, that the guys building the ranch for bullied LGBTQ teens and the doctors with the retreat in South Carolina have far more compelling backstories compared with Holly and Robert's relatively lame, if noble, goal of building an energy-efficient home that'd be totally out of reach to most people.

Holly's oblivious about his concerns, Erika can tell. She thinks they're guaranteed to win because they're a couple in love and everyone loves lovers, right? They fell in love while working on this project. Viewers watched their romance blossom in real time. And now they've gotten married on the very site in a wedding that Holly's sure will catapult them into stardom.

Except, that's not the way social media's tracking.

Erika checks her phone again, refreshing the r/ToThe-ManorBuild subreddit, the most honest touchstone of Holly and Robert's popularity, since, unlike the official *TMB* social media site, it's not moderated by the network. Her thumb flicks down the screen searching for the comment that will right this ship that appears to be dangerously listing.

Everyone working on the show is banking on the wedding going viral, that *People* magazine will splash the beautiful couple across its next cover, à la Christina Haack of *Flip or Flop* when she married Ant Anstead after divorcing Tarek El Moussa and then divorced Ant and married Josh Hall. That's the kind of publicity they're desperately hoping for.

Unlike Christina, Holly's not trending on Twitter, however. She's getting bashed on Reddit for spending way too much on a "simple Vermont wedding" during the height of a crazed real estate market when most couples their age can't afford rent on a cramped apartment, not to mention a three-bedroom secluded retreat with an attached guest suite and massive outdoor entertainment area on eighty acres. Talk about out of touch.

But that's not the worst part. The worst part is that they've committed the online-unforgivable sin: perfection.

Crap. Erika empties her glass. This is on her. Everyone knows that intentional insertion of a flaw only elevates the value of an art piece. She should have suggested the couple make a newsworthy gaffe à la Jennifer Lawrence tripping on the steps to accept her Oscar. The halftime show of Super Bowl XXXVIII would have been forgotten had it not been for Janet Jackson's unfortunate clothing malfunction. Those are the blunders that make headlines.

If only Robert's kilt hadn't been properly secured. If only she'd made a fool of herself by declaring her love midway through the ceremony. *If only the stalker on the hillside . . .*

No. She immediately shuts down that grim thought seconds before reading the comments about the deleted post.

> I bet he's vengeanceismine92 who got blocked on the TMB Q&A thread, too. What does he have against these guys? One seriously f'd up dude *shudders*. Reporting him for breaking the rules with that shit.
> Even if his comment was deleted, I can't unsee that. Sick MOFO. Stay safe H&R 'cause he's out there, somewhere. Prayers for their safety.

Vengeanceismine92. Erika racks her brain, trying to recall what he wrote or if she'd even read it. She vaguely remembers LuAnn, their producer, mentioning there was a sore loser who hadn't been chosen for the contest being so green with envy that he went around sabotaging the selected contestants. Though she's never heard of Sam Chidubem and Concita Jimenez running into this problem. Fans adore them and their dimpled cheeks, their twee seaside cottage painted in pastel colors with its sleeping porch and cozy reading room.

Ditto for Joel and Sean. If there are homophobic nutcases out there—and there definitely are—they don't pop up on the *TMB* subreddit. Nothing but gushing praise for those two, former teachers who could be enjoying their retirement traveling the world but who, instead, are constructing safe places like "therapeutic stables" to home horses who otherwise would be dogmeat. Joel and Sean get extra points for rescuing abused animals as well as humans. The word most often used to describe them is *heroes*.

She wonders if it's possible to contact Reddit to see the deleted quote from Vengeanceismine92. Maybe she could mount an argument that it's necessary to ensure Holly and Robert's safety, a pitch that, on second thought, might not be that much of a stretch. Because she has the feeling something is going on behind the scenes that Robert knows about—and is refusing to share.

He reacted so bizarrely when she showed him the photo of the wedding arch sent by the anonymous contact. She expected him to brush it off and advise her to block the number and forget it. He didn't. Not at all. What he did was clench his jaw and suck in his cheeks, his dark brow furrowing.

"Keep that to yourself" was all he said before whipping out his own phone and making a call to his father. Erika lingered, dying to eavesdrop, but Robert turned his back to her and walked off. Hours later, the place was flooded with ex-military dudes with reflective sunglasses and coiled earpieces fanning the perimeter and even inspecting the woods from where the photo had been taken.

Did the wedding make Robert paranoid or was he going overboard for another reason? He never got a chance to answer her whispered question, thanks to her mother's dick move. A pinch. Seriously?

Ugh. She wished she hadn't thought of that.

Skip it. Tired and achy and fed up with the whole cruel online culture, Erika slides from the couch and carries her glass to the kitchenette. She needs a break from *TMB* and her butt-insky of a mother. Good thing tomorrow's Sunday and she doesn't have to fix last-minute wedding snafus. She plans on sleeping until noon and watching *The Office* on an endless loop all afternoon.

A warm shower does wonders. Wrapping herself in a thick, clean towel, she's brushing her teeth and debating whether to save the dress Holly bought for her or to list it on eBay when the tiny hairs on her arms rise, her body sensing what her brain has yet to process: the sound of footsteps crunching on the gravel driveway below her open window.

She shuts off the toothbrush and goes stock still, bubbles of Crest foaming on her lips as she cocks her ears, tuning in.

There are two more slow, heavy steps. Definitely not a deer. Her pulse begins to pound hard. Whoever's here is right under her bathroom window, even though it's midnight. It couldn't be her mother; she's asleep.

Shit!

She spits out the toothpaste, shuts off the overhead light, and peers out the small octagonal window. There, partially illuminated by the moonlight filtered through the trees, she can barely make out the silhouette of a man. He is broad shouldered and staring straight up at her.

Shit. Shit, shit. Whoever he is, he might be lurking in the woods outside her apartment and waiting for her to go to sleep so he can attack. Her mind races as she tries to remember if she did or didn't lock the downstairs door. It's a blur.

Should she check? If he hears her on the stairs and the outside door is, in fact, unlocked, that'd be the perfect opportunity for him to sweep in and get her. If she doesn't check, she'll never get to sleep. Move or don't move? Hide or run? She can't think.

Once he's in the garage, the carriage house, there'll be no escape. Now she understands why her mother's battle-tough assistant, Doreen, keeps a loaded pistol in her purse.

Tiptoeing into her studio, Erika quietly slides open her drawer, her hands trembling as she removes a pair of underpants, sweatpants, and a T-shirt just in case she has to make a run for it. Grabbing the baseball bat she keeps near the upstairs door to pummel would-be intruders, she sits on her bed and prepares herself for the worst.

There's no one she can call for help. Certainly not her mother, who makes it a habit to turn off her phone at night so she doesn't have to listen to tourists whine that their cars got stuck on some poorly maintained dirt road or locals complain about some barking dog disturbing the peace. The nearest Vermont State Police barracks is all the way in Westminster, a forty-five minute drive. Even if they do have troopers on duty—and that's doubtful at this hour—it'll take them forever to get to her. By then, her throat will be slit.

And then her phone lights up with a message:

I'm outside. Let me in.

◇ ◇ ◇

"You scared the crap out of me," she says, leading him up the stairs to her apartment. "Do you want to explain what you're doing skulking around on my driveway . . . on your wedding night?"

"I need a favor." Robert Barron opens the door to her studio. "A big one."

He has been in her apartment only once, to drop off fabric samples. That was in the middle of a Wednesday and he was in a rush, running an errand for Holly, who wanted Erika's advice about upholstery. His presence in her private quarters while the world is sleeping feels awkward, like he's too big for this small space, for their tight intimacy.

She wishes she hadn't taken off all her makeup. She remembers she's not wearing a bra.

He shrugs off his Barbour and tosses it onto her couch. He's changed out of his wedding attire into jeans and a gray sweater. It appears he, too, has recently showered. His hair is damp and he smells of expensive soap. Also, of alcohol. Nothing too strong. But enough that he probably shouldn't be driving.

Has he come to admit his mistake? Is he suffering buyer's remorse? *I just realized tonight that you're the one I love, Erika. You're the one I want to be with for the rest of my life.*

"I need to get Holly out of here tomorrow," he says, pacing the room. "We need a break."

Erika blinks back to reality. They must have had a fight, that's it. That's why he's here. They've had a blowup and he's come to cry on her shoulder. "Did something happen?"

"Not exactly." He crosses his arms, still pacing the short distance her apartment allows. "Well, yes. Yes and no. Mostly yes, in a way."

He's not making any sense. He's uncharacteristically agitated and manic, his eyes darting back and forth, and what's with this constant pacing? It's like he's possessed. He might be more intoxicated than she thought. Or, geesh, could be he's on drugs. Wouldn't put it past those preppy groomsmen to have snuck in a bit of coke.

Rubbing his face, he says, "I can't go into it now. I'll explain when I get back next week."

Next week? Erika shifts her weight. Now she knows he's really lost his mind. "When next week?"

"Wednesday."

Impossible. Absolutely out of the question. "But Hector's coming Tuesday to—"

"Fuck Hector. He's a two-bit reality-show director. He's not Coppola, for chrissakes. He can deal. I'm taking Holly to Montreal for a last-minute honeymoon and that's that. It's only two and a half hours away, but it's got an international border crossing. Best of both worlds."

Her thoughts are spinning. This last week is crucial to the show's success, to their winning the contest. Hector the two-bit director is scheduled to shoot all the canned scenes in preparation for Monday's finale—Holly and Robert "seeing" their new kitchen for the first time (if that damn Lacanche range is ever unloaded from the barge in Newark). Robert grilling kabobs of colorful vegetables in the outdoor entertainment area with "close friends" while Holly bobs in the geothermally heated pool.

That's not all. Holly and Robert are supposed to be using the week to promo the heck out of the finale, with daily YouTube teasers and Instagram posts ad nauseum. This is not the time to be antiquing arm and arm in Les Quartiers du Canal or lingering over espressos in Café Myriade. There is work to be done. Tons and tons of work. There'll be a million decisions to make and who's gonna make them if Holly and Robert are off the grid biking through fallen leaves in the Parc du Domaine Vert?

"Can't you be back by Tuesday morning?" she asks.

"That's hardly a break."

"But what if there's a crisis?" She's beginning to panic more than a little. "What if the Lacanche isn't delivered or the landscapers walk off the job?" *Because you still haven't paid their last invoice*, she adds to herself.

"No problem. You can handle it." He comes over and places his hand on her shoulder. She's getting the impression this is his signature move. "I have total faith in you, Turnbull."

Not fair! She's only an assistant, a grunt hired to pick up cigars, answer email, and nag vendors. She's not supposed to be in charge of the whole enchilada. "We need you and Holly. You're the talent!"

"Right. And we'll be back by Wednesday. Possibly Thursday at the latest."

Thursday! That'll be way too late. Hector needs time to edit prerecorded scenes to trick the viewers into thinking they're happening real time. Shooting these rehab projects requires multiple takes, hours and hours that end up on the cutting-room floor. "Thursday's not going to work."

"Sure, it will. I'll be a phone call or text away. Holly and I will post every day on the *TMB* site. She's already put up a week of posts. Viewers will never be the wiser."

"LuAnn will know," Erika bites back, suddenly feeling abandoned.

"No worries. I've already texted LuAnn about our change in plans. I explained that, upon thoughtful reconsideration, Holly deserved a honeymoon. She'll understand."

Oh, she will not. Whether LuAnn's star rises or falls at *TMB* depends on her project winning the contest. She will hit the roof. She will declare mutiny, and rightly so. But, clearly, Robert is dead set in his ways and cannot be talked out of his impulsive decision.

If Robert and Holly bag out this week, they might as well stick a fork in their odds of winning the *TMB* contest and call it done. That's all folks. Peace out.

"One last thing," he says, leaning in close. Close enough to kiss her. "I need to borrow your car."

This is too much. She gently pushes him away. "Why do you need my car? You have two. Take one of yours."

"Unfortunately, the Range Rover's at Perry's getting winter tires and they're closed tomorrow. No way can I risk taking the Tesla to Montreal. It's too far and there are no reliable charging stations in that dead zone between the Vermont border and the city."

"What am I supposed to drive?"

Opening his wallet, he removes a black card. "This is the key to the Tesla. I'm leaving it with you so I can take your car tonight."

Aha! Now we get to the actual reason for his impromptu late-night visit, Erika thinks, taking the keycard. She's not liking Robert so much right now. She'll be glad when he leaves, quite frankly.

"My Kia has only three thousand miles on it. Be careful," she says, tossing him her car keys just as Robert's phone vibrates with a text. She braces herself. "Holly?"

Reading the message, he grimaces and says, "Yup. She wants me to come home pronto."

"Can hardly blame her. It's her wedding night. You're supposed to be with your wife, not your assistant."

"Not just any assistant. *You*. That's why she's upset."

Heat shoots up her neck. "What's that supposed to mean?"

He opens the door and hesitates. "What do you think?"

Erika doesn't dare say; she wants him to be the first to spit out the truth. "I, I don't know, Robert. I'm exhausted and confused. I'm not following."

"Well, I'm not going to spell it out for you," he shouts, taking the stairs down two at a time. "If you can't figure it out, go ask your mother."

FOUR

KIM

SATURDAY NIGHT

I'm drifting off to sleep when an eerie noise passes outside my first-floor bedroom window. Could be a car—except there's no purr of an engine. My immediate thought is my daughter's sneaking in late and doesn't want to wake me so she's driving really slowly. Then I realize that makes no sense, since she left the wedding before I did—in a snit, mind you—and was already here when I got home, pouting.

Now my Spidey sense is on alert and I get up to peek through the venetian blinds. That's when I see the Mass plates on a car parked in front of the garage and steam comes out of my ears. Robert Barron's freaking Tesla in my driveway—on his wedding night!

I'm so outraged by this brazen display of infidelity and disrespect to his sweet bride that I am about to go over there and rattle their cages when I stop. Now what's he doing? He's sitting in the car having a conversation on the phone, and a pretty animated one, too, judging from his waving arms and elaborate hand gestures.

Probably he's lying to Holly about having to run out for an emergency, as if anything's open at this hour in Snowden. Or maybe they've had their first marital spat and he's come crying to my daughter. I'm riveted, parked by the window, waiting to see what he does next.

It gets weirder.

He ends the phone call and exits the car. Then he pops open the front trunk (no engine) and removes a black plastic bag, quietly unlatches the lid of the garbage can Erika and I share, deposits the bag, lowers the lid—again, super quietly—latches it, and goes back to his phone. A minute later, there's my sucker of a kid letting him in the downstairs door.

I don't know what game he's playing, but I do not appreciate him dumping trash in my can without my permission. We don't have curbside pickup here in our neck of the woods, and even if we did, I wouldn't sign up. The local service charges forty dollars a month for service every other week. Highway robbery.

The landfill charges four dollars a bag, also steep, but between composting and the burn pile, I can get our garbage down to two bags per month and then I take them to the mystery truck parked at the local Stop'n Go on Saturday mornings. I save about two bucks that way. Not enough for a steak dinner, but it's the principle.

Robert Barron, on the other hand, is loaded. Plus, with all that construction, they must have a Dumpster on site at the house. Maybe two. I don't know if he's hiding wrappers from a McDonald's feeding frenzy or vodka bottles, but I'm not gonna let this slide. I'm about to knock on Erika's door to break up the party and tell him to take his detritus elsewhere when I have a think.

No matter what, he's the guy who signs her paychecks, and I don't want to embarrass my child any more than, *apparently*, I already did at the reception.

To be clear, I was acting only in her best interests. Someone needed to rein her in and no one else was stepping up to the plate. What else are mothers for if not to remind you to straighten your posture, keep your elbows off the table, say please, and not outwardly flirt with the groom?

It's not as though I was the only one whose eyebrows were raised by Erika's transformation into a flaxen replica of the newly minted Mrs. Holly Barron. During the cocktail hour, I caught more than one guest pursing her lips at Erika's bridal-ish outfit, and I even overheard someone describe her as "Robert's *nubile* young assistant."

Nubile.

Of course, I'd already said my peace earlier and, in so doing, lit the grenade about to explode between us. She was barely speaking to me when we took our assigned places next to each other at the lovely sit-down dinner. And then Holly and Robert came over to thank our table and it went downhill from there.

You could sense the trepidation as the bride and groom approached. Glasses were lowered. Forks and knives were set down on the plates. Conversation stopped. The other guests at our table sank into mortified silence as Erika took Robert's hand and pulled him to her, cupping her mouth to his ear to whisper a question the rest of us weren't privileged to hear. I couldn't believe the child I'd raised to be constantly considerate was being so rude.

Poor Holly. I was devastated on her behalf. She tried to be a trouper, pasting on her biggest grin, flashing her blindingly white teeth, finger waving to the guests at the next table. She asked us if we needed anything and we gushed about the ceremony, how beautiful she looked, the giant floral arrangements on each table.

Still, Erika continued to clutch Robert's hand, staring up at him pleadingly, waiting for his whispered response. Robert was clearly very uncomfortable and in no mood to engage in a private conversation with his fawning assistant while his bride was inches away, justifiably peeved by the interruption.

Finally, I couldn't take it a minute more. My fingers shot out under the table and squeezed the flesh on my daughter's thigh. *Pinch!* Erika flinched and shot me one of her fierce looks of hate, but it did the trick. She loosened her grip on Robert, who took the opportunity to escort Holly to the next table. Erika watched him go and sighed.

Good. Get used to it, toots. This is the new regime. While Erika sulked, I turned my attention to the delicious pumpkin ravioli and continued my conversation with the elderly man on my other side, another friend of the groom's family.

By the way, that was another strange thing about this wedding. No one from Holly's family was there. No parent, sister, cousin, you name it. No friends, either. Not even a college roommate, which was why Erika, her paid assistant, ended up being the only attendant. I found that very unusual and, also, sad. In my opinion, to have no one from her past in attendance on this special day to launch her future either meant there was something off about Holly's family or there was something off about Holly.

The band started up and that's when I noticed Erika's chair was empty, her dinner hardly touched. I thought maybe she'd gone to the bathroom or was out on the dance floor. Nope. She split, according to the parking attendant, who had to move several cars in order to allow her to leave early. I knocked on her door when I got home to give her a piece of the wedding cake I'd wrapped up in a napkin, but she didn't answer. I assumed she was beat and went to bed early.

Except now it's after midnight, Robert's upstairs in her apartment, his trash in my can, and I'm brewing with curiosity. What was so awful he felt the need to store it in our garbage instead of his? Well, I'm going to find out.

Pulling on my blue fleece robe and slipping on my boots, I shuffle outside and lift the lid. Sure enough, there's the bag. I give it a poke, open it a smidge, and close my nose. There's a faint metallic odor that's somewhat earthy.

Intriguing.

Lifting the bag out of the garbage, I go back to my mudroom, where I leave it on the boot cardboard by the entrance. Then I fetch a pair of rubber gloves from under the sink along with some barbecue tongs, prying apart the plastic tags gingerly. I'm betting roadkill or a dead rat he found in the garage, something too gross to sully his bins.

What I do not expect to uncover is a set of blush-colored women's pajamas made by Lunya in washable silk. Extra small. Each delicate piece spattered here and there with sopping patches of rust-red blood. I don't know what this is about, but I've watched enough Investigation Discovery to know I'd better preserve this just in case.

I wrap it up in the bag, stick the whole thing in my downstairs freezer, and return to bed. Then, like most parents of adult children who make questionable life decisions, all I can do is close my eyes and hope for the best.

Despite the worst.

TMB: LOVE AMONG THE ACTUAL RUINS

POST #63: FOR BETTER OR . . . WORSE?

Hi, I'm Holly Barron, a contestant on *To the Manor Build*, a super-popular rehab show.

This is my unfiltered, no-holds-barred, honest, behind-the-scenes peek at the craziness of turning a run-down Vermont log cabin into a net-zero awesome house with a hot, sexy guy I ~~am about to~~ just married.

My motto: Whatever I can do, YOU totally can do better!

Follow me to see how!

It's a wrap, folks!

Robert and I finally did the deed yesterday. We promised to love and honor till death do us part on a blazing golden autumn afternoon in our very own Vermont backyard. (And by backyard, I mean eighty hilltop acres—*squeee*!)

Duran at <u>Snowdrops Florists</u> assembled the most amazingly awesome wedding arch of fragrant eucalyptus and dark green olive leaves interspersed with pink, orange, and purple dahlias in full bloom along with delicate roses. Everything smelled so dizzyingly fresh!

Robert was drop-dead, be-still-my-heart GORGEOUS in a kilt of Clan Barron tartan custom made for him by Agnes at Loch Kindlich Kilt Shop in Edinburgh, Scotland. Jamie Frasier had nothing on my ma-an as Dave MacLaren, bagpiper extraordinaire, from Rutland, played a soulful rendition of "The Skye Boat Song." I'm getting teary thinking about it. Honestly, people, I am now crying buckets.

Okay, okay. Phew. Pulling myself together. Right.

The most *amaaazing* part is knowing all you lovely viewers were with us from the beginning. Some of the more savvy among you saw our romance blossoming before we did. How awesome is that?

Remember, Robert and I started off as strictly business partners who met in person for the first time shortly after Christmas (Yup. Ten months ago, folks!) He had the house; I had the vision. With my communication skills and his, um, *cash*, we embarked on this transformative *TMB* journey with one goal in mind: to build a beautiful, on-trend, energy-efficient, net-zero house, in an affordable way so you could, too.

We didn't realize our feelings were growing until we planned out the guest room that could double as a nursery. That sparked conversations about someday having kids (we each agree on no more than two for the planet) and how we wanted to raise them so they could be free to roam and explore nature's bounty. We might have killed a few bottles of wine during these late-night talks and, naturally, one thing led to another.

One night in particular stands out. It was during the full moon in June, the pink "strawberry moon." Robert and I were out in the field watching fireflies dance in courtship under the stars, sipping prosecco. He got down on one knee and said, "I have never loved anyone more than you and I never will, Holly. If you don't marry me, I'll die."

The next I knew, there was a sparkly ring on my finger and just like that, all my dreams came true. If you told me back when I was sixteen and living out of my car in Homosassa, Florida, that someday I'd meet and fall in love with a stunningly handsome, dynamic man while rehabbing a hilltop New England estate that would become our home, I would have told you to lay off the crack.

But that's what happened and I'm floating on air.

Okay. Getting back down to earth, A LOT of you have been asking about my wedding gown. "Simply elegant," one commenter said. "Brilliant in simplicity," though there was one snarkster who noted it wasn't exactly *white*. Look, you cannot put a Florida girl with a Vermont tan (i.e., skin paler than alabaster) in a white dress. YOU JUST CAN'T.

That's why Bailey Cho, Wedding Dress Design Queen!, of Mariée et le Marié in Montreal, chose a sexy, body-hugging gown of beige silk (pro tip: Shapewear!) with off-the-shoulder sleeves and a sweetheart neckline and THERE WAS NOTHING SIMPLE ABOUT IT. People, that dress had more hidden support than Bernie Sanders at a Dem Party fundraiser. (Vermont joke: as you know I am TOTALLY 100% apolitical!)

A sweet, dear local town clerk performed the ceremony, which went by so fast. I was afraid Robert would forget his lines because of that dress. (Every bride wants the man/woman she's marrying to admire her with that kind of awestruck gaze, amiright?)

Afterward there were lots of photos and then Bobby Ray and the Jazzhounds started up the band while Sprouts Abundant (don't you just LOVE that name? Believe me, they are EXCELLENT vegetarian caterers who serve way more than sprouts) produced tasty hors d'oeuvres (eggplant crostini and Vermont cheeses with figs, dates, and olives, among others) and entrées of roasted Vermont pumpkin ravioli, sautéed broccoli in chili crunch, and portobello mushrooms with chèvre and wild herbs. To top it off there was the wedding cake to end all wedding cakes: Grand Marnier–infused triple chocolate with a tangerine white-chocolate ganache frosting that was TO DIE FOR! (Thank you Alice's Bakery on Church Street, Burlington).

As the bride and groom, Robert and I couldn't tuck our napkins under our chins, pull up our chairs, and stuff our faces on this feast. We had to MIX and MINGLE and thank all the wonderful friends, family, and staff who'd traveled from near and far to celebrate our joy. We wanted to sincerely let our guests know how much we appreciated them being there.

That's when I heard *it.*

I can't go into details about what *it* was except to say it was an offhand remark made behind my back, after we'd moved to the next table, about a certain woman at the reception whom the guest speculated (wrongly) had designs on my husband. This guest went on to support her upsetting thesis by noting how the "femme fatale" had gone so far as to transform herself into a mini me, right down to the roots of her newly blond hair. Apparently, this love-starved doppelgänger of mine followed Robert everywhere with her eyes.

Readers, I knew exactly to whom this sadly misinformed guest was referring and lemme tell you, the guest couldn't have been further off the mark. I count this woman among one of my closest friends, a loyal and unquestioning ally who's been a tremendous support through the rocky road of property rehab. It was all I could do not to admit I'd overheard the snarky comments and set the record straight.

Since then, I've learned there's been similar trash talk online. (I'm not going to name the subject of this scrutiny, because I don't want to cause her further embarrassment.) All I'm asking is that if you've read comments opining the above on social media, that you discount them immediately. Like I said, this woman is a friend of mine; she would never, ever, ever hit on my husband.

Phew. Thank you so much for having my back on this.

Anyway, gentle reminder, we're one week out to the Big Reveal! Please, please, please don't forget to tune in a week from Monday to vote for Team Holly & Robert on *To the Manor Build*. We'll be live-streaming on YouTube at 8 p.m.

Robert and I want to thank each and every one of you from the bottom of our hearts, not only for voting for #TeamH&R, but for literally bringing us together. Smooches!

Signed,

—Mrs. Robert Alan Barron III (a.k.a. Holly!)

This post may contain affiliate links, which means I earn a small commission when you make a purchase through those links, at no additional cost to you.

FIVE

ERIKA

MONDAY MORNING

Shortly after her alarm goes off, Erika lies on her bed staring at the wooden ceiling of her carriage house, listening to the gentle autumn rain falling on the roof. *Pitter-patter-pitter.* This is her last week of working for Holly and Robert and she's not sure she has the fortitude to handle what's ahead—a jam-packed schedule with camera crews, Hector the director, and LuAnn constantly chattering in her ear.

All of which she must now deal with alone.

It's too much. Less than a year ago, her most pressing duty was checking the half-and-half levels in the steel carafes at the Bon Temps Café, where she was a part-time barista. Now the entire fate of Holly and Robert's *To the Manor Build* outcome rests 100 percent on her shoulders.

Clutching her churning stomach, she rolls over and shuts her eyes, wishing she could stay right here under the covers in her cozy room in the cozy rain. Sunday's sleep-in was a disappointing bust. She tossed and turned, tormented by dreams of Robert crashing her Kia, then her crashing the $100,000 Tesla and the pretty new house on which so many futures hinge burning to ashes due to a wiring error she overlooked.

Robert's left her to fend for herself. She feels abandoned and wobbly. He reassured her he'd be only a phone call away, except . . . he's not.

His last text was the one on Saturday night, when he was standing outside her window. Since then there's been nothing. No calls. No texts. Not one of his perfunctory emails asking her to check on flooring prices or shoot off a thank-you note to a contractor who lost out on a bid.

It's disconcerting and, frankly, disrespectful. No one appreciates being treated like a dirty tissue, tossed in the trash after being used.

She checks her phone, which she checked two minutes ago and two minutes before that. She calculates the number of checks in the past twenty-four hours: 720

Meanwhile, she's sent six messages, each of which deserved a response:

ERIKA: FYI, the Kia's a lease so I need to be mindful of the mileage, K? How many miles are you traveling?

ERIKA: Were you able to reach LuAnn? How'd it go? (Cringing)

ERIKA: Did you make it to Montreal?

ERIKA: Any trouble on the border?

ERIKA: How's my car holding up?

ERIKA: Need advice re: outdoor entertainment area. At your convenience. IMPORTANT!

Zip. Zero. Zilch.

She'd been kind of hoping for a personal response, a *Hey, thanks for coming through last night, Turnbull. Yer the best.* Or, at the very least a straightforward, *Thanks for switching cars. You're a savior.*

Initially, she was disappointed, then worried not to hear from him. Now she's beginning to get annoyed. Robert asks her for this *huuuuge* favor and doesn't have the decency to thank her properly? It's like he feels he's entitled to her car because she's a lowly employee.

Then it occurs to her that there's a very logical reason why he hasn't responded. They're on a road trip and he doesn't want Holly to pick up his phone to search for directions, see his late-night text to their assistant, and get the wrong idea. It'd be easy to do, what with Holly being so sensitive these days.

That post she put up this morning about a femme fatale at the wedding was really off brand. As a rule, Holly never lets the public peek behind the curtains to see her dirty business. It's all sunshine and roses when it comes to the rebuild—and her relationship with Robert. The vendors are fabulous! The contractors are on schedule! Robert is *soooo* romantic and sweet! They are soul mates!

It's as if the knock-down, drag-out fight that stopped production in its tracks the other day never happened. Or that they never bickered about money, which they did constantly.

As recently as Thursday, Robert raked Holly over the coals for blowing the budget on a hand-turned table she ordered from Erika's ex-boyfriend, Colton.

Robert was right that she'd paid too much for the table, but he was wrong to blame Erika for taking Holly to the Snowden farmers' market supposedly to show off her new celebrity friend.

Erika resented the implication. She was simply trying to be supportive of local artisans, since *TMB* was big on that. She figured Holly would purchase one of Colton's hand-carved cutting boards and display it on the kitchen counter out of politeness. She didn't expect her boss to go gaga over every stinking wooden spoon, which were nice but, frankly, a dime a dozen at any Vermont farmers' market.

It was Colton's sales pitch that won over Holly. He explained slowly and seductively his process for choosing which tree to carve, how he spent weeks wandering the local forests until he found the perfect maple, whereupon he would meditate at its roots until the tree gave him "permission" to cut. It was all Erika could do to keep her eyes from rolling out of her head as he recited the prayer he chanted in the original Pawnee before bringing out the ax and delivering the first blow.

"The noise of chainsaws terrorizes nature," he said, running a hand through his sun-bleached bangs. "The decibels upset the audible harmony so trees can't communicate."

Holly nodded in fawning awe. "That makes so much sense. I read a book all about how trees talk."

It didn't hurt that Colton was super cute. Far cuter than when he was plump and pink from being boxed in a cubicle at Edward Jones. Now his skin was leathery brown and his baby fat had disappeared into chiseled muscle. He'd ditched the polyester purple dress shirts with coordinating ties in favor of a worn moss-green tee that showed off his toned biceps. A thin, braided bracelet of ocean plastic in the same deep blue as his eyes circled his wrist, and when Holly made a comment that was mildly profound, he'd twitch his Cupid's-bow lips in deep, spiritual understanding. He smelled faintly of patchouli mixed with goat soap and his most recent bong hit.

"Feel this." He took Holly's hand, extended her index finger, and traced it along a watermark at the bottom of the bowl. "That's the original wood grain and it tells a whole story of the tree's history, its age, even the weather in which it grew."

"Oh, wow," Holly moaned. "I'll never look at another piece of wood the same way again."

Colton gently released his grip while maintaining her gaze. "Not just any wood . . ."

Do not say it. Don't you dare say it, Colton Whitcomb, Erika thought, grimacing.

"My wood."

Yup, he said it!

By the end of their visit, Holly had commissioned a massive Vermont farm table for $7,500 and even wrote out a check for half as a deposit. Colton promised to keep her apprised of the table's progress with regular updates; Holly said she'd like that. Before they parted, he gifted her a pine cone pendant he'd made himself that was supposed to bless the wearer with eternal life and fertility.

Robert hit the roof. He didn't care about the stupid fertility necklace that cost about five bucks, tops, given to her by a stoner woodland hermit. He was livid that they'd budgeted $1,700 for a dining room table, not four times that. Holly burst into tears and Robert had to rustle up flowers and a diamond tennis bracelet to get back in her good graces.

All this ruminating about Holly gives Erika an idea. She texts

ERIKA: Tell Holly it was a beautiful wedding. Don't worry about the project or . . . anything else. We'll be fine.

She waits. No dots. There should be dots. If Holly saw this message, she'd respond with her three-exclamation-point minimum. *THANK YOU!!!*

Okay, this is getting really frustrating. Perhaps she should try another approach, a text that will demand Robert's immediate attention:

ERIKA: So, not quite sure how to use this credit card to start the Tesla. Wanna call and give me a walkthrough?

She glares at her phone screen, summoning a response. Nothing.

A new explanation! International roaming. Robert probably turned off mobile data so as not to be dinged with high charges. Would he do that, though? He's in the final heat of a massively popular property rehab contest. Surely those types of fees would be factored into the cost of doing business. He could write them off on his taxes, probably. He writes off everything else—lunches, ski trips, his car.

In light of that revelation, she's back to email. He can get email anywhere if he has a Wi-Fi connection. Erika calls up her mail app and puts IMPORTANT in the subject line.

> Hi, Robert:
> I assume you crossed the border with no problems. When you get a chance, could you call and give me some directions on how to operate the Tesla? I tried Googling it, but I don't want to screw up whatever.
> Also, we need your contact info: hotel phone, email, dates you will be there. LuAnn will want to get in touch and I'll need to reach out to you if we run into a glitch.
> Thanks and stay safe. We'll keep you apprised on the progress
> E
> P.S. do you have text-messaging ability? Do you want to try WhatsApp?

She presses Send and waits, her heart sinking as the clock ticks. A gloom comes over her, a general sense of anxiety that something might have gone wrong. It's a foreboding, a premonition heavy with evil. There's no rational basis for this onset of the heebie-jeebies—aside from Robert's jumpy behavior in her apartment and the way he called in security for the wedding—but that doesn't allay her mounting fears.

Could he and Holly be in danger? Is that why they needed to leave the country all of a sudden? Robert has been super worried about money lately. The house is mortgaged to the hilt and his own dad cut off his line of credit. This is a crazy idea, but maybe in desperation Robert took out a loan from Boston's organized crime underworld and he's behind on his payments. That would explain his twitchiness the other night. He definitely was acting like a man with a target on his back.

Erika's chest tightens and the muscles in her legs begin to ache. She needs to move, to expel some of this excess nervous energy from lying around the apartment on Sunday, working herself into a tizzy. Exercise. That's the ticket.

Pacing the same short path as Robert did, she counts to one hundred. If she doesn't hear from him by one hundred, she's calling. Screw the roaming charges. It's now almost nine and the Monday workday has officially begun. Robert should be up and about, requesting a report on the day's events.

Her call goes straight to voicemail. She tries again. Voicemail. She calls fifteen times and gets the same result.

Voicemail.

She inhales through her nose and exhales slowly through her mouth, practicing her calming techniques, calling to mind the words of her therapist, Jill. *Examine the evidence*, Jill would tell her. *There's no reason to jump to the most dire conclusion.*

She refreshes her inbox. Nothing. Her heart continues to sink and sink and sink.

On a whim, she sends an email directly to Holly, just to confirm they're alive.

Hi, Holly:
What a beautiful wedding! The best. You looked GORGEOUS.

Erika bets after she's done getting dressed for work, her phone will be lit up with messages from the two of them. She turns off her phone and places it facedown on her bed to resist temptation.

An hour later, an AirPod in her right ear, her iced coffee sloshing in her pink metal travel mug, her laptop in its case over her shoulder, Erika turns on her phone, bursting with anticipation. She'll be so relieved when Robert writes back or—better yet—calls. Then she'll scold herself for being so silly to fret over a nonissue.

She inputs her password and waits for her phone to load, holding her breath.

Nothing.

Okay, this is ridiculous, she thinks, stuffing her phone into her bag. She's wasted the entire morning obsessing about those two, and they're so into their lovey-dovey selves they haven't stopped to consider others might need their attention. Wrapped up in their own little world, they are, the bougies.

On her way to stomping out the door, she notices Robert's Barbour on the floor by the couch. Again, another perfect example of his sense of entitlement. Just leaves behind an expensive coat like it's one of those plastic ponchos they distribute at outdoor concerts.

Well, some of us weren't born with silver spoons in our mouths, she thinks, picking it up and brushing it off and noticing, as she slips it onto the hanger, strange red-brown splotches on both cuffs. Funny. If she didn't know Robert is extremely fastidious and physically adverse to physical labor that might result in any sort of flesh wound, she'd say it looks like blood.

She tries to scrape some off with her thumbnail, her gel polish manicure sliding across the material, thwarting her ability to get a good sample aside from a dusting of tiny dark flakes.

Not blood. Definitely. She's not sure what the stuff is, exactly—perhaps that red paint used in the mudroom? But definitely not blood.

At least, that's what she tells herself, because, as Erika is beginning to learn, the truth doesn't set you free—it makes you crazy.

SIX

KIM

MONDAY MORNING

The Snowden town hall dates all the way back to the nine-teenth century. A creek runs through its dirt basement and the floorboards are four feet wide, hewn from virgin pines logged before Vermont was almost completely deforested. A black soapstone counter runs the length of my office and the walls are paper thin, meaning there's no privacy, either for the ghost occasionally moaning in our attic or for Doreen, my brittle assistant, who's had it up to here with our noisy—and nosy—Listers.

"I'm about to go in there again," Doreen says, thumbing over her shoulder to the conference room where the Listers, our town's elected tax appraisers, are holding a contentious hearing. "You should have heard them earlier. Had tell them to keep it down and they got all pissy. Could have used some backup but no one was around . . ."

Ah, yes, the daily dig about my tardiness. Hanging my coat on its peg, I hand her the Barrons' marriage license for processing and go to my desk. I've learned to ignore my assistant's gripes about my coming in late. What can I say? I'm a night owl. I can't help it if she's up at the crack of dawn, in by eight and out by three. That's her nutty schedule, not mine.

Doreen's from northern Maine, where she spent her youth hauling lobster traps with her brothers on bitterly cold, rainy, miserable mornings at sea. She and her husband, Elliot, moved to Vermont for the warmer climate, the way normal people retire to Orlando. On her off hours, they trap and hunt and traipse through the vast Green Mountain National Forest foraging for mushrooms, morel and psychedelic.

A toned marathoner with close-cropped red hair and a grin that makes babies cry, Doreen can be unintentionally and intentionally intimidating. She once scared a bear by sprinting at him buck naked. Her lower back tattoo proclaims IF YOU CAN READ THIS, YOU'RE TOO CLOSE. From our twelve years of working side by side, I've reached the conclusion she is half raccoon.

"How'd the wedding go?" she asks more civilly as she shakes the license out of the envelope.

"Fast and furious. Great food. So-so music." Booting up my computer, I check my phone for any word from Erika. None.

I tried phoning her yesterday concerning the bloodied PJs that are now a frozen, hard ball in my basement freezer, only to discover I've been blocked by my own daughter. Nor did she answer my subsequent banging on her front door.

Yet again I ask myself, Was she worth twenty hours of back labor?

"Who's grieving today?" I ask, scrolling through my work emails. We're not talking death here, unless it's the death of a property owner's bank account. Grieving is the statutory process of disputing the taxable value of a property as determined by a town's elected board of Listers.

"*The dentist*," Doreen whispers.

The dentist needs no introduction, since Snowden has only one. Dr. Emmons lives in a large Victorian at the edge of town. Never married, no children, no significant others to speak of, he keeps the shades drawn and his lawn unmowed, an instant red flag to certain members of our community.

Historically, our Listers have never been allowed inside the dentist's house for a property assessment. That changed last month, when a maid sporting a dog collar and apparently not quite conversant in the English language graciously served them iced tea and gingersnaps in the parlor. Bingo!

Listers are like vampires. Unless property owners or their agents grant them permission to enter, they have to stay outside. When they have to stay outside, they have to make guesstimates of what's inside and, by law, are directed to assume the quality of the interior and fixtures are the absolute best. Top notch. You really screw yourself over when you don't let in the Listers.

Case in point: Dr. Emmons. After their interior inspection,

the Listers reduced his assessment by $100,000, thereby lowering his taxes by at least two grand. But Dr. Emmons was incensed, not grateful, since during the inspection Dex and Morty, our dynamic duo of tax appraisers, happened to stumble on a basement of "exercise equipment."

Hence, the esteemed doctor's request for an immediate grievance hearing, which, judging from his thundering voice and table pounding, is going about as well as might be expected from a medical professional humiliated by the outing of his private sex dungeon.

"I'll sue the town until it's bankrupt!" Dr. Emmons yells from the other side of the wall. "You know damn well I'd never allowed the Listers in my house and never will!"

"And because of that, you've been overassessed," replies Dex, a retired farmer and himself the owner of a million-dollar estate. "Look, Morty and I counted only twelve fixtures, not twenty, as we'd had to estimate previously because you denied us access. That's a savings for you right there. As for the, er, remodeled playroom downstairs, even with the new wall-to-wall and recessed lighting, you'd be surprised. We downgraded the room since some prospective buyers might find the anchored handcuffs, you know . . . off-putting."

"Haylee Dawn Beauregard?" Doreen frowns at the license. "So that's why she keeps calling."

"Who?" I ask absently, deleting a slew of junk mail.

"Tammy Beauregard. She's called here a number of times asking if we know how to reach someone named Haylee Beauregard. Had no idea who she was talking about."

"That's odd."

Doreen flips through her desk calendar, where she keeps a written log of calls, including phone numbers, by date, a habit she picked up while serving in the US Navy. I used to tease her about being so antiquated, but once or twice her scribbled notes have turned out to be surprisingly helpful.

"Let's see. Twice. August thirtieth and then again just last week. Thursday. Claimed the matter was urgent." Doreen neatly replaces the pages of the calendar.

"What did you tell her?"

"I said I was sorry, but there wasn't anyone in town by that name. Nothing in the land records or voter rolls, either. I checked. How the hell was I supposed to know Haylee Beauregard was Holly Simmons? I'm not a mind reader. Should I tell Erika?"

"Better you than me. I'm giving her some space. She's not exactly happy with me these days."

"Again? You're always on her shit list." Doreen types out a recording statement to imprint on the back of the license. "She's just manipulating you, you know."

Here's the thing: Doreen's never had kids. Yes, she's a supremely generous aunt who's a second mother to her nieces and nephews, whom she loves with all her heart. But that's not the same as surviving the turbulence of daily coexisting with a teenager who hates your guts. I tend to take her parenting advice with a grain of salt, and maybe that's a mistake. Doreen has a tendency to be 100 percent right about everything. Eventually.

"Relax, Bob," Morty is saying now to the dentist. "Our only interest is in making an accurate assessment of taxable value. We don't care about anyone's dirty laundry."

Those two don't know from dirty laundry, I think, my thoughts gravitating magnetically to the frozen ball of blood-ied PJs. I find them really disturbing, especially the way they're wedged in my freezer between a turkey roast and a bag of peas that will someday be thawed and consumed. If only there was someone I could talk to about this, seeing as how Erika is giv-ing me the silent treatment.

At the sound of scraping, I look up from my emails and see Doreen sharpening her pencil with a pearl-handled buck knife.

"Pssst!"

She whips around. "What?"

I nod to our concrete bank vault where we keep the land records, our own cone of silence. I get up and go in. Two seconds later, Doreen enters and shuts the door. "What the fuck's up?"

"I've got a problem."

Doreen nods. She loves problems. "Bring it."

I tell her about Robert's visit to Erika's apartment and my discovery in the trash. "Whaddya think?"

"Well, it definitely meets the definition of creepy." She studies the spines of our black vital record books as though they might contain the answers. "Maybe Holly had a heavy period and he was being the gentleman, disposing the evidence, so to speak, in a container where the paparazzi wouldn't find it during their Dumpster dives."

"They have paparazzi?"

Doreen shrugs. "These days everyone who's anyone has paparazzi, right?"

"No clue. I'm so out of it."

"Tell you what I do know," Doreen continues. "If I forgot to change a tampon or whatever, I sure as hell wouldn't throw away perfectly good PJs. Didn't you say they were washable silk?"

"Not cheap, either. I looked them up online. Like two hundred bucks."

Doreen lets out whistle. "Dunk them in cold water and baking soda. Good as new. Where are they now?"

"In my freezer."

"Remind me not to come to your house for dinner. Why'd you put them there?"

"To preserve them, in case they turn out to be evidence."

She half smiles, tolerating my paranoia. "Here's some more oil you can throw on the bonfire of conspiracies I see you got burning in your noggin. While I was processing that marriage license, I remembered that last fall a woman who said her name was Haylee, *ahem*, spent about two hours going through our property records. She was a brunette then, but approximately the same build. Trim and tidy, kind of like your daughter. And, as we all know, anyone can change their hair color, right?"

"I don't remember a Haylee coming to the office."

"Probably because you were home, late again that morning. Anyway, now I'm thinking she might have been Haylee Dawn Beauregard. What're the chances they're two different people, huh?"

"Slim. I read in a *To the Manor Build* Q&A that Holly's first-ever visit to Vermont was last winter. You have any idea what was she researching?"

"Our policy is don't ask, don't tell, right? So, I didn't."

Then an arresting thought crosses my mind. If that really was the same Haylee, then the only reason she would have been in the office would be to research a certain tax sale in which her future husband ended up with a plum piece of Vermont real estate for a pittance.

Lately, I've had some regrets about how I handled that sale as the collector of delinquent taxes. My intentions might have been noble, but because of my bold decision to go outside the law, a struggling young family was booted from their homestead, losing the log cabin they'd built by hand.

It's almost too painful to think about. I remember when Zeke Strickland dropped off his building permit at the office. Muscled and tanned, he was such a rugged, hardworking young man full of big plans to live off the grid on land he and his wife, Gretchen, had scraped together all their pennies to buy. He dug the foundation, put up the walls, and even built a chimney for the woodstove. It was straight out of Laura Ingalls Wilder.

And then random tragedy struck. While shingling the roof, Zeke fell off the ladder and hit his head, supposedly causing permanent damage to his brain. I don't know how that injury affected their finances except that they stopped paying their taxes. Gretchen was trying to make ends meet, I'd heard, by selling honey from their beehive and crocheted washcloths at the farmers' market. With Zeke out of commission, whatever she was earning from a few jars of honey and some cheap cotton dishcloths would barely cover the cost of cereal for the twin toddlers they now had.

When they fell into arrears after a year, I tried to contact the Stricklands to see if we could work out a payment plan. Zeke was unpleasant, to say the least, a far cry from the grinning, determined man bursting with enthusiasm when we first met. He was surly, angry, and every other word was a crude expletive.

Gretchen had left, he said, and taken the kids with her. I could go fuck myself and my payment plan. The town was going to take his property over his cold, dead body, because he wasn't leaving without a fight. They'd have to drag him out. It was a little after ten a.m. when we chatted and I'm pretty sure he was blind drunk.

Eventually, the sheriff did literally drag him from the cabin per the eviction order secured by the new owner, Robert Barron, and, as he promised, he made quite a scene. Zeke was kicking and punching wildly, vowing to burn the place down and to make Robert pay if it was the last thing he did. Fortunately, the sheriff was able to slap him in handcuffs before he was able to reach for his guns.

None of that would have happened if I hadn't done what I did. It'll haunt me forever.

"You okay?" my assistant asks.

Rousing myself back to the present, I see her giving me a crooked smile, like she knows exactly where I've mentally gone, which is definitely possible. She's Doreen. Nothing happens in this office without her knowledge, and just because we haven't discussed the illegalities of the tax sale doesn't mean she's unaware of what I did. She's really, really good at holding her cards close to her chest, which might explain why she's the reigning poker champ down at the Legion.

"You seem lost in thought. Anything I can do to help?" she coaxes.

"It's nothing," I lie, pointing to the permit binders. "I remembered I forgot to send in the town hall's water-system renewal application to the state DEC. It was due Friday."

"Pssh. The state doesn't care. They're all working from home, out taking hikes with their dogs. Submit it and you'll be fine. It's not like it'll land you in jail." She pulls down the black marriages record book from the shelf. "At least, not for that."

SEVEN

ERIKA

"Silver Sage? This isn't Silver Sage; this is mint and I *haaaate* mint!"

Erika can't help feeling the mismatch is somehow her fault as Vanessa, the interior designer with a shock of blue hair, stomps her foot in frustration. If only Holly were here. She's the one who selected the color.

"I dunno," says a painter working his way through a small bag of Fritos, waiting for this sage/mint dispute to be resolved. "To me, it looks kinda like gray."

"That's even *more* depressing," Vanessa declares. "We're not decorating a prison. We're supposed to connect with Vermont's natural outside beauty. Get it?"

She flaps a hand back and forth between the gray/mint

trim and the huge floor-to-ceiling thermal window, beyond which landscapers are busily plugging in drooping Sawara cypress and blue holly to coordinate with the red of the brilliant winterberry. It's a mad rush to beat an unexpected early frost. Anything that could go wrong is going wrong fast. They are experiencing Murphy's law on warp speed.

The weather, for instance. Sleet is now in the forecast. Somehow in all the planning, no one stopped to consider the possibility that they might not be blessed with blue skies and jewel-toned foliage for picture-perfect exterior videos in the third week of October in northern New England. Now Team H&R is in a mad dash to lay the sod and spread the cedar mulch so they can film the house before the shiny new build is dulled with dark clouds.

Vanessa spins around to Erika. "Holly needs to make the call. Put her on speaker so we can all hear what she has to say."

Erika tenses. She's been dreading this request. "The thing is, I've been trying to reach her and can't."

"What do you mean?" Vanessa pulls out her phone, her blue fingernails flicking over the screen. "Where is she?"

LuAnn, chiming in from LA via the laptop on a side table, answers that. "On her spur-of-the-moment honeymoon, apparently. Out of the country."

Vanessa yanks off her trendy, orange cat's-eye glasses. "No one told me they were going on a honeymoon. For how fucking long?"

"Robert said he'd they'd be back Wednesday," Erika replies weakly. "Maybe Thursday, at the latest."

Vanessa tosses her glasses onto the borrowed teal velvet sectional. "You have got to be fucking kidding me. We are *sooooo* behind. They should be on site prepared to put in ten hours every day at the minimum. There are tons of details they need to sign off on. What's Hector have to say about this?"

"He was not pleased, to put it mildly." LuAnn taps into her own phone four-thousand miles away. "Look, people, I'm as upset as everyone else on the team, especially since I was given no notice. Found out when I touched down yesterday in LAX. Robert shot me a short text with hardly any explanation. Haven't been in contact with them since. Erika, have you had any luck at all?"

"Texts. Calls. Emails. Nope." Erika shakes her head, also baffled by the couple's silence. "No luck." Which does not sit well. Not at all.

If anything, Holly is an overcommunicator who automatically texts and calls before she thinks.

Is the red in the mudroom too ocher?

I'm thinking maybe a turkey wrap for lunch. No, one of those cucumber salads. I feel bloated.

Did I have something in my teeth on the Zoom. I saw later in the mirror there was a piece of cilantro.

Oooh, did you catch Love Island last night? Craaazy.

Is it my imagination or is there more space junk?

I'm soooo tired. My feet are KILLING me.

Hey, have you ever done mushrooms? Robert has a guy . . . Very "mind opening."

Don't forget to order more of that cardamon tea. I am addicted!!!

So, not hearing from Holly going on forty-eight hours raises more alarms than it would for most people, even if she is on her honeymoon.

"I can't understand why they left to begin with," LuAnn says. "Holly and I spoke at the wedding. They planned to recover Sunday and then throw themselves full throttle into the final days. She was totally pumped. It doesn't make sense that all of a sudden they'd leave the country and, apparently, cut off all communication."

Erika debates whether to relay how agitated and manic Robert was acting the night he came to the apartment to borrow her car. But she decides sharing those personal details would be disloyal, like she'd be bad-mouthing her boss behind his back. Besides, as their assistant, Erika feels that her job is to put Holly and Robert in the best light, not to sow seeds of doubt in the minds of *TMB*'s producers.

"Well, that's it! We've lost the contest." Vanessa flings herself onto the couch, even though no one's supposed to sit on the velvet. "Go with the prison-green paint. I'm booking the next flight to London to handle clients who actually care. And pay."

"We're all disappointed," LuAnn says. "But that's the risk you take when you're dealing with nonprofessional talent. If we don't hear from them soon, we might have to announce that the Vermont project is out of the contest in order to allow Holly and Robert space to address the proverbial 'personal issues' et cetera, et cetera . . ."

Erika laughs at the absurdity until she notices LuAnn's not smiling. Wait, she can't really be serious. *TMB* wouldn't pull the plug so late in the game, not after the hundreds of thousands of dollars Robert's sunk into this house and their back-breaking efforts to make it a winner. *Would they?*

"Totally. Better to cut your losses now," Vanessa adds morosely. "The vendors will be pissed, but at least *TMB* will get a write-off."

"*No!*" Erika hears herself shout. "We are not going to give up. We can't!"

Vanessa props up on her elbows. "My, my. What's gotten into Miss Mouse?"

"I've got an idea," Erika says, though she doesn't quite. Not yet.

"Oh, please." Vanessa flops backward. "Spare me the can-do 'tude."

"Give her a chance, V.," LuAnn chastens. "Go on, Erika."

Finding herself suddenly on the hot seat, Erika feels her armpits dampen as she furiously brainstorms. "Okay, so, this may sound whacked, but how about I sub tomorrow when Hector comes to shoot? I'm about Holly's size and now we have the same hair. I can raid her closet to find an outfit Holly can wear during the reveal, for continuity." Her mind is racing and her body feels disassociated, her lips moving faster than her thoughts. "Hector can use me in the prerecorded scenes. No facial close-ups, naturally. No voice. Production can do their magic and Holly will be back later to do the live-streaming. Problem solved!"

LuAnn nods slowly. "A body double. Interesting. Let me run this by Hector. I'm not sure it'll fly, but I applaud your ingenuity. Meanwhile, leave no stone unturned trying to reach out to these two." She holds up her phone, pointing to a message.

"Just heard from legal. Off the cuff, they say Holly and Robert are in breach of contract if they don't get on set pronto and that'll be grounds for cancellation as well as a lawsuit to recoup *TMB*'s costs. Pass this along to Robert when you reach him. That'll get him out of bed."

Erika's stunned. Was she mistaken or did the producer actually consider her suggestion?

"What about the sage?" Vanessa finds her glasses on the floor and slips them back on. "Who's gonna sign off on that?"

"Go with your gut," LuAnn says. Then, pausing thoughtfully, she adds, "What's your take, Erika? Is the green too minty?"

Erika chews the tip of her pen and squints, as if a powerful producer asking for her opinion is as common as LuAnn asking her to whip up a soy latte. "V. might be right. Farrow and Ball makes a lovely sage called Calke Green that won't turn gray against the Slipper Satin on the walls."

"Not bad," Vanessa concurs. "But you can't get Farrow and Ball around here and we need it pronto."

"I can color-match it to Benjamin Moore at the hardware store downtown. I could have a gallon here in a half hour, ready to go."

"Works for me," says the painter, crunching his Frito bag into a ball.

LuAnn nods again. "Good job, Erika. You have certainly earned your stripes today."

Don't speak too soon, Erika thinks. *The day's not over.*

EIGHT

ERIKA

After returning from the hardware store with a gallon of Benjamin Moore's Saybrook Sage in pearl for the painters and a small container of vanilla Greek yogurt for her lunch, Erika enters Holly's office and closes the door.

Erika likes this room because Holly insisted on keeping a log wall, the only remnant of the original cabin built by the Stricklands, over Robert's protests that the logs were energy inefficient. To Erika, the logs are authentic Vermont and homey, especially juxtaposed against Robert's cherished concrete.

The three other walls are painted a calming blue—Healing Aloe—that goes well with the wide-plank floors in southern pine. Holly brought in wrought-iron daybed with a locally stitched quilt in a print of pale yellow flowers to match the pots of kalanchoe by the one window, and once Erika found her napping there, hugging a worn stuffed bear. She looked like a little girl, small and vulnerable.

A bamboo standing desk with Holly's iMac takes up most of the far wall. Erika lowers it to a sitting position, pulls up a chair, and goes to work, buoyed by her unexpected success with LuAnn this morning.

First on her to-do list is checking the status of the Lacanche Cluny Classique model gas range in french blue with brass hardware. It was ordered in June with the understanding that it could not be delivered for six weeks. Now it's October and allegedly the range is being held up in a container port outside Newark. This has been an ongoing headache. Customer service has started answering her calls with, "Sorry, Erika, no developments," before she even has a chance to speak.

To her delight, the news is for once positive. The French range has been sprung from captivity and is on I-91 rolling toward Vermont. All Erika has to do is beat the bushes for skilled laborers to install the foreign stove—no easy feat with this short notice. Fingers crossed, the $16,000 range will be front and center by the reveal.

Next up, Colton and the table. This has her worried. He was supposed to have it delivered before the wedding. However, he messaged her *during* the wedding that he'd run out of the heirloom beeswax he uses to finish the wood, so it wouldn't be ready until Tuesday.

His attitude was annoyingly blasé, which might mean the table's as exquisite as he's been boasting or it's still a pile of sticks in his mother's basement. The longer Colton takes to produce the goods, the more Erika fears it's the latter. She has her reasons.

For starters, he didn't take measurements of the dining area until last month and even then the lumber wasn't cut. He told Holly he was trying to choose between two maples to determine which wanted to be immortalized as a center of familial "break fasting." Instead of Holly cracking the whip, as any right-minded customer would do, she poured him a cup of yerba maté and they discussed wood spirits and modern Druidism. One of those maples could have been down and split in the time it took to hold their impromptu tea party.

Despite Colton's promises at the farmer's market to keep Holly apprised of his progress, it's been mostly crickets since then, though not for lack of trying on Erika's end. She leaves yet another message on his mother's home phone urging him to confirm he'll deliver the table tomorrow, but she's not holding her breath. Colton went AWOL when he dumped her via text last year, too. When it comes to confrontations, Mr. Naturalist prefers to hide under a rock.

Those tasks done, Erika devotes the rest of the afternoon to hunting down Holly and Robert. On LuAnn's advice, she launches her search by calling Montreal's choicest hotels. None of the top ten hotels on Tripadvisor claims to have guests registered under those names, though Erika realizes that might be because Robert booked them under pseudonyms to avoid being spotted by fans . . . or maybe the head honchos at *TMB*.

On a hunch, she loads Holly's app for the security cameras at the house and is puzzled to find all four have been deactivated. The last images are from Saturday morning around eight a.m., when the rental company arrived to deliver the folding chairs.

Because of the wedding activity, Robert or someone must have turned off the cameras and then forgotten to turn them back on. He's usually hyper alert for saboteurs, a holdover from working on his father's gentrification projects in Roxbury, Massachusetts, where the elder Barron's cameras regularly caught protestors trying to tamper with equipment. Perhaps there was an electrical malfunction or maybe Holly accidentally switched them off. Erika moves on, another question to ask the couple when they return.

Having exhausted all other options, Erika debates calling their parents. She doesn't want to unnecessarily spike alarm by reaching out to Robert's father, but she is running out of ideas. As for Holly's mother, that's a dead end. Those two haven't spoken in ages, apparently.

Holly must not totally hate her mom, though. Otherwise, why would she keep a small silver-framed photo of her on the shelf?

Erika picks it up and runs a finger along the silver frame. Tammy Beauregard looks not much older than Holly herself in this picture. Thin with the sun-kissed skin of a lifelong Floridian, she's at a beachside bar, her lips a coral pink smile, her french-manicured nails stroking the stem of a chemically green margarita. She looks nice enough. Kind of fun, actually.

Too fun, perhaps. Holly once quipped that her mother "was always out drinking and entertaining clients, never at home taking care of me" when she was growing up. Erika didn't know Holly well enough then to press for more details and didn't want to upset her further by trying, especially since, after making the comment, her boss grew very quiet.

The office phone rings, jolting Erika out of her revery. Her initial hopeful thought is . . . Robert!

"I'm looking for my son, is he there?" The dictatorial tone is unmistakable. The two men sound identical when they're in a mood.

"Hello, Mr. Barron," Erika says, relieved he, not she, is doing the reaching out. "Robert's not here right now."

"Where is he? He's not answering my calls or texts and I've been trying since Sunday."

Well, that answered *that* question. "He's on his honeymoon, though no one appears to be able to contact him or Holly. I suppose they want to be alone?" She puts that in a question to avoid an argument.

"That's no excuse. I've got a bone to pick with him about underpaying the security team I brought in at not inconsiderable effort at his insistence. Of course, the eleventh-hour security wouldn't have been necessary if he'd taken my advice weeks ago and nipped the problem in the bud."

Having never had a father she remembers, Erika isn't used to the startling effect of a man in full-throttle indignation demanding accountability from an offspring. It's almost as if she were his daughter and he's furious at her for something *she* did wrong. It's not fair.

"I'm, I'm sorry," she stutters. "I don't know anything about this. Was there a problem weeks ago?"

"I thought for sure you knew. Robert said that jackass sent the photo to your phone. You're his assistant, no?"

"Yes, but . . ." Her head is swimming in confusion. "Robert said he requested security out of an abundance of caution. He never mentioned anything specific."

"Because he was ashamed of being outed as a wimp and rightly so. A Barron would handle this himself like a real man, I told him. We don't go running to the police so they can air our private affairs in a public report. Go root out this Strickland fellow and show him who's boss. That's how you deal with bullies who are too chicken to meet you mano a mano, who have to resort to sending anonymous letters in the mail for chrissakes!"

A cold, clammy sensation is rippling through Erika's entire body as the elder Barron gleefully goes on and on about how he would have taken "the hillbilly" in hand. She can barely pay attention; all she can think is . . . *What letters?*

A tickle rises up her neck. Robert never mentioned anything about Zeke Strickland other than referring to him as "the prior owner," and that was usually in the context of the rehab: "The prior owner's well is inadequate." "The prior owner should have put the stone wall here." "The prior owner butchered that orchard."

Most of what she knew about Zeke Strickland was from conversations with her mother at the dinner table, and that wasn't much, except that he'd suffered a traumatic brain injury from falling off a ladder and lost his ability to work. Then he lost his family and finally his property. Her mom felt really bad about his string of bad luck.

Bert down at the general store was far less generous.

Months before, when he learned Holly and Robert had hired her as their assistant, he said, "I'd think twice about working for them flatlanders, dear. They had the sheriff drag the guy who lived there out of his own cabin and from what I heard he vowed to get back at Barron for stealing his land and may I say I can't blame him. Still, he ain't right in the head, you know. Used to take potshots at hikers for trespassing. No telling what he might do to Barron." Then he mimicked a shiver.

Erika had dismissed him as Bert being Bert, as usual trashing his favorite targets—flatlanders—despite their being his best customers.

After assuring the elder Barron his son will call him as soon as he gets in, she hangs up and goes to her purse to fetch her keys, one of which is small and made of silver metal. It fits in the bottom drawer of the filing cabinet reserved for Robert's Robber Barron material. Not even Holly has access.

She wouldn't have access, either, except Robert gave her the key so she could leave the contraband Cuban cigars there. With all that was going on with the wedding, she never had a chance to give it back. The drawer slides open partway, far enough to see the cigars are gone.

Robert's black Dell laptop is there, but she can't wedge it out, because the drawer appears to be stuck. Papers sticking out of a manilla folder under the laptop have gotten caught in the groove on the track, making it impossible to open. She pushes the drawer in and out, trying to dislodge them, and winces at the sound of the paper tearing.

Frustrated, she sticks her hands under the laptop and yanks

out the whole file. It's not thick, but it's messy, filled with envelopes shoved in haphazardly, as if Robert had to hide them quickly and shut the drawer before anyone saw.

All are addressed to THE SO CALLED ROBBER BARRON in dark blue ink, the author pressing his pen so fiercely into the paper, it's made tiny holes. She's come across them before in her daily mail runs. They're the ones that instantly turn Robert's mood sour, worse even than when he has correspondence from the IRS. These must be the letters Robert's father was referring to.

These might explain why Robert was so antsy and restless throughout the ceremony, eyeing the hill as if a sniper were lurking there and then rushing Holly away from the arch once her mother pronounced them husband and wife. Perhaps more disturbing was how he'd arrived unannounced on her doorstep at midnight, demanding to borrow her car so he could hustle his wife to Canada.

What was it he said exactly? *"It's got an international border crossing . . ."* As if the restrictions of going through customs at Highgate, Vermont, were the appeal of the trip instead of visiting a romantic European-style city.

And now he and Holly have gone dark.

Erika gets up and flips the lock on the office door. She's not sure why she did that, except she has a prickly sense she's not alone. Returning to the file, she opens one of the envelopes and removes a piece of graph paper. She does the same with the next and the next. Hands shaking, pulse racing, she lays them out on the southern pine floor, where they make a square of monomaniacal madness.

Though they're unsigned, she can see why Robert told his father they were from Zeke Strickland.

"He's moved on," Erika overheard Robert comment once when he and Holly were discussing whatever happened to the "prior owner." "Heard he went back down south somewhere. Or was it out west?"

But this most recent envelope, like all the others, was mailed from Burlington, Vermont, and only days before the wedding. And, like all the others, it's spelled out in letters cut from magazines and pasted onto the graph paper, old school.

aRM FoR aN aRM
eYE FoR aN EYE
yoU sTEAL MY hoUsE
i KiLL yoUR WiFE
ThEN TAKE yoUR LiFE
ThiEVEs RULE

NINE

KIM

At 5:01 p.m., I lock town hall and pull down the shades, though I realize that's overkill. Everyone has left for the day and there are no meetings tonight, so I don't know why I'm being paranoid. It's not as though people have nothing better to do than spy on the town clerk.

Doreen's revelation about "Haylee's" visit has knocked me for a loop. I can't take any chances. Either I toss the file with the damning evidence into my burn pile or hand it over to Gretchen Strickland with a full mea culpa and request for mercy. Intentionally destroying public records would cost me my job. Revealing the truth to Gretchen would cost me my job *plus* legal fees and possibly my house. But I'll sleep better.

I haul the aluminum standing ladder from the damp basement utility room to our second-floor vault where the historical society keeps its archives. At the very top of the metal fireproof cabinet, in the banker's box marked SNOWDEN VILLAGE SCHOOL REGISTERS, 1930–1939, I stick my hand between 1932 and 1933 and retrieve the red file with the notices, certified returned receipts, and supporting documentation of the tax sale I conducted nearly two Januarys ago.

It burns a hole in my bag as I cross the lot to my car, my nerves brittle enough to crack. The mantra hammered into me from when I was an assistant clerk about Erika's age plays on repeat in my brain: *Above all, never remove public records from town hall. Never.*

And, yet, here I am, breaking the law.

Again.

I make a pit stop at the Snowden general store to rustle up food for dinner. In my lifetime, the store's transitioned from a dusty dispensary of basics to a beloved destination for second-home owners who've brought with them demands for french roast, avocados, and daily delivery of the *New York Times*. Its refrigerated cases stock an eclectic assortment of delicacies, from fancy cave-aged Cabot cheese to repurposed plastic margarine containers containing earthworms for fishing, freshly dug by the owner, "Mayor" Bert.

Thankfully, the aisles are still lined with dusty cans of pork and beans way past their expiration dates and jars of green olives stuffed with almonds because Bert's late wife adored them for martinis. Bert recently expanded the cooler to accommodate the vast and, to him, ridiculously named, if profitable, array of Vermont craft beers. In the summer, he is known to light a grill by the front steps from where serves hotdogs for $1.50 while delivering treatises on how he would solve the world's issues. Tourists take photos.

"It's only Monday, Kim," Mayor Bert says as I plunk down a box of chardonnay along with a ready-made Cobb salad. "Tough day?"

I run my card through the machine and give him a look. "Just the twenty percent who cause eighty percent of the problems."

"Amen to that." He rips off the receipt and lays it on top of the salad's plastic cover. "Guess that was quite the wedding you performed. You know, I offered to write up a beverage quote for them and include some local cheese, but they didn't return my calls. Supposedly went with that pricey caterer up in Burlington instead." He presses his generous belly against the counter and leans close. "Word is, the marriage is a sham for ratings."

I fake an innocent smile. "Oh, I don't know about that. They seemed mighty in love to me!"

"Dunno." Bert shrugs. "That's what I heard."

Lifting the boxed wine by the handle, I say, "This should hold me for the night. Thanks!"

He tips an invisible hat. "Be careful driving. The deer are everywhere. It's like they have a sixth sense hunting season's right around the corner and they're going bonkers."

Mayor Bert's not wrong. This is the time of year when deer and their pursuers get a little stir crazy. As a matter of fact, I pass a six-point buck boldly standing on the side of the dirt road not far from a group of camo-covered men sighting their rifles at a white target. They'd better watch it. Dusk is falling, and Fish and Wildlife doesn't take kindly to discharging firearms after sunset.

Out of habit, I check to see if the lights are on in Erika's apartment when I get home. The garage is dark and the driveway is carpeted with fallen leaves. No indication of tire tracks.

Getting out of the car, I lug my belongings into the house, fretting about my daughter. Breaks my heart she's giving me the silent treatment just because of that stupid pinch at the reception. She's not being very mature, but I can't force her to talk. All I can hope is for a crisis to emerge where she'll have no one to turn to aside from her mother. I know that's sick, but that's why boxed chardonnay was invented.

It's now officially dark outside and cold inside. I don't bother starting a fire in the woodstove, since I'll be lighting the burn pile. Shrugging on my late husband's old brown canvas Carhartt for comfort, I grab the file, camp lamp, and matches. Erika makes fun of me for refusing to wash her father's coat even though he died nearly a quarter-century ago. What she doesn't understand is that this ratty Carhartt with its lingering scent of woodsy cologne and Craig's stale sweat is the last remaining intimate connection to the love of my life. We all have our totems.

I pour a Solo cup of tepid subpar wine and head out the door. The burn pile is hidden slightly in the woods, about one hundred feet from the house on the other side of the driveway. Close enough to be convenient and far enough to not be an eyesore. At least the day's rain has ensured I won't be risking a brushfire. A brushfire ignited by the town clerk burning public records. Now there's a local headline.

The gray evening light is sufficient to light the path to the ring of rocks. I kick off the damp cardboard covering the charred remains of the last fire and squat down to search for dry kindling.

That's when I notice the torn magazines.

There are at least four or five, decades old. *Popular Mechanics. People. Bride* and *Us Weekly.* They're sliced up, as if they've been used for a school project. Did some kid dump them here? The culprit could be my elderly neighbor Janice McWilliams, who's a bit of a hoarder. Her basement is stacked with *National Geographic*s going back to 1962 and, I bet, that's not all. Her kids have been up here, trying to clean out the house in preparation of sending her off to assisted living, so maybe they were the ones who dumped this stuff, figuring I'd burn it eventually.

I'm studying an impossibly airbrushed image of Christie Brinkley on the cover of a 1980s *Sports Illustrated* when I hear a twig snap.

I wait, holding my breath. Another snap. It's a deer, I tell myself. That's all. But my primal instincts, already alert in the gloaming, urge me to take heed as the proverbial hairs on the back of my neck rise, alerting me to an intruder. I'm being watched.

In my peripheral vision, there is a shadow on my driveway about fifty feet away and up a slight incline, a figure dressed head to toe in black. Before I can turn my head for a closer look, a sharp crack pierces the tranquil silence of the woods.

Another crack, even louder and closer than the one before, follows.

Instinctively, I throw myself belly down to the hard, leaf-strewn ground, covering the back of my head with my crossed arms. It takes a minute for my disbelieving mind to wonder if I'm actually being shot at. And, if so, what to do?

My heart pounds, pumping me with an overload of adrenaline that's far from helpful. I'm unaccustomed to being a target, so I have no way of discerning if someone's trying to kill me or if I'm overreacting. I feel like the panicked deer who in his fright doesn't know whether to leap left or right, to be frozen in place or kick into a run. My thoughts are muddled.

Another crack ripples through the air and now I'm physically shaking. I can't see him on the driveway and my confusion is transforming to pure terror. He might be obscured by a tree or maybe he's circling around for better aim. I have no choice. My only hope of survival, as dim as that might be, is to be a deer, to hightail it, zigzag, into the woods.

But as soon as I make my move, the piercing whine of a bullet whizzes past my ear and, klutz that I am, I trip over a stone, falling flat onto the burn pile, a sharp rock hitting my solar plexus and knocking the wind out of me with such force, that my face is in the ashes and I'm unable to move.

That's when I hear the shuffling of footsteps coming through the fallen leaves. I could try crawling on my hands and knees, breathless, but it's no use. I can't. I am paralyzed, pinned to where I am.

A goner.

TEN

ERIKA

Erika spent the afternoon sweating about the threatening letters she found in Robert's locked drawer, vacillating between showing them to LuAnn or the police or keeping them secret, as Robert did. There has to be some justification for why he hasn't taken them to the cops, because, according to her brief research, Zeke Strickland has committed multiple felonies.

From what Erika's been able to find out on Google, threatening via the USPS to kidnap or injure someone is punishable by up to five years in prison and $250,000 in fines. And they had to have been sent from Zeke since no one else implied in his letters got his house stolen out from under him. Only him, and, by extension, Erika supposes, his wife, Gretchen. Seems like a slam dunk to her.

The most sensible conclusion Erika's been able to come up with is that Robert was saving the letters to use as evidence in case Zeke followed through with his threats. If this is Robert's rationale, then it's not her place to turn them over to the police prematurely. She might not even have the right, considering they were sent to her employer, not to her, and she discovered them only because she was snooping in his private, locked file cabinet.

On the flip side, Robert and Holly still haven't responded to anyone's emails, texts, or calls. It's been forty hours since they've come up for air. Robert's own father doesn't know where he is. And Erika hasn't been able to confirm that they've checked into any of the higher-end hotels in Montreal, thereby raising the almost unthinkable question: Has Zeke Strickland somehow gotten to them already?

Erika can barely concentrate on the mundane tasks of being an assistant with the thought that somewhere out there this maniac is on the warpath. He could be camped out in the woods using the same long lens he—*might have*—used to take the photo of the wedding arch to spy on her at this very moment.

What if he's lumped her in with Robert and Holly as the thieves who stole his property?

What if he's holding them at gunpoint and precious minutes are slipping away because Erika's too chicken to make a move?

To save her own sanity, she settles on a plan. She will hold the file until she reaches Robert and Holly or until Wednesday evening, whichever comes first. If she doesn't hear from them after that, or if they don't return as Robert promised, then she's going straight to the Vermont State Police with the letters and the mysterious photo. If those aren't enough to get the cops to launch an investigation, she has the advantage of claiming her car has been stolen because Robert took it and he's missing.

Her previous experience with the police around here hasn't exactly inspired confidence in their professionalism or abilities. One cop in particular—a Vermont state trooper she actually went through high school with named Andre Picard—is on her radar as particularly untrustworthy, especially when it comes to discretion. He's known for spilling secrets all over this small town. That said, surely he and his colleagues can handle a basic case of grand theft auto.

In the meantime, there is blessed work to keep her mind occupied. It's fun work, too, since finally she has permission to do what she's always dreamed of doing: raiding Holly's fabulous closet.

Since being hired as their assistant, Erika's been given free rein to roam through the house in all phases of construction and decoration. She's familiar with the functional mudroom, with its authentic barn door and antique soapstone sink, the gleaming kitchen and two-story great room and the loft that overlooks it. She's washed towels in the sunny laundry and once took a nap on the Murphy bed in the guest room. She's tried her hand at billiards in the basement man cave with its mahogany bar and seventy-inch television. And of course she has access to all of Holly's office, even her iMac.

The only area that's been off limits is Holly and Robert's suite on the second floor.

Until now.

LuAnn and Hector approved Erika's proposal to dress like Holly for the prerecords. Having already cleared his schedule and arranged his flight and rental car to arrive on Tuesday, Hector, especially, was not inclined to change plans to accommodate a couple of millennials who didn't have the discipline to honor their commitments. Though he put it much more colorfully.

With tacit permission from the *TMB* powers that be, Erika is off to shop the stash, as giddy as a kid in a candy store.

Her employers' bedroom suite takes up one upstairs wing of the house and was the first area to be completed and filmed. Since Holly and Robert took up residence there, they've kept the door locked and the cameras out. Last month, Hector shot footage of them pretending to be surprised by the finished rooms, snippets of which have been posted online as a tease to the final reveal.

Erika reviewed the footage to recall what Holly was wearing so she could be sure to don the same for their prerecording. *To the Manor Build* has clear rules about the talent's attire. No white or black tops. No green. Jewelry is to be understated so as not to draw the viewers' interest away from the most important aspects—the appliances and fixtures which will be featured on accompanying, lucrative, advertisements. *TMB*'s prime sources of revenue.

In the bedroom shots, Holly is wearing a french blue silk button-down blouse over slim camel-colored leggings. Her hair is half-up, half-down and her earrings are the two-carat diamond studs given to her by Robert as an engagement present. Surely Holly will have taken those with her, Erika thinks, secretly hoping she hasn't, because she would LOVE to try them on.

Not that the camera will be zooming in that close.

With a master key in hand, Erika ascends the floating stairs, stepping quietly on the thick wooden treads as if not to alert Robert and Holly. She hesitates at the balcony, taking in the view of the great room. The setting sun illuminates the twenty feet of windows facing Snowden Mountain, seeming to set its red, orange, and yellow trees ablaze. Here is the aha effect Holly and Robert and their architect struggled to achieve.

Here is what makes their house the winner of the *To the Manor Build* contest.

She checks the time—five o'clock—and makes a mental note to tell Hector that's when he should shoot the final scene at the outdoor entertainment area. Robert will be manning the grill while Holly pulls herself from the heated pool, the setting sun glistening on the glasses of wine and beer being hoisted in salute by their fake friends. The entire *To the Manor Build* run has been leading to this coup de grâce, and Erika is determined that Holly and Robert will not disappoint.

Turning left, she walks along the balcony to the southern side of the house where a set of white double doors marks the entrance to the primary suite. Erika inhales deeply and tries the knob. It opens easily.

Hmm, odd. If Holly and Robert planned to go away for the week, surely they would have locked their bedroom, considering they lock their bedroom when they're out for a jog.

Erika checks her phone again. A brief text from Robert or

Holly would set her mind at ease. A simple "hello" or "checking in" or "thanks."

Nothing. Always *nothing.* Maybe she should stop expecting anything else.

Sliding her phone into her back pocket, she follows a short hallway to the bedroom, most of which is taken up by a king-size bed. The bedroom's relatively modest square footage is offset by the high-pitched ceiling and workable skylights, to let out heat in the summer. Two walls are painted a light dove gray. One wall is lined with six small mullioned windows. The accent wall is a darker gray to coordinate with the zigzag Nordic pattern in the authentic rya rug. The opposite wall isn't a wall at all but a pair of thermal-paned french doors leading to a private deck.

The deck is big enough for only a glass table and two cushioned chairs and faces east to take advantage of the morning sun. There's even a weatherproof cabinet with a built-in coffee maker so the lord and lady of the manor can enjoy their first cups of the day without the interference from guests—or children.

Back inside, a narrow unlit Scandinavian gas-fired stove stands in the corner next to a geometrically stacked triangle of polished logs. In the other corner is an antique mahogany fainting couch, so minimalist you wouldn't want to lie on it if you were actually fainting. Robert made a big joke about the fainting couch on the YouTube snippets, bringing his hand to his forehead as he collapsed and immediately rolled off. He had a point.

The bed is unmade. A half-drunk bottle of champagne lists to one side in a bucket of what was once ice and is now warm water, an empty flute on each side table. Erika leans down to pick up what she mistakes for a tissue and discovers to her horror it's Holly's white lace thong, perhaps flung in a moment of passion.

Her cheeks go hot as she catches sight of Robert's plaid boxers tangled in the Egyptian cotton sheets. Witnessing the aftermath of their lovemaking makes her feel slightly dirty, as if she's a scummy Peeping Tom. She should leave immediately before she stumbles upon another personal item she has no business seeing. Her employers would be furious if they had any idea she was invading their privacy.

Then they should have locked the door, her inner voice says.

No, that's not right. This is their house. They can do whatever they want, Erika thinks, focusing on the task at hand—getting Holly's outfit and getting out—as she rounds the corner into the walk-in closet.

The his-and-hers closet isn't so much a walk-in as a walk-through, connecting the bedroom to the primary bath. The closet is the only part of the house to be degraded with wall-to-wall carpet in a fragile beige and was installed at Holly's insistence. Because carpeting negates the benefits of a radiant-heated floor, Robert had a fit.

Or, rather, pretended to have a fit.

Staged, harmless disagreements are a cornerstone of *To the Manor Build*, and Robert and Holly have not been above repeating the standard fare. When shown this expansive walk-through closet, for example, Holly asked where Robert was going to keep his clothes. They've "bickered" about his "need for a man cave" and Holly's "need for a massive European stove" even though, as Robert noted, the only things either of them can make are reservations. They've gone tit for tat over whether the tiled backsplash in the kitchen should be in a herringbone or subway pattern. (Erika wanted herringbone; Robert didn't want tile at all.) They chose a hand-painted blue and yellow fleur-de-lis to match the French range.

That said, Robert's side of the closet is indeed half the size of Holly's side. It's constructed of manly, dark mahogany with tidy rows of suit coats and wool pants on wooden hangers. Abutting the built-in chest of drawers is a stack of cedar shelves, each displaying a neatly folded thin cashmere sweater in a rainbow of colors.

Erika sinks her nose into the stack of sweaters, inhaling a trace of Robert's citrusy bergamot cologne. She used to make fun of her mother for sniffing her late father's coat the same way, but now she gets it. She picks up a sweater and gives it a squeeze, but it's not the same. He's not wearing it.

Wait. This is Robert's favorite pullover, a heathered gray guernsey he bought in London when he was in grad school. He was wearing this sweater when they met in her mother's office last winter. He would never think of taking a trip to Canada in autumn without it.

Which is when she notices his socks, balled up on the floor next to his Santoni suede chukkas. Okay, now something really is off. Robert's style for kicking around a city like Montreal would be that guernsey, dark, slim-fitting jeans, and those expensive Italian boots. Also, he would definitely wear his beloved leather jacket, which is still on its hanger. He never would have forgotten that.

On a hunch, she pokes her head into the spacious bathroom of floor-to-ceiling marble. The door to the steam shower is still open, one white fluffy towel bunched onto a rack. Robert's razor and shaving soap lie in a small puddle of dried suds by the sink. The couple's matching electric toothbrushes are in their respective chargers next to opened tubes of Colgate.

They're slobs, Erika tells herself. That's all. They were in a rush, packed only a few things for a short stay, and left the place a mess, never expecting their assistant would be in their secluded quarters nosing about. It's nothing more sinister than that, she thinks, going to fetch the next day's outfit.

Holly's side of the closet runs the entire width of the bedroom. The shelves are painted bright white with strips of LED lights under her exquisite shoes, museum pieces in their own right. Holly's wedding dress has been replaced in its white plastic zip-up cover, the veil in its own case.

The kicky plum-colored minidress she changed into for the reception is piled in a careless heap. Erika steps over it and goes to the shirts and pants.

The blue blouse and camel leggings are hanging in their dry-cleaning bag. That makes sense, Erika thinks, taking them down and looping them over her arm. Holly knew they'd be the first things she'd wear upon her return from her trip.

Having retrieved what she came for, she can't resist one last peek. Carefully laying the blouse and leggings on a cushioned bench, she goes over to the French Empire bureau Holly purchased off the internet. "An antique," Holly explained to viewers, fingering the brass lion head pulls. "From the 1990s." All Erika could think was how the drawers would stick in Vermont's summer humidity.

Not today, however. The top one slides open with ease to reveal neat rows of jewelry boxes in gray, blue, and black velvet. Long boxes for necklaces and bracelets. Smaller ones for earrings and rings. But that's not what catches her interest, oddly enough.

It's Holly's passport.

Erika's pretty sure you need a passport to cross the border into Canada. Perhaps this one is expired. She opens it to Holly's smiling face across from her real name: *Haylee Dawn Beauregard*. The passport expires in two years.

She has a thought and goes back to the top drawer in Robert's built-in. She pulls it open and finds a navy billfold. Cufflinks. Someone's old WWII medal. A few loonies. (Could have spent those in Canada.) A Magnum condom in its gold foil packaging. (She will not allow herself to go there.) A photo of him in boarding school wearing a maroon blazer. And a US passport. Also current.

Erika's phone buzzes and she jumps, the passport flying out of her hand, scooting under the bench where she's laid the clothes. Robert, is her first thought. Robert is always her first thought when an unknown number streams across her screen.

"It's my lucky day!" gushes a female voice in a southern drawl. "I'm so glad you answered, Erika. You're not an easy gal to get hold of."

The number might not be familiar, but the voice is. Erika's heard it almost every day on the house landline answering machine. She fetches the passport from under the bench and steels herself for an inevitably awkward conversation ahead. "Hi, Tammy. How are you?" Holly's mother.

"I'd be a heck of a lot better if my daughter returned my calls. I get she's a busy gal who doesn't have a minute to chit-chat with her mama, but I must admit, my maternal meter's been off the charts with worry lately. I got a sixth sense about shit like this, ya know? It'd be such a comfort to hear my baby's voice. Can you put her on the line?"

Erika deflates as she sits on the bench next to the display of designer bags. "I'm sorry, Tammy, but Holly's not here. Really."

"Dang. You got an ETA?"

For once, Erika doesn't have to lie to run interference for her boss. "To be honest, I don't. She and Robert left for a spur-of-the moment honeymoon to Montreal."

"Montreal? Well, that accounts for the incommunicado. With the exchange rate the way it is in Canada, Haylee's probably up there shoppin' till she drops." She lets out a slight laugh, as if this news is a relief. "She'll come up for air when she maxes out her Amex."

Maxes out her Amex.

Shoot. Why didn't she think of that?

Erika snatches up the clothes and hurriedly exits the suite, phone to ear as she rushes down the hallway. "I'll have her call you back when she gets in," she says, practically skipping down the floating stairs. "First thing."

"I do so appreciate that, Erika. And you make sure to take care, too. Don't let my daughter work you too hard. I can hear the stress in your voice all the way down here in Homosassa."

That's not the half of it, Erika thinks, ending the call and rushing into Holly's office. Tossing the dry-cleaned clothing on the daybed, she boots up Holly's iMac, opens her browser, and clicks the bookmarked tab labeled Chase.

Holly doesn't have an Amex—Robert does—but she has a Visa Freedom Unlimited card from Chase she monitors with such regularity her desktop has saved its password. Holly uses the Visa daily, for gas, groceries, online shopping, you name it. Everything except for expenses related to the rebuild. That has a separate, dedicated card. Erika clicks Login and the page automatically populates.

Navigating to Current Activity, Erika scrolls to the most recent transaction, a $462.34 debit from the spa where Holly got a facial hours before she got married.

Since then, absolutely nothing.

TMB: LOVE AMONG THE ACTUAL RUINS

POST #64: WE LOVE TO ENTERTAIN!

Hi, I'm Holly Barron, a contestant on *To the Manor Build*, a super-popular rehab show.

This is my unfiltered, no-holds-barred, honest, behind-the-scenes peek at the craziness of turning a run-down Vermont log cabin into a net-zero awesome house with a hot, sexy guy I ~~am about to marry~~ just married.

My motto: Whatever I can do, YOU totally can do better!

Follow me to see how!

Hey, fellow manor builders! Hope you're all enjoying this yummy autumn, the coziest time of year. I just adore donning a thick wool sweater, lacing up the hiking boots, and heading to the mountains for an invigorating day of clean, fresh air and healthy exercise. The bugs are history. The leaves are falling and the views are spectacular.

Afterward, there's nothing more rewarding than a cup of <u>hot spiced apple cider</u> and a few laps in the outdoor pool.

Whaaaaat?

Yup, you read that right. You can take a Florida girl out of Florida, but you cannot take her out of her (heated) swimming pool. New England's frigid winters and gray skies were bitter-enough pills to swallow. As I explained to Robert, if I was going to move up here permanently, then I needed to incorporate some Sunshine State lifestyle into our rebuild and that meant outdoor entertaining ALL FOUR SEASONS.

Like, don't even argue. This was nonnegotiable.

But how do you create an outdoor entertainment center complete with sauna, jacuzzi, heated pool, and strategically placed firepits for ski-in/ski-out evenings without running up the fuel bills? Remember, our aim here is to show how anyone can construct a net-zero house without sacrificing comfort or needs. Because, let's face it, I *need* to swim.

Here's the AMAZING thing: since we incorporated the pool into the rebuild's design, the geothermal pool I demanded will actually cool our house in the summer and heat our house in the winter through radiant floor heating using the energy extracted from the earth. I know, it's crazy complicated. I'm not sure I understand it myself, but it really works. Click here for more information from a trusted geothermal expert.

Fellow manor builders, I was SO EXCITED about discovering that what at first seemed like a petulant whim on my part turned out to be an energy-saving breakthrough. Think about it: no fossil fuels will be burned to heat/cool our home or heat our outdoor pool. I'm stunned.

Now that we were going forward with the outdoor pool (which would also heat our sauna AND jacuzzi), Robert and I were gung-ho to finish off the entertainment center with a complete kitchen. This meant a powerful grill and pizza oven.

In the end, we chose this island six-burner (marine grade) black stainless steel grill with white granite-topped side cabinets. In addition to the (115,000 BTU) grill, there's an additional infrared side burner and infrared rear burner. It comes fitted with halogen lights in the cooking zone to make grilling in the dark a lot easier.

Robert insisted on an authentic Italian wood-fired pizza oven capable of baking two pizzas at a time and up to thirty (!) pizzas in half an hour. You might be wondering why so many pizzas?

Because Robert and I LOVE to entertain.

Before moving to Vermont, we didn't have the room to welcome guests of any number into our cramped apartments. We'd have to meet in restaurants. Here, it's a different story. Our friends and family will be treated like kings!

To top off the arrangement, we constructed a pergola around the elevated dining area/bar, which will provide shade in the summer and shelter in the winter. Hydronic radiant heating underneath the bluestone-terraced space means we'll never have to shovel snow from that area, ever. (Antifreeze is actually in the pipes.) Finally, we bit the bullet and installed two fire tables AND a hearth with sturdy outdoor furniture to withstand the most brutal storms a Vermont hilltop can deliver.

I cannot wait for when those near and dear to us can come up for a weekend to hike, ski, swim, or just open a book, relax on the hammock under the apple trees, and get away from it all. Our outdoor entertainment center will be where we gather for delicious meals served hot off the grill. I can see us sitting on our new comfy couches sipping our favorite Vermont craft beers and nibbling on artisan local cheeses while the sun sets over the hills and the stars come out. After the sun sets, we'll light the firepits and toast our good fortunes, friendships, and blessings.

So many blessings. Who'd have thought that I, who'd spent many lonely nights in the back of my mother's car while she went to work at a job she detested, would end up building a dream house in heaven? Robert and I couldn't have done this without your support.

Anyway, gentle reminder, we're LESS than one week out to the Big Reveal! Please, please, please don't forget to tune in a week from yesterday to vote for Team Holly & Robert on *To the Manor Build*. We'll be live-streaming on YouTube at 8 p.m.

Until then . . .
—Holly

This post may contain affiliate links, which means I earn a small commission when you make a purchase through those links, at no additional cost to you.

ELEVEN

KIM

TUESDAY MORNING

"This is how we get Lucky." Vermont state trooper Andre Picard removes the dirty plastic milk jug of mysterious yellow fluid from the back of his pickup truck. "Brace yourself."

His warning doesn't prevent the assault to my senses as he pours out the vile-smelling fluid procured from a farmer down the road. The delicate lining of my nostrils sears at the stench of musk, stale urine, ammonia, and dirty sneakers. I have to swallow a reflex to vomit.

"Liquid gold." Andre smiles as he soaks some rags in nanny goat urine. Or, more specifically, urine from a nanny goat in heat.

Baaaaaah.

Lucky, the elusive billy goat who's been terrorizing Snowden the past week, destroying compost piles, uprooting newly planted fall bulbs, trampling gardens, and chewing on garages, regards us with new interest from his perch on top of the metal roof of Esther Bolduc's toolshed. He chews his cud silently, his satanic eyeballs gleaming yellow with intrigue.

As the outgoing town clerk herself, my mother prepared me for the worst when I took over her job: midnight complaints about random animal and/or weapons discharges, angry confrontations over delinquent tax notices, overflowing toilets due to the ancient town hall plumbing, and, lately, unfounded accusations of elections tampering.

But nowhere in her list was assisting the animal control officer in trapping an angry, destructive, and now horny goat, ironically named Lucky, who's jumped his fence and gone on the lam. I've read the town clerk handbook and I have a good inkling this is above my pay grade.

Nevertheless, Lucky needs to be captured and I happened to be in the wrong place at the wrong time when I showed up at Andre's house this morning to report last night's shooting. The trooper was halfway out the door, chasing a tip on the fugitive farm animal, when I knocked.

"I could use an extra hand, if you don't mind," Andre said, stepping into his official Vermont State Police dark green pickup. "Jump in and you can tell me about it on the drive over to Esther's house."

As I detailed the events, however, I began to feel increasingly foolish. I couldn't describe the shooter or if it was a male or female, because he or she didn't speak. When Andre asked about a vehicle, I said I hadn't seen or heard one. The only injury I'd suffered was a scraped knee from falling.

"So, you tripped and fell and got the wind knocked out of you," he said, one hand on the wheel, his elbow out the open window. "Then what happened?"

What I *thought* would happen was I'd meet my executioner. What *actually* happened was—"Nothing." I stared my hands in my lap, silently adding bruised self-confidence to my list of injuries.

"Any footprints? Tire tracks?" Andre pressed.

"No and no."

"Bullets you could find, maybe lodged in trees?"

"Nope."

"Shotgun shells?"

"Nuh-uh." I thought about this. "You know, the Campbells next door were sighting their rifles. Do you think it could have been them?"

"Could be," Andre said diplomatically. "We've had complaints about that crew before, getting liquored up and discharging firearms after sunset. I'll go talk to them."

"That's okay." I didn't want to get my neighbors in trouble. Nor did I want to confess to Andre that, more than likely, I'd worked myself into a frenzy getting paranoid about the Stricklands' possible reaction. The cheap wine probably didn't help my mental state, either.

"Tell you what. I'll alert Fish and Wildlife about the incident once we're done here," Andre said, after picking up the milk bottle of urine from a farmer's house along the way. "My bet is what we have here is a poacher getting a leg up on the season. Every year, illegal takings get to be a bigger and bigger problem because they know we're short staffed and won't catch them. In the dark, he might have mistook you for a deer."

I considered how I must have appeared in Craig's soft brown coat while I was leaning over the burn pile on all fours, inspecting the cut-up magazines. "I should have known better. Should have been wearing blaze orange."

"Naw. You were on your own property. There was no reason to think you'd get shot at before rifle season." He stopped at a light and stared straight ahead. "Then again, when you're driving down the road there's no reason you'd expect to be hit head-on by a reckless driver, either. But it happens."

I shifted on the hard seat, uncomfortable. Goddammit, Andre, I wanted to say, why'd you have to bring that up?

After that little bomb of his, we were silent until we reached Esther's, where I'm actually glad for the distraction of the horny goat.

Andre dips the rag in the urine and squeezes. Good thing he's wearing thick rubber gloves.

"Stand back." Holding the rag above his head, he begins to swing. With his military haircut and built physique, he reminds me of a male stripper who's just ripped off his chaps and is giving the girls a show until I'm rudely shocked to reality when I'm hit by a spray of urine. There is no choice. I will have to cut off my head.

"I told you to stand back," he says, slowly approaching the billy goat.

The buck requires little persuasion. Sniffing the air, he

clambers off the roof and gallops toward Andre, who climbs into the pickup's bed, dangling the rag of romance just out of the goat's reach.

"Get behind him, Kim. Give him a push if you can."

Clutching the animal's furred butt, I lean to the side to avoid a rear kick. Andre instantly grabs him by the horns and yanks him up and in, tying him securely with a rope affixed to the cab. I glance down at my lovely jacket smeared with mud, urine, and lord knows what else.

"Excellent work." Andre jumps off the truck, closes the rear door, and tosses the rag into a bucket. "I'll take this guy back to his home and cite the owner for violation of 20 VSA section 3341, and that'll be that." He rips off his gloves. "You still interested in filing an official report?"

"I'm good. You guys have enough on your hands. And you've gone above and beyond already for the town."

Andre isn't Snowden's official animal control officer. Our official animal control officer used to be a wonderful woman who "got done," as we say around here, after fielding too many calls about an animal hoarder's "petting zoo" down on the River Road. Cows, pigs, ducks, chickens, an obnoxious tom turkey, rabbits, one peacock, and Lucky the goat proved to be too much last summer, and she handed in her notice.

Like other troopers, Andre ends up doing jobs that used to be left to local authorities, whether that's catching dogs or goats or responding to nighttime noise complaints. Those responsibilities use to fall to the constable, but we haven't had a constable in years, which means it can be like the Wild West in this part of Vermont.

On the drive back to his house so I can get my car, he says awkwardly, "I'm sorry if you took what I said the wrong way. I didn't mean to upset you."

"I took it the way you meant it." I've known this kid since he was in kindergarten. He can't pull one over on me. He used to hang out at our house snarfing down boxes of Hot Pockets with Erika and their close circle of friends—every single one of whom eventually dropped her like a hot potato after the accident. "You're still angry. I get it."

"Not angry." He parks in his driveway, shifting into neutral, the engine running as he keeps his gaze straight ahead. "Just sad."

◇　◇　◇

"Thank you for coming to work today," Doreen deadpans as I arrive at town hall a little before noon.

"Andre asked me to help him catch a runaway goat." I hang up my bag, the Stricklands' tax-sale file, intact and complete, inside. "Had to go home and stand under a hot shower for twenty minutes to get the stink off."

"These people want to talk to you and only you." She hands me a piece of scrap paper with a list of phone messages from the morning. "Too bad you weren't here a few minutes ago to see me put a couple of trustafarians in their place."

I wince. This is the danger of leaving Doreen to her own devices. While she's the most warmhearted person when it comes to helping humble folks in need, she has no truck with our more privileged visitors. "What happened?" I ask, dreading the answer.

"Don't worry. Nothing bad. The couple who bought the Rothmans' house came in complaining about the internet around here, said they worked remotely from their jobs in the city and a three-megabyte DSL was unacceptable."

This is exactly the kind of urban whine that raises my assistant's hackles. "*Aaaand?*"

"And the woman in the North Face jacket said, 'Who do I call to get it upgraded?'" Doreen snickers. "Big mistake."

Yes. Yes, it was. The woman was probably perfectly nice and had absolutely no idea that complaints about our primitive internet happens to be one of Doreen's triggers.

"I said, 'Have you tried calling God? Maybe he'll flatten the mountains for you if you slip him an extra twenty.' Then I told her to contact Bill Iverson, who's doing that whole internet co-op thing, and she left satisfied."

"Sounds like you handled it well."

"Of course." Doreen points to the last name on the list. "Andre the cop called right before you got here."

I turn my attention to ANDRE VSP. CALL ASAP. "Must have left something in his truck." I pick up the phone to dial the first number on the message list: Dr. Emmons, the dentist with the S&M parlor. Not a call I'm eager to make, especially since there's nothing I can do for the man.

"It's not about something you left in his truck." Doreen taps the ASAP. "Apparently, it has to do with Erika."

I freeze and hang up the phone just as someone answers the dentist's number. Cops + kid is every parent's nightmare equation, and, from personal experience, my thoughts shoot to the worst. "Oh, my god. Is she okay?"

"I'm sure she is. I mean, he'd have been here in person if she were dead, right?"

Doreen's bluntness sometimes can be a little much to take. "What did he say, exactly?"

"He said exactly to give him a call." She taps the message again. "He needs to know how to reach Erika. He wouldn't say why or what it was about, but he did say it was important. Like, urgent."

TWELVE

ERIKA

Erika awakens full of high hopes. Sitting in the lotus position on her bed, she runs through the morning meditation that's become part of her daily routine, reframing all potential challenges into positives.

The shoot will go well. The weather will be perfect. Lu-Ann will be pleased. Colton will deliver the Vermont farm table. Wayfair will come through with the staging furniture. Most of all, Holly and Robert will call to say they'll be back tomorrow and Erika can forget about those letters locked in the office filing cabinet.

At least the weather is cooperating! Yesterday's rain has erased the ozone, leaving everything sparkling and bright, if not nearly as warm as the wedding day. They will definitely be able to film the exterior of the house with the newly planted landscaping and fresh mulch. The wind hasn't blown off all the leaves, so there'll even be a touch of Vermont fall foliage hanging by a thread. The outdoor entertainment area will be glorious with that fading Fruity Pebbles mountain for a backdrop.

Humming to herself, she showers and dresses in Holly's clothes, relieved to see her ass looks just fine in the camel leggings, thank you. Calling up a screenshot from Hector's earlier take, Erika carefully pins back her hair so it's half up, half down, like her boss's. She shellacs it in hair spray specially chosen for its nonreflective qualities.

She slips into a stylish black belted raincoat almost identical to a designer version Holly owns, grabs her pink coffee cup and laptop bag, and goes downstairs prepared to slam whatever curveball the universe is pitching today as she slides into Robert's Tesla.

Her phone buzzes, but she doesn't answer, even if it might be Holly or Robert. Distracted driving is just as dangerous as a DUI. Look what happened Saturday when she almost got clobbered by that deer.

Look what happened ten years ago, the annoying voice in the back of her mind taunts.

"The past is not the present," she reminds herself, pulling up to the Holly Hill gate and punching in the code. "Keep your nose to the grindstone and your eye on the prize."

The camera crew's van and Hector's rented Audi are in the driveway. They're already setting up to make the most of the morning sun currently blessing the small porch off Holly and Robert's bedroom. Yup, everything is A-okay.

That is until she enters the house, dumps her stuff, and boots up the office computer to check Holly's inbox.

TEAM H&R IS FINISHED! screams the subject line of the email LuAnn sent at 1:00 a.m. Vermont time.

"Crap, what now?" Erika mumbles, clicking on the first of two YouTube links under the message: "Watch this and then Zoom me immediately! We've been blindsided!"

The video is a promotional teaser for *To the Manor Build* contestants Dr. Sam Chidubem and Dr. Concita Jimenez—affectionately nicknamed "Doctor Samita" by their devoted legion of fans. Some genius marketeer came up with a brilliant scheme to post brief bios of the valiant healthcare professionals who will be the first guests to christen the doctors' rehabbed beachside home in Charleston, South Carolina. The images are set to the haunting music of French composer Erik Satie.

Erika is riveted by a nurse detailing months of not being able to hug her children, so fearful was she of passing on the virus to her family. An emergency room doctor says he studied hard and devoted his best years to saving lives only to find he was powerless against an invisible foe that brought him so low he actually considered suicide.

The heartbreaking stories are interspersed with shots of the therapeutic retreat. Flashes of rooms painted in pastel hues, hammocks swaying in the ocean breeze, hurricane lamps, shelves of escapist literature, and a puzzle table on a porch accompanied by a nice cold glass of lemonade.

It's clean and fresh and soothing. The retreat is exactly what a troubled world needs to heal, Erika thinks, simultaneously crestfallen that their own project can't compete and wishing for all the world she could teleport to that porch.

"Congratulations, docs. You win," she whispers, logging out of YouTube and logging into Zoom.

LuAnn jumps into the meeting right away, though it's three hours earlier on the West Coast. Braids tied back under a pink headband, sweat glistening on her brow, the producer appears on the screen breathing hard from a workout.

LA glamorous, Erika thinks. Another place on her bucket list—California.

"You watch the video?" LuAnn asks without introduction.

Erika tells her she did as she multitasks by scrolling through Holly's outbox, on the slim chance Holly may have accessed her email to contact someone. *Anyone.*

"The montage is fantastic." LuAnn swigs from a water bottle. "It's moving and touching and stylish. Totally on brand for *TMB.*"

The most recent message in Holly's outbox hasn't changed from when Erika last checked. It's the one she sent Saturday morning to the caterer asking about staffing.

But wait, what's this?

Erika blinks at a series of messages Holly sent to Colton Whitcomb in rapid succession on Thursday, between 1:17 and 1:35 p.m. Apparently, he told her boss the table would be delayed, but no one told her, the assistant in charge of organizing delivery. She didn't find out until Colton emailed her Saturday while she was busy with the wedding.

"The bottom line is we're falling behind because those two are off on their honeymoon," LuAnn is saying. "Holly's cued post this morning about the geothermal pool is indulgent in comparison to that video. It's also stale. You can tell it's been in the hopper. They should be present and accounted for on Instagram Live. That's what Joel and Sean in New Mexico are doing. Do you know in the past twenty-four hours they've added seventy-six thousand followers? Do you know how many we've gained during that same period?"

Erika's only half listening, so focused is she on the email thread between Colton and Holly.

COLTON: Thanks for taking time to come up here and check out the table last night. Sorry about the delay, but I believe it's worth waiting for the beeswax. I don't know if I mentioned this, but I special order it from a melittologist in Colorado who harvests limited supplies based on the energy of the colonies. The bees are on their own schedule. They cannot be forced.

HOLLY: The table's exquisite, Colton. I am sooooo excited to get it into the house. Once Robert sees how magnificent it is, he'll come around about the cost. I know he will!!!

COLTON: I'd like to meet him.

HOLLY: Hmmm. Better if we orchestrate our own reveal.

COLTON: Bee (pun intended) that as it may, I always enjoy our visits, Holly. I find connecting with the client on an intimate level imbues my craftsmanship with meaning.

HOLLY: That's great!!!

Erika has two thoughts. The first is that, yay, the table really is done and Colton's not as much of a space cadet as she feared.

The second thought is far more troubling: Holly and Colton apparently have been meeting on the side, without Robert's presence. Which wouldn't be a big deal—Holly meets with lots of contractors and vendors on her own—except that she's deleted this email thread from her inbox.

Why?

"Are you listening, Erika?"

Erika hurriedly switches to LuAnn, who's frowning from the laptop. "Sorry. Multitasking."

"This is most important so I need your devoted attention. I'll tell you how many followers Robert and Holly have gained in the past twenty-four hours. None. *Zeeeerooo.*"

"That can't be true," Erika says, calling up their Instagram page. "We picked up tons from the wedding."

"Not as many as we'd anticipated, unfortunately." LuAnn massages the bridge of her nose. "Anyway, we can't turn back time. What I need now are three solid suggestions on how you're going to reverse this trend immediately and up our numbers. Otherwise, there's no reason whatsoever to keep the production going."

Almost on cue, Hector shouts, "Cut!" from somewhere outside. Erika inwardly groans. There are so many fires to extinguish and loose ends to tie. It's overwhelming. Hector will demand multiple takes and she has yet to cut the vegetables and spray them with glycerin. She doesn't have a minute to spare noodling around Holly and Robert's Instagram account.

"I'm not sure what I can do," she tells LuAnn. "I have to go soon. Hector has me standing in for Holly, remember?"

LuAnn lets out a long, slow sigh. "Right. Shit. How long will that take?"

"I don't know. The weather's good here. Hector will probably want to cram it all in."

"*Eriiiikaaaa!*" He's calling her name from the living room loud enough for LuAnn to overhear.

"I get it," the producer says. "Call me later so we can brainstorm. I'll see if I can lasso in our social media coordinator. In the meantime, remember—if we don't hear from Holly and Robert or from their representatives by the end of the day, that's it for this project. We have got to cut our losses to avoid a debacle."

Erika pulls on her fingers, trying not to freak.

"I will add that I lost sleep last night over those two," LuAnn says. "They may be nonprofessional actors, but it's not like them to go completely silent. Between you and me, do you think there's a reason to be concerned, like, for their safety?"

"*Where is that assistant?*"

"Concerned?" Erika's thoughts instantly shoot to the disturbing letters locked in the bottom drawer a foot away, to the disarray in Holly and Robert's bedroom upstairs, to the passports in their drawers, to their stone silence. All bright red flags waving alarm.

WWRD? What would Robert do? The question requires no hesitation. He's sunk hundreds of thousands of dollars of his own money—and his father's money, too—into this project, on the risky gamble he'll win the contest and recoup their investments and then some in product endorsements and influencer deals.

Robert would want her to fight for Team H&R. He would want her to save his bacon by assuring LuAnn and the *TMB* honchos breathing down the producer's neck that everything will be fine, that this house is a locked-in winner.

What would Robert do?

He would lie.

"Not yet!" Erika says brightly. "Robert said they'd be back by tomorrow and I'm sure they will. I mean, what's the worst that could have happened?"

Wrong choice of words. She realizes her mistake as soon as LuAnn leans into the camera, suspicious. "What's the worst that could have happened? I get the feeling, Erika, that there's something you're not telling me."

Erika shakes her head, but says nothing. She doesn't trust her tongue not to tell the truth.

"Let me remind you that as their producer, I have to be apprised about every detail of this project, good or bad, especially bad. If I find out you haven't been forthcoming, I will see to it personally that you never work in this business again. I hate to be a jerk, but that's reality. So let me ask again: Do you know something I don't know?"

This time, Erika's tongue comes through with one word that she innately senses will seal her fate.

"No."

THIRTEEN

ERIKA

LATE TUESDAY MORNING

"What the hell are these?"

Hector Aldridge, *To the Manor Build*'s goateed director, waves angrily at the colorful strips of red and yellow bell peppers interspersed with white mushroom caps and slices of cooked sausage Erika has cut with meticulous precision.

"Vegetables," she replies, wiping her palms on her apron, wishing people would stop yelling at her. "Kabobs."

"Kabobs! Kabobs! Always fucking kabobs. That's all the talent ever does on these shows is stir fry or kabobs. Slicing peppers. Occasionally a stupid zucchini. Do you know how fucking sick I am of peppers?"

She did not know, but she is now up to speed.

The morning so far has been a blur of retakes and tantrums

and delays. Wayfair arrived with the staging furniture right when they were set up to shoot the great room windows and ceilings. Erika thought Hector would be happy the furniture was in place so they could film the room in its entirety, but he only stamped his foot onto a can of Diet Coke, sending brown soda spewing onto the beige sisal rug.

Filming the downstairs guest suite went slightly better since it faced south and benefitted from favorable lighting enhanced by the white shiplap walls and yellow-and-white quilts. Hector was able to get a shot of Erika from the back opening the sliding door to the small patio located directly underneath the private deck off the primary suite above. He was also able to move freely above the room with its two queen beds and generous sitting area complete with functional kitchenette, avoiding the relatively cramped guest bathroom. Vanessa the interior designer had installed a wall of mirrors to make the space appear larger than it was, forgetting—or, perhaps, blatantly ignoring—the fact that reflections are the kiss of death on reality rehab shows.

Hector had a few choice words about her, though he did compliment Erika gruffly on the pains she'd taken to pass as Holly. "You'll do," he said, taking a swig of a new can of Diet Coke. "In a pinch."

The bonhomie was short lived when he discovered the fancy French range had yet to be delivered. "How am I expected to shoot the kitchen without a goddamn stove!" he yelled, sweeping the required wire basket of lemons Erika had carefully arranged on the marble counter onto the concrete floor. "Bush league, I tell you. Bush league!"

Now they're in the outside entertainment area shooting close-ups of the grill and Hector is throwing another fit. It's almost one thirty and none of them have had lunch. Everyone's hangry, not just the director. They've been working nonstop. They need a break.

A crew member leaning against the slate-topped stone half wall gives her a reassuring wink as he hands the director a vape from his shirt pocket. Hector brings the vape to his mouth, inhales as if it is the breath of life itself, and exhales slowly, closing his eyes to savor the effect. Within just a few minutes, he returns the vape to the cameraman and regards Erika with a beatific expression.

"You've done a wonderful job, my dear, cutting them so even. Shall we spritz the lovelies with poison and position them just so?"

Baffled, but relieved, Erika twists the knob on the grill. Instead of blue flame, however, there is nothing. Not even a click of the electric starter.

The cameraman pulls a Bic out of his pocket, turns the knob, and lights the gas. Success! "Bum igniter," he says. "For ten grand, you'd expect better. This ain't a Weber. Call the manufacturer and tell them to get up here. This needs to be fixed by Monday."

Add it to the list, Erika thinks, exhausted. She steps aside so the camera can close in on the flames flickering out of the grill, precariously close to the skewers that've been doused in highly flammable glycerin for shine.

Hector yells, "Cut!"

Erika dumps the tainted vegetables and meat into the trash,

taking several photos of their placement first. She will have to replicate the exact same order of peppers, mushrooms, and sausages for Monday's reveal. Provided Holly and Robert have returned and LuAnn hasn't canceled the project.

The crew members check their phones or go to the bathroom as Erika checks her own phone. Two messages from her mother, one from a private number, and a call from the town office. Nothing from Holly or Robert. However, the landline has a voicemail.

"Hey, Holly and crew, Colton here."

Erika crosses her fingers. Not exactly the priority level of Holly or Robert, but welcome nonetheless.

"Good news. The beeswax arrived earlier than I anticipated so the table's finished. Got it in my van and ready to deliver. Holly, I left a couple of voicemails on your cell, too. Thought you might want to give Robert a heads-up so he can be there to kick the proverbial tires . . ."

And write the proverbial check, Erika thinks, nonetheless thrilled he's come through.

"If I don't hear from you, I'm swinging through the area and will drop it off tomorrow afternoon, if that's okay. Until then, fare thee well!"

Tomorrow? She checks and finds left the message was left at 6:10 p.m. last night, shortly after she closed up the house for the day. That means Holly and Robert likely won't be around for the delivery. Bummer! No matter. The table's done. Another bullet dodged.

"Erika Turnbull?"

She jumps, startled to see two Vermont state troopers: a

woman with a light brown complexion, her black hair neatly pulled into a bun, looking extremely serious, and Andre Picard, whom she knows all too well.

Unfortunately.

No words have yet been exchanged, but Erika has a foreboding their sudden presence must involve Holly and Robert. Her palms go damp.

"Your camera crew let us in," Andre explains. His gaze is shifting up, down, left to right, as he mentally adds up the costs of the marble countertops and matching flooring, the custom-made mullioned windows and $18,000 programmable refrigerator. "If you have a moment, Trooper Yasmin Kashi and I would like to ask you a few questions."

Kashi whips out a notepad and pencil. "Ms. Turnbull, do you own a late-model red Kia with Vermont tags ABX 25C?"

"My *car*?" Erika's chest squeezes. Ominous images of twisted metal, two injured passengers slumped in the front seats, flash into her thoughts. "Oh, no. My boss borrowed it late Saturday night to take his wife on a honeymoon to Montreal. Has something happened? Did you find them? Are they okay?"

"That's an affirmative, then." Kashi writes this down. Turning to Andre, she says, "Can you secure confirmation on the operators, Trooper Picard?"

Andre nods. He asks Erika to spell Holly and Robert's names, though he must know who they are. They're Snowden's reigning—and only—celebrities. He can't be that out of the loop.

Erika fumbles through the spellings of Robert Barron III and Holly Simmons, a.k.a. Haylee Beauregard, her thoughts jumbled. It seems the cops have no idea Holly and Robert were with the car, which means they must either still be missing or . . . *unidentifiable.*

The possibility fills her with terror. Tammy Beauregard was wringing her hands just last night, panicked about not having heard from her daughter. Maybe her maternal instincts were not simply superstitious.

"Robert has a driver's license from Massachusetts," she says, doing her best to be helpful. "Holly got her Vermont one about six weeks ago. I don't know if it's under Holly Simmons or Haylee Beauregard. She goes by both."

Kashi and Andre exchange knowing looks. Putting away his own notebook, Andre says, "I wonder if you wouldn't mind accompanying us to the scene. We'd like you to identify possible objects of interest."

This is not good. Not good at all! What does he mean by "objects of interest"?

"Just tell me if you found Holly and Robert," she begs. "That's all I care about. Come on, Andre!"

He waves her toward the door. "At this moment, I'm afraid the situation is unclear. Now, if you'll just step into our SUV—"

"I can take my own car. I mean, Robert's. He loaned me his Tesla to drive while he borrowed my Kia."

Andre, annoyingly, takes out his notebook and writes this down, too.

"Not advisable," Kashi responds, unblinking. "You need four-wheel drive. A Tesla wouldn't make it where we're going."

"Where are we going?"

"The middle of nowhere."

FOURTEEN

KIM

"Any word from your kid?" Doreen asks before taking a bite of her peanut butter and Fluffernutter sandwich.

I stir my lemon water, my pulse only now slowing to normal. "Not yet. I texted. Left a phone message, but she's probably with the police."

"Gotta say. I'm surprised you're so calm. Aren't you dying of curiosity? I am."

"Of course! But now that Andre let me know she's okay and in the back of his SUV, I'm just glad to be relieved. That cryptic message you took gave me a freaking heart attack, Doreen. I had no idea if Erika was alive, injured, or dead. Next time the cops call and ask how to reach my daughter, will you do me a favor and confirm everything's okay?"

"How many calls like that you expect to get?" She takes another bite and chews, unrepentant.

"God willing, I've reached my quota." In Erika's lifetime, there've been two urgent messages from the state police. That's enough.

Finished with her sandwich, Doreen rolls up the crumbs in cellophane, tying it in a knot. The clock above the copier reads 12:45 p.m. We are fifteen minutes into the daily lunch half hour, which Doreen approaches with the solemnity and ritual of a Benedictine monk at vespers. First, there is the clearing of the conference table and the banishment of all visitors or, as Doreen calls them, "intruders." Most lawyers and researchers familiar with our office wisely schedule their hours in our vault so that they're out by noon.

Today, unfortunately, a newbie fresh out of law school was forced to exit blinking and disheveled, with his yellow legal pad and wrinkled notes under his arm as Doreen escorted him to the door, which she locked, flipping the sign from OPEN to CLOSED. That's the second part.

The third part of the ritual is the official drawing down of all blinds in the conference room, followed by the official laying out of the cloth napkin, sewn by Doreen's mother, onto which is laid the following items: one peanut butter and Fluffernutter sandwich on white bread, the crusts removed; one small bag of Cape Cod potato chips; one carrot, cut into three-inch sticks; one seedless clementine; two Fig Newtons; and, finally, a box of Hershey's 2 percent chocolate milk, complete with little straw.

My assistant has the palate of a preschooler.

She eyes me warily. "Are you gonna eat actual food?"

I check the clock again, coughing to hide my stomach rumbling. "In three hours and ten minutes."

"Intermittent fasting is total bullshit. You know that right?" She crunches on a carrot stick. The potato chips are already toast, the packet squished into a little ball. "You probably make up for all the calories you aren't eating during the day by stuffing your face in the four-hour window."

"No, I don't." My mind hearkens to the dark chocolate brownies I baked last night, consuming two with bare seconds to spare. In all fairness, it'd been a tough day. I was shot at and then there was the gnawing soul-searching to do with the folder from the Strickland tax sale.

Actually, I have that poacher to thank for my change of heart. If he hadn't scared the bejesus out of me, I might have burned the file, which would have been wrong and unfair on so many levels. The piper must be paid, I decided as I sat in my kitchen, licking dark fudge off my fingers. I've got to do right by Gretchen and Zeke Strickland—I've got to give them a chance to get back the house Robert Barron took.

Getting up and fetching my bag off the hook, I remove the file and slide it to Doreen. "Here. Can you make two copies?"

She pauses peeling her clementine. "What's this?"

"The Strickland tax file. I'm gonna give one copy to Gretchen and, if I can find him, another to Zeke."

"What for?" She resumes her peeling, maintaining her face in poker mode.

"When you told me about that woman you think might

have been Holly coming here to do research, I realized there were a few loose strings about that sale I need to tie up."

She picks off a segment and pops it in her mouth. "What kind of strings?"

Oh, she's good. I bet she's only waiting for me to confess. "Let's put it this way: if the Stricklands were on the ball before the tax sale, they wouldn't have lost the house."

"That so." Doreen swallows and picks off another segment, displaying not a hint of emotion. "By the way, Elliot and I were discussing Haylee or Holly's visit . . ."

I can feel my neck flush warm with mortification. "You discussed this with Elliot?"

"No worries. He's a fucking hermit. He doesn't have any friends aside from old farts at the Legion and, trust me, they don't give a tinker's dam about 'what goes on' in this office." She finger-quotes *what goes on*. "Anyway, I remembered that Holly or Haylee or whatever showed up with a guy. Also, she was in pantyhose. Beige taupe. Like from CVS. Seems kind of strange for a style influencer, right?"

Doreen has a way of veering off track. "Agreed. But I don't care as much about the hose as I do the guy. Was it Robert?"

"Nuh-uh." She swallows the last of the clementine, scraping the discarded peels into the Tupperware container she'll take home and dump into her compost. "Medium height. Stocky. Blond and tanned, the way you are when you work outside in the sun. Like a construction worker, maybe."

Medium height. Stocky. Blond and tanned, the way you are when you work outside in the sun. Like a construction worker, maybe. The exact opposite of Robert, who's tall, pale, and almost gives the impression of being willowy due to his long black hair. I can't envision him wielding a hammer, much less nailing up two-by-fours.

"He didn't come into the office, but I saw him through the window," Doreen continues. "He was sitting in the passenger seat smoking a blunt."

I blink in amazement. Marijuana's legal in Vermont, but I haven't adapted to people openly consuming what the federal government still considers a Schedule I drug. "A blunt, you say. Is that what the kids are calling weed these days?"

"Spleef. Joint. I dunno. I don't touch the stuff, personally. I'm more a gin gal. But I sure as hell could smell it. He had the window down and the smoke was wafting into our vent system. Skunk odor all over the place. I was about to go out there and make him move."

I press my temples, wrapping my head around the vision of Holly showing up in drugstore pantyhose chauffeuring a strange stoner. Doreen must be mistaken. "That means the Haylee couldn't have been Holly. She wouldn't be driving around with some loser getting high in the middle of the day. On *TMB* she's all about exercising and healthy eating and nontoxic living."

"Pot's not toxic," Doreen says, finishing her final carrot. "If you grow it yourself in organic soil like my grandma."

"Forest for the trees, D. Stick with the program."

"Just saying."

I steer us back on track. "This is what's been bugging me. Like I said yesterday, I read an interview with her and Robert where she said they didn't meet in person until after the Stricklands failed to redeem and he took her to Vermont to show her the property. That would have been ten months ago. But, according to you, she was in our office the previous September. That's four months before Robert took possession."

"That article's gotta be wrong."

I pull out my phone and go to the pertinent Q&A on the *To the Manor Build* site, scrolling down to the key part and reading it aloud. "'Then, out of the blue, he called me last winter and asked if I wanted to go skiing in Vermont and check out this kooky property he'd just acquired for a song at a tax sale. Thought maybe I might be interested in making a video of it.'"

"So?"

"So, your timeline doesn't make sense."

"I know how to settle this." Doreen gets the clipboard of signees we keep in the middle of the table next to the stapler and jar of pens. Everyone who comes into the office to do research must sign in with a name and telephone number, just in case someone walks off with a zoning file or forgets a pair of glasses. As with her desk blotter, my assistant retains every page going back a year. Older pages, she stores in a file. Say what you will about the wonders of modern technology, there is no substitute for old-fashioned paper and pen.

"Here it is. Last November twenty-eighth. Right after Thanksgiving. Later than I thought. Still, before Robert officially got the property." She runs her clipped-short nail under the scrawled HAYLEE. "First name only, but spelled the same. Not the traditional h-a-y-l-e-y." Then she takes my phone lying between us and punches in the number written next to it.

"It has an 802 area code. Vermont," I note.

"The car she was driving had Vermont plates, too." Doreen holds up a finger, listening to the message on the other end, then hangs up.

"Where does it go to?"

"Bob's Bait and Tackle on Bear Swamp Road. Thought it seemed familiar."

"Maybe to you," I say, now totally flummoxed. "But not to Holly Beauregard."

"What about the stoned dude waiting in the car? To be honest, he didn't give off a good vibe, and that had nothing to do with him stinking up the vent with weed. I got the sense she was in here to look up records on his behalf."

"Because he didn't know how?"

"Possibly." Doreen rearranges the clipboard in its holder on the conference table. "Or he's a local who wanted to keep a low profile so he got Holly, who was from out of state, to be his front. That way, none of us would be the wiser."

FIFTEEN

ERIKA

TUESDAY AFTERNOON

Andre is riding shotgun; Kashi's driving, so short her nose barely touches the top of the steering wheel, which would be humorous if not for the fact she's goosing it on the switchbacks, making Erika dizzy in the back.

"Excuse me," she asks, knocking on the Plexiglas, "but could you slow down? I'm getting carsick back here."

Kashi meets her gaze in the rearview. "Almost there."

Almost where? They've been driving for forty minutes. Now they're on a service road in the Green Mountain National Forest, having just passed a sign marking a wilderness area. Erika has always thought of wilderness areas as thick, deep woods for hard-core hikers. No snowmobiles or ATVs allowed. Moose country.

To calm the butterflies in her stomach, she taps her collarbone, a trick she learned from her therapist. She wishes Andre would show her some mercy and slip her a hint of what's going on. No doubt in his training he was taught to keep witnesses oblivious so their initial impressions wouldn't be prejudiced by subliminal subjections, or some such police BS. Whatever, this journey of not knowing is torture, especially since Andre would have mentioned if he spoke to Robert and Holly.

Erika calculates it's going on sixty hours since anyone's heard from them. There are no comforting explanations remaining for why they've gone dark. If something's happened to them that she could have prevented by sounding the alarm yesterday when she first became concerned, she'll never forgive herself.

"Is this where we turn?" Kashi asks Andre.

He points to a yellow tape tied to a tree. "There."

Kashi swings into a barely discernible pull off in the overgrown underbrush and kills the engine.

"Can you make it in those?" Andre asks, nodding to the pair of Holly's thin leather driving loafers on Erika's feet.

They'll be trashed in the mud. The least of her problems, Erika thinks.

"Not like she has a choice," Kashi says, brushing off her own sturdy boots. "Do you have a spare key? It might come in handy."

Erika fishes through her bag with no luck. "Not on me. Robert has the original."

Kashi and Andre lead the way. A set of tire tracks has forged a path through the dense vegetation, damp from the recent rain. Erika follows, stepping on logs and avoiding mucky boobytraps, head down. She doesn't want to see the so-called scene. She wants to go back to her apartment and hide under the covers.

The cops quit walking and Erika looks up, her heart plummeting. The Kia's listing to one side, its left tires flat, a gaping hole ringed by shards of glass where her rear window should have been.

"Oh, no," she moans. She aches for it as though it were her own child beaten and abandoned in the woods. "*Oh no!*"

Andre says, "I'll take that as a positive identification of your vehicle, then."

She can't speak. It's awful. So *violent*. If this is the state of her car, she can't bear to think about the state of its passengers. It makes her sick.

"A hiker found it this morning," Kashi says, as Andre slides a thin rod down the window and breaks the lock. "Reported a suspicious vehicle. I assume this was not the condition in which you saw it last."

The car is covered in leaves, dirt splattered along the sides. "No. This was not the condition in which I saw it last."

"There's glass all over here," Andre cautions as they move closer. "You'll cut your feet in those slippers."

"Do you think Robert got carjacked?" she asks as Andre unlocked the door.

"Carjacked?" Kashi asks "What do you mean? Like held at gunpoint and forced to drive to this location?"

"Yes," Erika says. "That's exactly what I mean." Was she missing something? Isn't that the very definition of carjacking?

Andre clicks on a flashlight and inspects the interior, reading off the contents of the car. "Bottle of Diet Coke in the cupholder. A couple of unopened bills on the passenger's seat. A pen. Lots and lots of glass."

"If they were headed to Montreal, is it possible they might have taken a train? Now, I usually hop on the Adirondack in Whitehall 'cause that way you don't have to cross the lake, but they could have picked it up as far north at Rouses Point if all they were trying to avoid was that never-ending road construction in Montreal," Kashi suggests. "If they left the Kia in Whitehall, then this vehicle might have been stolen from there and dumped here. The station's only an hour away."

Erika brightens. She hadn't considered the train. Robert wouldn't have wanted to leave his pricey Tesla in a strange area, but he wouldn't have thought twice about ditching the Kia in an unsecured lot. "He didn't mention a train, but it was all very last minute. Do you think that's what happened?"

"There are no visible signs of foul play. No blood. No signs of a struggle. No tracks leading from here to deeper in the woods. We've done a thorough search of the immediate area," Kashi says. "It'll be easy enough to check if they purchased tickets."

"They might have used pseudonyms."

"Why would they use pseudonyms?" Kashi asks.

"For privacy? They're in this online property rehab contest, a really popular show called *To the Manor Build*. They have hundreds of thousands of followers. Robert and Holly are on their honeymoon. They wouldn't want to be pestered."

Kashi writes this down.

"This is interesting." Andre is holding a plain, brown cardboard box. "Yours?"

"No," Erika says, warily. "What's in it?"

He holds up a length of rope. "This and these," he says, fisting a handful of plastic zip ties.

They look so sinister, a sour sensation rises in her throat. "Gross."

"And one knife." Andre's latex-gloved hand pinches a folded knife with a wood veneer. "Also not yours?"

Her mind is swimming with hideous images. *Rope. Zip ties. Knife?* It's like a serial killer's emergency prep kit. "I've never seen any of this stuff in in my life. What would I do with a knife and a rope and zip ties?"

Kashi says, "I don't know. What would you do?"

Erika's confused. Surely, they don't think she's lying. "These aren't mine. That's the truth. I don't know whose they are."

"Could they have belonged to Robert and Holly Barron?" Kashi regards her with that weird unblinking stare.

What was she suggesting? "No! Absolutely not. Robert and Holly aren't like *that*."

"Then who do they belong to?"

"Whoever stole the car?" Erika suggests. "That seems the most logical explanation."

Unless . . .

Andre sets the box on the trunk, clicking on his light as he inspects the rear through the broken window. "Actually, it appears our earlier assessment was incorrect, Trooper Kashi. Is this blood?" Andre shines his light on a dark red patch in the corner behind the driver's seat.

Both women peer inside and for one horrific, nauseating moment, Erika leaps to the same conclusion. That is until she spies the silver case glinting under Andre's light and she goes weak in the knees.

"Not blood," she says, light headed with relief. "Candied Tomatoes."

"Candied tomatoes?" Andre frowns.

"A shade of lipstick called Candied Tomatoes by Florasis. Cost me forty-nine bucks. Must have fallen out of my purse and then with the car closed and the sun . . ."

"I hate when that happens," chimes in Kashi, letting her cop mask slip.

Andre shakes his head. "We should have it towed to the barracks regardless. Have it swabbed and dusted. Do an odometer reading . . ."

That's when she remembers something that might be helpful that won't require her to violate her employer's privacy. "This car's leased, you know," she blurts. "The company that owns it might have a tracking program installed. Like, they know how many miles I'm putting on it and when's the next oil change. They might be able to tell you where it's been and when it got here."

"Good thinking," says Kashi. "Meanwhile, do you have any contact information for Robert and Holly Barron?" Kashi flips to another page in her small spiral notebook. "The name of the hotels they're staying in in Montreal or Airbnb?"

"No idea."

Kashi lifts her pen. "Pardon?"

"We've been trying to reach both of them for a couple of days. We assumed they were on their honeymoon and wanted to be alone so we've been trying not to worry. Robert said he'd be back by tomorrow at the latest. Or maybe Thursday. But he didn't leave any forwarding information."

"When was the last you spoke to either Mr. or Mrs. Barron?" Kashi asks, a wrinkle of concern forming between her brows.

"Since after midnight on Saturday. I was probably the last person to see Robert when he came by my apartment then to ask if he could switch cars. My Kia for his Tesla."

"Midnight Sunday or midnight Saturday?"

Erika has always had trouble with that one. "Midnight Saturday. A few hours after his wedding."

"To Holly?"

"Yes, to Holly." What does she think?

Kashi pauses from her rapid note-taking. "You said you were the last one to see him? How do you know?"

Erika doesn't like the way Kashi asked that, as if she suspects her of lying. "I'm not certain I was the last. I'm just not aware of anyone else who's seen them since."

Kashi waits a beat and then says, "And there's been no contact since. No texts from them. No email. Not one phone call."

"That's correct. Which is strange, I have to say, because this is the last week before the big reveal on *To the Manor Build*. There're a lot of decisions to be made and scenes to shoot. Before he left, Robert said he'd be reachable by phone or text, but that hasn't been the case. No one's been able to reach them."

"Not even friends or family?"

"I spoke to Robert's father yesterday morning. He hadn't heard from him. As for Holly's mom, I spoke to her yesterday evening. She hasn't had contact, but, in fairness, my impression is they're not that close."

"I see." Kashi flips to a new page. "You have their contact info, though."

"Not with me, but I can get it to you."

"That would be useful. Also, any business associates."

"You might want to talk to LuAnn, the producer in LA. She's always emailing them and I know she's been concerned."

Kashi finally blinks. "Rightly so."

Andre quits snapping photos of the scene and joins his partner. "Why didn't you file a missing person's report?"

There's a hint of reproach in his question that pricks Erika's conscience, making her feel simultaneously guilty and annoyed. It's so like Andre to take advantage of the situation to pin some sort of blame on her, and she can't resist shooting back, "I didn't know I had to file a missing person's report because a forty-year-old real estate investor on his honeymoon didn't check in with his assistant."

Kashi's lips twitch in a snicker. "Is there any other information you can provide that'd be helpful?"

The threatening letters in the bottom of Robert's drawer. Holly's and Robert's passports which she found while pawing through their personal belongings. Erika keeps pulling on her fingers, unsure what to do. Now would be the time to tell the police everything. Her car's been trashed and found containing restraints and a knife. Robert and Holly are unaccounted for.

Erika has a horrible image of Zeke with a gun pressed to Robert's or Holly's temple forcing the other to drive, him ranting and raving about their stealing his house. They might still be alive. He might have them tied up, perhaps holding them for ransom. Then again, she doesn't know for certain Zeke sent the letters, but if she turns them over to the police, that would be their job to determine.

Robert would be livid if his hidden correspondence was made public without his permission. What was it his father said? Something about Barrons not running to the police with their private business. Guess that must be true, since she wouldn't know about the letters' existence—or the passports, either—if she hadn't been snooping.

Besides, Erika would rather not have to admit that while her employers were away she was violating their privacy. Not only would that reflect poorly on her, but Robert and Holly would dismiss her immediately without offering to write her a recommendation. And Robert did say they'd be back tomorrow, so better she should stay the course and wait for them to return as scheduled. That's what he'd want her to do.

"Not at the moment," Erika lies. "But I promise to let you know if anything comes up."

SIXTEEN

KIM

After speaking with Doreen and growing more certain that it was Holly who stopped by the office last year to look at the property records, I've finally decided Gretchen Strickland deserves to know the truth about tax sale before it's too late. Under Vermont law, she has exactly one year from the day of the transfer to contest the tax sale in court. That leaves roughly two months, plenty of time for someone comfortable with the system to hire a lawyer and get the ball rolling.

Not so much for a legal neophyte like Gretchen, who, I'm guessing, doesn't have a savvy real estate attorney on retainer, unlike Robert Barron or his father. Those two probably have a stable of blue-blood chiselers. That's why I've decided to bring the file to her myself and outline the steps she must take immediately, if not sooner.

It took some doing to hunt her down. Gretchen's address isn't listed anywhere on the internet. She has no Facebook, Instagram, or Twitter account. Nothing to do with LinkedIn, and her numbers don't automatically pop up on Google. It's like she doesn't exist.

There's a reason for that. According to the statewide voter registration system, Gretchen's address is available to me, as a town clerk, but secret to the public because she's listed as "safe at home." I take that to mean she's a victim of domestic abuse seeking protection from her batterer, her husband. She and Zeke are still married, I believe, but they weren't living together when the tax sale was happening. He'd gone off the deep end by then, and word around town was he was taking out his frustration on her so she fled with the twins.

Now I'm driving to Grandfield, a former railroad junction forty miles up 100B, to knock on the door of a former resident who probably despises me for putting her house up for tax auction. I'm dreading every minute.

Gretchen's apartment is in a weathered gray two-story house with a crumbling porch that appears about to collapse and chipped paint that should be tested for lead. I find a space on the street to park discreetly just as my phone rings. Erika, at last. I've been on pins and needles all day waiting to hear what happened with the cops and her car.

"Hey, honey," I answer casually, as if nothing's going on.

"Hi, Mom." Erika lets out a breath. "Sorry I didn't call sooner. I know you left, like, a hundred messages."

"Three texts," I clarify, sinking low in my seat as a small blue Ford pulls into a space in front of Gretchen's apartment. "And two voicemails."

"Yeah, like I keep telling you, no one my age picks up voicemails. The only reason I even have an answering message on my phone is for work."

"Duly noted."

"Anyway, I just want to fill you in that I'm fine. I'm not in any trouble. I wasn't kidnapped or murdered."

"Nice to know." The door to the blue car opens and a woman carrying a cloth grocery tote gets out slowly, the pink legs of her scrubs peeking out from under her zip-up coat. "So why did Andre want to talk to you?"

"About my car. Don't make a bigger deal about this than it is, but Robert asked to borrow my Kia over the weekend. He wanted to take Holly on a surprise honeymoon to Montreal and felt there might not be enough charging stations for the Tesla."

I do not ask about Holly's Range Rover. Nor do I mention that I saw Robert dump a bag in our garbage that turned out to be woman's PJs lightly spattered with blood, a bag currently stuffed in my freezer. The goal here is to regain my daughter's trust while surveilling the woman I'm now certain is Gretchen slowly climb the uneven wooden front steps and push open the downstairs door without using her key.

"Anyway, it was found this morning abandoned and vandalized in the national forest down in Peru."

"Peru!" All thoughts of Gretchen fly out the window. "What was your car doing in Peru?"

"That's what the police are trying to find out. The going

theory is maybe it was stolen from a park 'n' ride? I dunno. They're checking it out. They're checking into whether Holly and Robert might have left it in Whitehall and taken the train to Canada. The bummer is, the Kia's a total loss. My insurance is covering it but there'll be a five-hundred-dollar deductible."

I can't believe this. If it weren't for bad luck, my kid wouldn't have any luck at all. "What do Holly and Robert have to say about this?"

There is a pause and then Erika says sheepishly, "That's the other thing. We haven't been able to locate them. I'm assuming they've totally unplugged, but if they don't return as scheduled by tomorrow night, I'm gonna freak."

I don't blame her. The mystery of their whereabouts aside, Holly and Robert's absence must be ratcheting up the tension on the set and, therefore, my daughter's stress. From what Erika's been telling me, the stakes are never higher than the week before the reveal, with daily live promotion and teasers online to lure crucial viewers. I don't see how Team H&R has a chance of winning the *TMB* contest if they're choosing these last days to "unplug."

But I try to comfort her with my go-to line. "It'll all work out in the end. If it doesn't work out, it's not the end!"

"That's what I keep telling myself," she says cheerfully, even if, as I suspect, the positive attitude is forced. "Anyway, what are you up to tonight?"

I'm grateful she's willing to move past our tiff from the weekend without requiring a postmortem. Sometimes, all mothers and daughters need is a little space to cool off. "Running an errand."

"At this hour? What kind of errand? Don't tell me some idiot needs emergency notary services."

No, but that would have been a good excuse. "I'm meeting up with Gretchen Strickland." That's about as honest as I'm going to get. I'm not sure if Erika grasps the complexities of tax sales, but she might understand enough to realize what I'm about to tell Gretchen will be bad for her employers.

"Gretchen Strickland!" Erika repeats, sounding alarmed. "You mean, *Zeke Strickland's* wife? The people who used to own Robert and Holly's place?"

She might be aware of more than I give her credit for. "Yup."

"Are you meeting with *him*, too?"

"I'm not sure . . ."

"Oh, my god, Mom, you can't. Zeke's, like, messed up in the head. He's super dangerous."

This catches me off guard. "What makes you say that?"

"Just take my word for it. Zeke is a very, very, very bad dude. Tell them to meet you during office hours when there are other people around. You're all alone down there. It's not safe!"

A light goes off in the upstairs apartment I suspect is Gretchen's. I haven't the heart to break it to my excitable daughter that I'm nowhere near the office, that I'm on Gretchen's territory, miles away. "Relax. We're gonna have a brief chat and then I'll be home. No big deal."

"Okay. I hope you're right. Though, hold on." There's a pause. "If Zeke doesn't happen to show, ask his wife where he is, okay? But do it subtly. Don't tell Gretchen I'm the one who wants to know."

"Why?" Now I'm suspicious. If Zeke Strickland is the devil's spawn, why is she trying to find him?

"Call it a hunch. Or, as you would say, no big deal."

◇ ◇ ◇

The entryway to the building reeks of musty carpet and stale cigarette smoke. I pass by two cinched white plastic bags of garbage deposited outside the grimy door of an apartment from which a TV blares and take the narrow stairs to the second floor. Not sure what the building codes are in Grandfield, but this chopped-up house would be a death trap in a fire.

The door to Gretchen's apartment is decorated with orange pumpkins and black cats cut from construction paper and sprinkled with silver glitter. Halloween is right around the corner and someone's making an effort. My guess is it's Gretchen.

Gathering my strength, I rap softly.

There's a muffled shuffling on the other side and then a woman's cautious, "Who is it?"

"I'm here to see Gretchen. It's Kim Turnbull, the Snowden town clerk."

"*Who?*"

"I need to speak to Gretchen about a property she and Zeke own in town. I have . . . new information." Hopefully, that will be enough of an enticement.

The door opens a crack, enough for me to make out a woman in sweats and dark hair tipped with purple. "What are you doing here? It's late."

No argument there. "I'm really sorry. I just want to give

this to her." I hold up the file. "Documents from the tax sale. If I could speak to—"

"Let her in, Nicole."

Gretchen steps into view wearing a blue robe and thick glasses, her head wrapped in a towel, indicating she just got out of the shower. There's something about her that's vaguely familiar. Then I remember she came to the office once with a babe on each hip to bring me a gift of raw honey as a thank-you for helping Zeke fill out the building permit for his cabin. Though that couldn't have been more than five or six years ago, with the dark circles under her eyes and her sallow skin, she seems to have aged decades. Or that could be the harsh effect of the overhead fluorescent.

"How'd you find her?" asks Nicole, closing and locking the door behind me. "She's supposed to be on the safe-at-home list."

I avert her excellent question with a "Just did." I can't risk being interrogated by a roommate. "Gretchen, I won't be long. But it'd be a good idea if we could go over these documents together, so you understand what they're about and what you have to do to get back your Snowden property."

Gretchen blinks once or twice. "Are you serious?"

"That's why I'm here. Is there someplace where we can sit?"

She pulls out one of the folding chairs around a plastic table, pushing aside a plate of congealing microwaved frozen pizza. To our left, the blue screen of a TV flickers in front of a threadbare couch. The floor is a minefield of plastic toys.

Nicole folds her arms, her belly button protruding through a thin T-shirt. She's pregnant. "You good, Gretch?"

"It's okay. Yeah."

"Five a.m., you know. That's when the little stinkers get up." Nicole shuffles in slippers to a door at the far end of the room, shoots us a parting glance, and disappears.

"We've got three kids sleeping so we need to keep it down. Have a seat." Gretchen gestures to the chair and goes to the refrigerator, her hand shaking slightly as she reaches for a green bottle of Mountain Dew. She sits across from me, the folder marked STRICKLAND TAX SALE lying between us like an unopened Pandora's box, its one saving grace being that there's still hope. "Did something change?"

I did, I want to tell her. "Nothing's changed. Except you're coming up on a really important deadline to reclaim the house and I wanted to give you copies of these records so you could start the process."

Gretchen drops her gaze to the folder, but doesn't touch it. "I thought it was a done deal. You signed over the deed to Robert Barron, right?"

"To be specific, the *town* actually deeded the property after you and Zeke failed to redeem."

"That wasn't my fault," she says, taking a sip of her Mountain Dew. "Zeke and I were separated by then. I wasn't getting the mail, he was. I didn't know anything about the auction. Didn't know it was coming up for sale or that the taxes hadn't been paid, even. I couldn't believe it when Zeke told me we'd lost the house. I was like, What? How? Shouldn't I have been notified?"

This is where I close my eyes and summon all my courage. "Yes. You're absolutely right. You should have been notified. I screwed up."

There is a calm before the storm. She is rigid, forearms resting on the table, fists clenched. "What do you mean you screwed up?"

"I mean, I should have sent you and Zeke notification of the tax sale by registered mail with a returned receipt signed by at least one of you for our records. I didn't. I didn't even send you a notice by regular mail. There was no way you could have known the auction was coming up unless you read the legal ads in the local paper, which no one ever reads, or happened to see one of the three postings around town, which no one ever sees. In other words, as collector of delinquent taxes, I did not comply with the law." I pause to inhale another breath. "On purpose."

Her fury builds. Eyes bulging, cheeks a hot red, she pounds her fist so hard it rattles the dishes in the cabinet. "Goddamn it. I knew it. I knew it wasn't our fault. I told Zeke you people were working with Barron. Did he slip you a bribe or what?"

"Guys!" Nicole hisses from the bedroom. "*Shhh.*"

"For the record," I clarify in a whisper, doing my best not to take her insult personally, "working with Barron was the opposite of what I was trying to do by not notifying you. Actually, I was out to skewer the sale on your behalf. What they call planting a poison pill."

Her jaw drops. "*On our behalf?* Well, you didn't do a very good job. We lost the fucking house."

"Look, you owed $8,462 in back taxes. I'd tried to work out a payment plan with Zeke—"

"Like he was even capable of working out a plan," Gretchen snaps. "My husband suffered a TBI after falling off the ladder while shingling our roof and his prefrontal cortex was shot to shit. Do you know what that means?"

"No, not exactly."

"It means he can be a pussycat one minute and one minute later he'll be threatening to blow off my head. It means he's lost the ability to control his rage, to tamp down his aggression. He's constantly in anger mode. That's his default setting now. He punched so many holes in the walls of his old apartment they looked like swiss cheese. He's in living hell."

I cringe thinking of the pain and fright she's endured, not to mention what Zeke's going through. "I'm so sorry. When I was dealing with him and the taxes, I had no idea."

"That's why you should have contacted me." Crossing her arms, she raises her face to the peeling ceiling. "Whatever. That was two years ago. It's too late now."

I shake my head. "It's not. That's the point of the poison pill. It's a baked-in fatal flaw, which is what these records show." I tap the red file. "You can appeal the sale based simply on the fact I failed to notify you, the owners, that your property was about to go to auction. The Vermont Supreme Court's made it clear in prior rulings that failure to notify is a sufficient basis in and of itself to reverse a tax sale.

"You're practically guaranteed to get your property back. Best of all, the property you'll get back won't be your log cabin; it'll be a million-dollar estate and the taxes will be paid. You won't just have your land—you'll be stinking rich."

Gretchen regards me with a wary stare. "There has to be a hitch."

"No hitch. I'm the only one putting my ass on the line

by coming forward. You could sue me. Robert Barron will *definitely* sue me and the town and I'll lose my job for failure to uphold my oath of office. It's all bad for me and the Town of Snowden and certainly the Barrons, but not for you."

Tears are pooling in the corners of her eyes. "I still don't get why you would do something like this to us."

"I didn't do it *to* you. I did it to *help* you. I wanted to give you an option to get back your land if the tax sale went through, which it almost didn't, since the locals who regularly bid at these auctions did their research and saw there wasn't a return receipt with an owner's signature. Why end up with a property only to lose it in court, was their attitude. So they sat this one out and it was almost yours again. Everything would have worked out as I planned—"

"You mean, no one would have bid on the house and we'd have had time to come up with the money?" Gretchen interrupted, beginning to get it.

"Exactly. You could have had extra weeks, months, maybe a whole year. I just never expected some out-of-state blogger would get wind of the auction and swoop into town with a bucket of cash."

For the first time tonight, Gretchen allows her lips to drift into a slow smile. She seems to have calmed down a bit. Perhaps her change in fortune might even be sinking in. "Does Robert Barron know what you did?"

"He didn't at the time. He thought he got a steal that the locals were too stupid to recognize." I think of the visitor from Florida riffling through our records a year ago. "If he's discovered the fatal flaw since, he's kept his mouth shut. It's in his best interests to keep this quiet until the deadline for appeal passes in January. That's why I'm here tonight, because you have about ten weeks to get a lawyer and start the ball rolling."

Gretchen opens and shuts the file without examining the contents. "I can't get over this." She rests her elbows on the table, massaging her forehead. "I can't believe there was no reason for us to lose our house, that it could have been ours all along."

"It can be yours again, even better than before. You'll own it free and clear. No debt. No back taxes. That's the good news."

"Good news?" She sits up. "You think this is *good news*? Now I have to hire a lawyer. How much is that gonna cost? How am I supposed to pay for one? You don't think Robert Barron with all his money and connections won't fight me tooth and nail?" She flicks away the folder. "It'll be a cakewalk for him. I don't care what you say, no judge is gonna hand over this so-called million-dollar property because you forgot to send one certified letter."

She might have a point, but I refuse to concede. "Have faith. I'm willing to testify in court that I intentionally failed to mail you the notice. It wasn't accidental oversight. The Vermont judicial system tends to be biased against property confiscation."

"Is it? Hmmm. I seem to recall a Vermont judge allowing a sheriff to show up unannounced and boot my husband from his own home in February during a snowstorm."

That's true. Also true is that Robert will hire platinum attorneys to run Gretchen Strickland into the ground. Yet, where there's a chance, there's hope. "Give yourself some time to think about what I said." I get up, slinging my purse over my shoulder. "If you need the recommendation for a good real estate lawyer, give me a call. I know a few."

"You'd recommend a lawyer to sue yourself?" Gretchen asks, with a laugh. "Why?"

"Because it's the right thing to do. And I happen to get a lot of pleasure from a clear conscience."

The other bedroom door opens and Nicole emerges again, annoyed. She's had it. "Okay, guys, you've gotta wrap this up. I'm not getting any sleep."

"She's going," Gretchen says, giving her roommate a thumbs-up.

Outside in the short hallway that smells of old cigarettes, I say, "I truly am sorry, Gretchen. It was never my intention for you to lose your house."

She leans against the doorjamb and sighs. "If I'd only known about the taxes being in arrears, I could have scraped up the cash, asked my parents for a loan, anything. You shouldn't have interfered. You should have followed the law. You're an elected official. That's what you swore to do, right?"

"Could not agree more, believe you me. But what's done is done. All I can do is make amends by admitting my mistake and doing what I can to correct it."

Gretchen nods quickly. "I appreciate that. I'm sure it wasn't easy for you to come here."

Not by a long shot. "By the way, I have a duplicate set of records for Zeke. You don't happen to have an address where I can send them, do you?"

She snorts. "An address? Hardly. Zeke lives out of his pickup."

"Any place in particular?"

"Nope. He's always on the move. Though, if you were waiting for me, you likely were pretty close to him and had no idea." Gretchen chucks her chin toward the street where my car is parked. "His truck was right under the Michaelsons' oak tree when I got home tonight. He likes the spot because it's shady. I ignored him like always. Got inside real quick."

I vaguely remember a white beat-up Ford behind me. I thought for sure it was unoccupied and the idea that it wasn't, that Zeke Strickland saw me but I didn't see him, gives me the creeps.

"I've caught him passing by the day care when I fetch the kids or in the parking lot outside the grocery store. Too wily for the cops, though. As soon as I call to report him violating his restraining order, he's outta there." She pulls her robe tighter, protectively. "Zeke always was a survivor. Doesn't need much to live on. Clean water. A tarp to keep off the elements. He's a good hunter so he can catch his protein. He never was one for going on the internet. He's got a cell, but it's prepaid in cash. When it comes to not wanting to leave a digital imprint, Zeke was ahead of the curve."

"Sounds like the Unabomber."

"Not far off. Do you know that when we first got the Snowden property, we actually spent an entire winter in the old root cellar? I swore I wouldn't live underground with only a trap door to the outside, but Zeke fixed it up really nice. We lay carpets to take the chill off the stone floor and put in a bed and a woodstove and a couple of pieces of furniture. We were snug as bugs in a rug. Being below the frost line, it was relatively toasty, too."

No. Out of the question. "I can't even think about living in a hole. Too similar to being buried alive, my ultimate fear."

She raises and lowers a shoulder. "You get used to it. There are way worse fates."

"Yeah?"

"You could be living in a house you have no business owning knowing somewhere out there is a family whose home you stole just because you could. My husband may have mental health issues and he might be so violent he's impossible to live with, but at least when he's on his own, he's not hurting anyone."

With that, she closes the door and turns the latch, ending the discussion before I can tell her more bad news that she definitely doesn't want to hear.

TMB: LOVE AMONG THE ACTUAL RUINS

POST #65: HOW DO YOU HIDE YOUR DIRT?

Hi, I'm Holly Barron, a contestant on *To the Manor Build*, a super-popular rehab show.

This is my unfiltered, no-holds-barred, honest, behind-the-scenes peek at the craziness of turning a run-down Vermont log cabin into a net-zero awesome house with a hot, sexy guy I ~~am about to marry~~ just married.

My motto: Whatever I can do, YOU totally can do better! Follow me to see how!

Hey, Fellow Manor Builders!

Hard to believe our Big Reveal is only (counts on calendar) five days away. I cannot wait to show off our energy-efficient, comfy home. I'm so excited, I'm half-tempted to pull back the curtain and let y'all see. But since I can't (contracts 'n' all), I'm gonna talk about dirt today. Specifically mud.

People, I'm gonna come right out and say this right now, no offense to you New Englanders, but when I was growing up on the shores of Florida, mud was not a thing. We left our sandals and shoes at the door, kicked the sand off our feet, and entered our house through a breezeway or, if you were fancy, foyer. We did not have mud. More importantly, we did not have rooms for mud. Mudrooms. Whoever heard of such a thing? It's not like we have "sand rooms" in Florida.

Lemme tell you what: all it took was one Vermont spring to nearly swallow my Rover in two feet of gunk and not only was I insistent we have a mudroom, but I insisted it be the first room finished in the house. Along those lines, there were also three nonnegotiables:

#1 A mudroom must connect the garage to the house in this climate. Look, I am not parking my car in a heated garage and then braving the elements outside before I can enter the house. Not gonna happen. Garage + Mudroom + House all connected. The way Good Lord intended.

#2 A mudroom must have a separate entrance to the outside. This is common sense. You don't want to have to pass through the garage to access the mudroom. Plus, when we have kiddos (hint hint, Robert), I like the idea of them coming in from playing in the backyard to clean off in the mudroom before setting foot in the house.

#3 A sink. See above: clean off. Every mudroom needs a serious sink. Ours is from Vermont Soapstone, a deep bump out with plenty of room for a good scrub and big enough to wash that Bernese mountain dog Robert's always threatening to get. (*No. Freaking. Way.*) Ours is situated under french double-casement windows that open onto the apple orchard. I just imagine a summer day, washing up after harvesting vegetables from our own garden as a warm breeze blows in off the apple trees. Heaven.

BLOG HIJACK!!!

Robert Barron here. My wife's adorable (yes, sweetie, we WILL get that Bernese mountain dog and you will LOVE him), but she's missed the most important quality in a functional mudroom, which is . . .

#4 Durable flooring. A mudroom floor's gonna get lots of traffic. Because I insist we make the most of our radiant heating system, I went with green slate tile. This is a metamorphic rock that was formed by eons of earth pressure. It's not gonna get scratched by Jasper's nails. (*That's what I'm naming him, Jasper. Or how about Hagar?*)

BLOG REHIJACK!!!

Bye, bye, Robert. See you later, honey.

Phew, he's gone. It's me, Holly, to close off the discussion with a reminder that a mudroom must be warm and welcoming. After all, this is the first part of the house to greet you after a long day.

That's why my interior designer, Vanessa, and I chose a cozy farm theme that's comforting and cheerful. We painted the walls in Farrow & Ball's buttery Snow White in modern emulsion so it's easier to clean and used Farrow & Ball's deep, rich Preference Red on the doors and benches crafted by a local carpenter who heeded my request for plenty of storage underneath. (Because you can never have enough storage in a mudroom.) A local seamstress covered the bench cushions in an exquisite Scandinavian fabric featuring brown nuthatches amidst falling green and red leaves and blue flowers. (I am DYING for you to see it Monday.)

But wait, here's the best part: Vanessa found an antiques dealer in Woodstock who had these amazing, authentic black early primitive pegs to hang coats and scarves. They add such a touch of class. Robert balked at the price. ("Three hundred dollars for ten wooden pegs?") I told him to get over it and deal. They make me happy.

And when Holly's happy, everyone's happy.

But when she's not . . .

Talk to you soon! In the meantime, please log on to ToTheManorBuild.com and let me know what you think of the mudroom. And whatever you do, don't forget to be there Monday to see it all, live! You are gonna flip your grits!

–Holly

This post may contain affiliate links, which means I earn a small commission when you make a purchase through those links, at no additional cost to you.

r/ToTheManorBuild: Talk about the episodes and your favorite rehab teams

Posted by vtayup26–50 min. ago

Hey Team H&R peepls–GF heard on VSP scanner yesterday that car driven by Robert was found trashed in forest. Supposably an active search for him. Whatthewhat?

(7 comments)

Agirlandherdog82–45 min. ago

Whatthewhat is right! Holy shit!

pennypinch2345–40 min. ago

See? I knew something was up. My woo-woo sense was tingling. Keep us posted u/vtayup26

Awwwsnap90–30 min. ago

VT911 FB site rumors that car owned by local woman obsessed w/R. Don't know if true or not . . . lots of whack cases on that page.

Agirlandherdog82–30 min. ago

Can relate. I'm obsessed w/R too. Only reason I watch the show

Handywithahammer56–20 min. ago

U people are pathetic, ya know! Just saying. Peace out.

pennypinch2345–10 min. ago

| If H&R are ok, they need to post ASAP!!!

Awwwsnap90–5 min. ago

| And if their not ok........?

SEVENTEEN

ERIKA

VT911 FB site rumors that car owned by local woman obsessed w/R

This is why you don't go on Reddit, not if you want to retain your sanity, Erika thinks as she does a quick search for
Awwwsnap90. Aside from the post using the grammatically
incorrect *their* instead of *they're*, he—or she—does not exist.

Andre. She'd put money on it.

Only the police know she owns the Kia Robert was driving, and it'd be just like her old high school nemesis turned cop
to fan the flames about her being some loser bunny boiler. Oh,
hey, no biggie. He's only the officer leading the investigation.
She wouldn't trust him as far as she could throw him.

Frustrated, she tosses her laptop onto her bed and peers out the window at the raw, gray day. Her mother's Subaru's not there, she notices with an uptick of alarm. It's seven thirty in the morning. Too early for her to have left for work, which raises the question: Did she even make it home last night?

Erika checks her phone and finds three hysterical messages from LuAnn asking her to set up an early Zoom meeting to "get on top of this cluster ASAP!" Crap. Their producer probably read the same Reddit BS and is raising red flags about her being the assistant who's slightly too dedicated.

Also, Kim has not replied to her texts asking how it went with the Stricklands and urging her to call as soon as she gets in. My, how the tables have turned, Erika thinks, sliding out of bed and going to the floor for her morning meditation on positivity and gratefulness.

Today's gonna be a toughie, she can tell. Four square breaths in and one mantra about looking forward to decorating Holly's dining room and her mind immediately leaps to Colton. That flake. She'd waited until eight for him to show up with the farm table he was supposed to deliver that afternoon, and he blew her off. She'd worried maybe he'd come and gone while she was with the cops, but the painters who were there all day said they didn't see him. Now they'll have to film a rustic dining room without its focal feature: the rustic farm table.

"I am looking forward to the French range arriving," she continues, inhaling deeply. "I am anticipating an easy, hassle-free installation."

At the sound of gravel crunching, she gets up and peeks through the window. The driveway is bare. She must have imagined it, she decides, returning to her lotus position on the floor.

"I am really looking forward to Robert and Holly returning from their trip today." She refuses to let herself go to the dark place where she wonders if they've been kidnapped and killed. Kashi's hypothesis about the train has saved her sanity, even if there's no word, yet, on whether the police were able to confirm the couple purchased tickets.

Also, she found some consolation online when she Googled "extra passports." Apparently, lots of people have two passports: one to store in the safe of a foreign hotel where they're staying (often at the hotel's insistence) and a spare to keep on hand while tooling around the foreign country. Having lived overseas while getting his MBA from the London School of Economics, Robert might know this kind of pro tip.

At least, that's her working theory.

An hour after her meditations, Erika is showered, dressed, and off to work, her printed to-do list in its plastic folder and her laptop case over her shoulder. No pink travel coffee mug today, though, because she left it at the house. That's okay. A coffee run will give her an excuse to stop by the general store to get a bead on the stories Mayor Bert's spreading around town like the Typhoid Mary of gossip.

First, she's going to knock on her mother's door, since she should be up and around, going off to work herself at this hour. But the curtains are still drawn and there's no answer.

Erika tries not to worry.

On the off chance there's been an accident, she calls the local hospital. For peace of mind.

◇ ◇ ◇

"What happened to your Kia?" asks Mayor Bert, ringing up her order of a coffee and one of Irma MacDougall's freshly baked cinnamon scones to give to her mother. "Heard the flatlander crashed it and trashed it."

You'd think the mayor would be rolling out the red carpet for flatlanders, the only ones naive enough to buy a $26 wedge of cheddar and a couple of cans of Heady Topper for $24. Yet every chance he gets, he's dissing the collective New Yorkers and Bostonians, as if the cash they rain into his bank account were mere Monopoly money.

"Robert must have really plummeted in your estimation if you're calling him a flatlander, Mayor," Erika says.

He rests his generous belly against the counter, unruffled by her quip. He does love to stir the pot. "Don't get me wrong. There are good flatlanders and then there are bad flatlanders. A good flatlander comes to town and respects the culture, keeps his mouth shut about a person's constitutional right to own a gun or eat meat. A bad flatlander comes to town and tries to force his ways on ours. We gotta drive electric vehicles and put in bike lanes and eat organic. You hear what I'm saying?"

What she hears is more sour grapes that Holly and Robert didn't hire him to cater the wedding. "To answer your question, I have no idea what happened to my Kia. Robert borrowed it to take Holly to Montreal because the Tesla can't go that far." Erika swipes her card. "How it ended up all the way in Peru is a mystery."

The machine beeps and a message pops up on the tiny

screen: DECLINED. Erika goes cold. Surely she has enough money in her own bank account for a coffee and a scone.

"Try it again, dear," Bert advises. "It's been wonky lately."

That had better be the case, she thinks, running the card again. Even though she's been flush these past few months thanks to her new job, she suffers from the PTSD of prior overdrafts. The machine ruminates and then almost begrudgingly announces APPROVED.

"Holly's got a Rover, though. A Westminster." The Mayor's not gonna give up this business about the car. "Last year's model. Why didn't they take that to Canada?"

Erika sips her coffee. "Robert said it was at Perry's getting winter tires switched."

"Perry's?" The mayor shakes his head. "Bad timing. Perry had a heart attack, dontcha know. Had to have major surgery. No wonder the Rover's still there. Robert should take it up to Burlington. Or put the tires on rims like I do and learn how to switch them himself. Then he'd be a true Vermonter.

On this xenophobic note, Erika takes her scone and coffee, effects a false nonchalant wave, and exits the store, crossing the green to town hall to surprise her mother.

Doreen's behind the counter filling out paperwork when Erika arrives with the pastry in its waxed bag. "For me?" she asks, putting down her pen.

"Sorry. It's for Mom. I should have picked one up for you, too."

"No, no. Please. I put on ten pounds the first few weeks on this job because of Irma's cinnamon scones." Doreen opens the bag and sniffs. "Oh, man. Stuff's like crack." Setting it aside, she says, "I'll make sure no one eats this until your mother gets in."

"She's not in yet?" Erika glances at her phone, which is lit up with messages, not one of which matters. No Colton. No Robert and Holly. No Mom. "It's quarter past nine. That's late even for her, right?"

"Meh." Doreen shrugs and goes back to the form. "Something on your mind? You don't usually come around here checking to see if she's punched the clock."

Erika sips her coffee. She really should fetch the mail and get to work, since all hell is breaking loose. But she's dying for her mother's report about the Stricklands and whether she learned anything more about Zeke. "I don't think she came home last night."

Doreen goes, "Huh."

"You know why?"

"Nope. What she does after hours is her business. I don't pry into her personal life."

"It has nothing to do with her personal life. She was meeting Gretchen Strickland and I just want to know why."

Doreen bares her teeth, the closest she can get to a smile. "No clue. Look, I've got some land recording to do, soooo . . ."

"I'm out," Erika says, taking the hint. "Please tell her to call me when she gets in, okay?"

"Will do."

Outside, Erika calls her mother's cell and then landline, relishing Kim's voice on the recorded greetings. If her mother's okay, she will never ever again ignore her calls and texts.

She even breaks her own rule and leaves another message on her voicemail. "It's after nine, Mom, and I'm growing a little worried that I haven't heard from you. You didn't come home last night and you didn't answer the door this morning. If you don't get back to me by noon, I'm calling the police."

Erika hangs up and is struck by a thunderbolt of self-awareness. She's done it. She's committed the unthinkable.

She has finally become her mother.

EIGHTEEN

KIM

"I don't see why you have to go through the whole house."
Gigi Rogers positions herself on the third step of the grand
marble staircase with her arms spread, a ringed hand clutching each railing as if she were a medieval queen or, perhaps, a
nightclub bouncer. "All I did was redecorate. We didn't *add* any
space. It shouldn't affect the taxable value."

Whether or not her "redecoration"—to use her amusing
description of a $2 million renovation—has added to the value
of a mansion for which there are no comparable properties in
Snowden or, perhaps, all of Vermont, is not for Gigi to decide.
This is the task for the subcommittee of the Board of Civil Authority of which I, as town clerk, am a member.

We are inspecting the property because Gigi, the third wife

of the Wall Street kingpin Harvey Rogers, was not satisfied with the taxable value set by the Listers. She and Harvey are going through the motions by appealing to our board because they must in order to contest in superior court.

Good luck with that. Vermont Superior Court is back-logged with genuine cases, and judges here tend not to rule favorably on billionaires pitching hissy fits over paying their fair share to support public education. I doubt Gigi has ever entered a public school or, if she has, pretends she hasn't.

Gigi proceeds to lead us on a tour of the twenty-thousand-square-foot house, the heels of her leather boots pounding the stone floors in sync with the strides of her long legs. I have to follow her bobbing platinum bun to keep up. I'm afraid my two partners in this committee, both justices of the peace and both men over sixty who are unaccustomed to mingling with former underwear models, are not paying attention to any other fixtures besides the pair of silicone traffic cones propping up the front of Gigi's cream-colored ribbed cashmere dress.

Actually, Gigi is a notch down on the class level from Harvey's second wife, Jaqueline. Jaqueline was an equally tan, if horsier, former debutante who went by the mannish name of Jaq, a nickname bestowed on her by her fellow chums at Asheville. Jaq made a big deal about being a doting wife to Harvey after stealing him from the first one, whose name I can't remember. And then Jaq trotted off with her riding instructor, Elise, so there you go.

Jaq's decorating tastes reflected her equestrian background. Very British country manse with polished wainscotting and gilt-framed paintings of dead ancestors standing atop moors with silky dogs pointing at foxes. Lots of deep reds and worn oriental carpets. Antique swords over the fireplaces (there are six) and mismatched floral couches with leather footrests. A library with books no one has read and a "children's wing" sufficiently distant from the parents' suite to guarantee uninterruption at adult parties and years of therapists' bills for the youngsters. There was a tack room and a "game shed," supposedly for letting blood run out the necks of decapitated fowl.

Gigi has done away with all that, stripping the priceless paneling and rolling up the carpets, painting the walls a stark white or, in the guest suite, a creamy beige. Gone is the wood, in is the stone. The more Italian marble, the better. The stable has been converted to a Roman bath space with a heated mineral pool and statuary of cherubs, tinted water pouring from their mouths like blue Gatorade. Call it modern-day Caligula.

"Don't forget, the quality of the materials factors into the assessment," Johnson Grant, one of our JPs, mansplains, his rheumy gaze squarely on Gigi's ass. We trail behind her as she begrudgingly lets us through the hand-tooled doors to the dining room with its 270 degrees of windows overlooking Snowden Valley below and the ski resort to the west.

The locals call this ridge of relatively new monstrosities "Hedgerow," shortened from the original "Hedge Fund Row." It's not a compliment, though Gigi and Harvey took it as one and christened their seventeen-acre estate and mausoleum of an abode as Hedgerow Manor. They rarely occupy the place more than three weeks a year.

I can't help comparing this wasted opulence with the two-bedroom firetrap where Gretchen lives with her kids—and her roommate's kids, too.

After visiting Gretchen, I am physically sickened by the Rogerses' endless, empty rooms, the ridiculous amenities serving no purpose other than to impress guests. Take, for example, Gigi's $40,000 Italian refrigerator in solid ash with a built-in coffee maker and TV. That doesn't even make any sense. Do the Rogers really need a rooftop helipad? Is a "golf simulator" room a requirement?

If I could wave a magic wand, I'd whisk Gigi to Gretchen's place so she could see up close and personal how the other half lives. I doubt that would bring her to Jesus, though. Listen to the way she talks. We're passing through one of two kitchens (not including the "catering kitchen," whatever that is) and she's back to griping about taxes.

"If you can believe it, we pay one hundred and twenty thousand dollars a year! For a vacation home! Outrageous!"

That's at an assessment of $6 million. I hate to break it to her, but with all this marble and the Roman baths, the new indoor swimming pool (does Gigi think for a moment we're gonna miss that?) as well as the exercise studio in the converted tack room and the new twenty-eight-seat movie studio in the basement, she should add another mil, according to my back-of-the-napkin calculations.

Which translates into another thirty grand to that tax bill, Gigi. You might want to give your accountant a heads-up.

We are about to take the elevator to the second floor when I pause to check my phone. It's been buzzing on and off all morning. I haven't answered, because I didn't want to be rude. But clearly something's exploding at work.

"You should know, "Gigi says, keeping the elevator door open, "that due to security concerns, we expressly forbid any photos of the interior."

I hold up a finger. "Duly noted," I say. "Please, go on without me."

Gigi doesn't seem to like that, but I step out onto one of her many terraces to take the call anyway.

"Hey," Doreen says. "Whatcha doing?"

For heaven's sake. She'd better not be bothering me because she's bored. "I'm with the BCA. We're touring the Rogerses' house."

"Oh, yeah. How is it? You can make it out from the top of Mount Snowden. Looks like the fucking Taj Mahal. Are there cherubs? I bet it's got a fountain. Does it have a fountain?"

"Two. One spits blue vomit."

"Classy. Didn't mean to interrupt your tour of Disneyworld on meth, but your daughter stopped by and brought you a scone. A cinnamon one from the general store. Irma MacDougall's. With frosting."

I'm touched. I can't remember Erika ever bringing me a pastry. This is a gold star day, as she would say. "How sweet. Literally."

"Full disclosure: I ate it."

"Shit, Doreen. Why'd you do that?"

"Because it was gonna get stale. It was delicious, by the way." She coughs. God willing she's choking on a scone crumb.

"Anyway, you should probably give her a call. I might be wrong, but I think she thinks you're dead."

"Dead?"

"Didn't see your car in the driveway this morning. Didn't hear you come in last night. She's all worked up. Tears in her eyes. Reminds me of the way you get when you don't know where *she* is."

It's the stress from this ridiculous *To the Manor Build* contest and then her car getting stolen and vandalized. My daughter doesn't do well under pressure. "You didn't tell her I had to leave early to do BCA inspections?"

"And ruin all my fun? Think of the hell she's put you through, not returning your calls or messages. The silent treatment. Let her see how it feels for once. Payback time, baby."

It's no use scolding Doreen. She'll only grumble about my being ungrateful for her wisdom and then make me feel bad. "Okay, I'll give her a ring."

"Also, Tammy Beauregard called here twice this morning. She's flipping out after reading online that the car her daughter and son-in-law were driving was found abandoned in the woods. She also wants to know if the rumors are true that the car belongs to Erika."

"Geesh. That's out there already?"

"I guess. I dunno. I stay away from the internet. Devil's playground in my opinion."

I send a text to Erika letting her know I'm okay and on Hedgerow for a BCA inspection. I wait for her reply and get a classic—OK. In a meeting—from her Apple Watch. Mark my words, those watches are perfect tools for serial killers. That's why she and I have agreed to emergency code words only we know in case one or the other of us gets kidnapped. Ours is "pistachio ice cream," the flavor of which we both despise with a passion.

When I return to the tour, I'm disappointed to find the inspection's over. I've missed the upstairs of Gigi's house, which is a pity and questionable, since there are twenty bedrooms and just as many bathrooms. Realizing I'm the hard-ass in this committee, the lady of the manor must have taken advantage of my momentary absence to race through the tour with claims of "nothing's changed." I can see the men going along with her commands, their sheepish tongues lolling out of their mouths.

"Thank you, so very, very much," I overhear Johnson gush. They're in the foyer, which is easy to find since the house is built in concentric circles. Just follow the floor-to-ceiling windows and you're bound to end up at the front door. "We'll be in touch."

"Actually," I correct, flying in before Johnson makes a promise Gigi will take as gospel, "our committee will deliver a report to the BCA in its entirety and then the BCA will issue a decision that will be delivered to you by certified mail."

Gigi's gold bracelets clink as she waves this off. "Harvey and I will be in Cannes by then. We'll leave it up to the lawyers."

Ah, yes. Those threats of legal retaliation never get old.

Halfway down the hill, I get three bars and park on the side to call Tammy Beauregard. I don't know what I can tell her. She probably has more info than I do at this point.

"Kim?" She answers like we're old friends. "Oh, I am so glad you called me back. Is this a bad time?"

Her southern accent is thicker than I expected from my brief interactions with Holly. "This is a fine time, Tammy. Not sure I can help you but—"

"I'm at sixes and sevens over Haylee. I don't know what to do. We don't chat regular and it's no secret I ain't been the best mother, but if I bring out the big guns and insist she call her mama right away, she usually does within the hour. But it's been days and now this news about their car—your daughter's car—and . . ." Her voice cracks into a sob. "I'm all the way in Homosassa. I'm so far away! Do you have any news?"

My heart aches. I, too, have paced the floors waiting for word from a child that she's okay. The gnawing angst is so crazymaking you want to crawl out of your skin. You feel you'll go insane if you don't get an all clear. And yet our kids are still alive and well. So far.

"I'm sorry you're going through this, Tammy. I'm sure your daughter and Robert are fine. You know how millennials are. They think they're the center of the universe . . ."

"Hmmhmm."

"Erika said they're supposed to come back tonight. And . . ."

"And if they don't . . . ?"

This is the looming question, isn't it? "No. Don't go there, Tammy. Don't borrow trouble."

There's a pause on the other end followed by the sound of nose blowing. "I just keep going over and over about what Haylee said when we last we spoke right before the wedding.

She was insistent I stay put. I said no way was I not gonna be there to see my baby get married. But she wouldn't hear of it."

More nose blowing and sniffling.

"She said, and this is a direct quote, 'Mama, I love you too much to lose you.' I said, what does that mean? I thought she was worried I was gonna die in a plane crash or something silly. But then she got real serious and said, 'We got a huge problem with the prior owner. He's a mean sumabitch, Mama. A snake in the grass. And I don't trust him not to show up and make a scene. I'd rather you watched the ceremony online at home where you're safe.'"

Tammy's tale sets my hair on edge. The mean sumabitch, obviously, is Zeke Strickland, described by his own estranged wife as irrational, prone to violence, and fueled by rage. Is this why Erika overreacted to my meeting Gretchen last night? Is this why she asked me to find out where he was?

In the past, when Holly and Robert were out of town, I have definitely worried about Erika staying late to work alone in that big house, the house Zeke claims was stolen out from under him, the house he's threatened to torch to the ground. If Holly was so concerned about what mayhem Zeke might have wrought in front of thousands of viewers that she wouldn't allow her own mother to be present, what might he do to my daughter?

After all, it's not like she has the protection of the security detail Robert hired for the wedding. She's defenseless, a sitting duck. I'm outraged that Robert has left her there to fend for herself while he zipped off on a romantic getaway *in her car*. How dare he expose a twenty-seven-year-old assistant to that kind of danger! He's exploiting his employee, frankly, and there'll be more than one of us reading him the riot act when he returns.

Trust me. I'll see to it Zeke Strickland will be the least of his problems.

Getting back to Tammy, I take a deep breath in an attempt to calm myself before I calm her. "If it makes you feel any better, I was at that wedding and nothing happened. Haylee was probably just being a nervous bride. Look, as soon as I find out anything, I'll call you. I promise. I have your number in my contacts. Meanwhile, try to keep positive, okay? Worrying doesn't add anything but wrinkles."

"You're right. I'll try to get a grip. Thank you, Kim. Here's to hoping the next time we talk it's to share good news."

"Absolutely," I say. Then I hang up and call Erika, going straight to voicemail. It's all I can do from calling again and again until she answers. I won't have a moment's peace until she does.

NINETEEN

ERIKA

WEDNESDAY AFTERNOON

"I, I . . . I don't know, know what to . . ." Erika cannot find
the words. Her mind is a swamp of shock and irritation and
spiking anxiety. Somehow, she has messed up. Messed up big
time. Could she have been that careless?

"Seems okay to me." Joe Marconi, possessor of kitchen
appliance expertise and a thick Boston accent, shrugs at the
Lacanche Cluny Classique model gas range. "What's the problem?"

Custom-made in France, the dual-fuel range with six
gas burners and two electric ovens cost a total, after taxes, of
$18,600, took four months to manufacture, another month to
ship and deliver (for $1,580), and is the focal point of Holly's
kitchen.

The white tile backsplash with blue and yellow fleur-de-lis has been specifically color coordinated to the french blue range. (The factory in France set a sample color chip to ensure perfection.) The back of the glass cabinets is accented with the same shade. The effect would have been stunning if the range were, indeed, blue.

It's not. It's black. And it looks awful. The clashing shades hurt the eyes.

"The problem is it's the wrong color," she says, folding her arms, partially to keep herself from falling apart.

"That's what you ordered." Joe unfolds a delivery notice and points to the English translation under the French description. "BL. That means black."

Erika closes her eyes. It's not Joe's fault. He's just the messenger. But she can't help almost screaming, "In no universe does 'BL' mean black. 'BLK' means black. Or 'BK.' Not 'BL.' BL means 'blue'!"

"What do you want me to do, pack it up and ship it back? That's not gonna be cheap. Not *shah* it's possible, not without contacting the company and *they-ah* probably closed for the day. Six *ow-ah* time difference. You know how the French *ahh*."

Time difference or not, returning it is out of the question. The reveal is now less than a week away and Hector held off filming the kitchen specifically because the range hadn't been installed. They must have a range. Could they paint it? Borrow a blue model from a dealer on the slim chance it had six burners? Or should she ignore the color mismatch and have it installed? The guys are here and they won't return before Monday. They made a special trip from Boston.

Again, this is the kind of decision that's way above her pay grade. Holly and Robert should be on site to deal with this snafu. Part of her is furious with them, even if that's totally illogical, since more and more it appears something truly awful may have happened.

Kashi hasn't been able to confirm they were on the Adirondack line to Montreal, and Erika would have expected to hear from them by now if they were on their way home either today or tomorrow. At the very least, they need to know there's no car waiting for them at the station—or wherever they left it.

"Erika, have we lost you?" LuAnn whines like a mosquito in her ear.

Before the deliverers arrived with the wrong range, Erika was in the midst of a heated Zoom meeting with LuAnn and Xavier, *TMB*'s vice president of "convergence and social media," who are in high alert over online chatter about Robert and Holly. Fires are breaking out left and right and she has only two feet to stomp them out.

"Be right there. Dealing with the range," she says into her AirPods.

"Okay. Do hurry," LuAnn says. "Xavier has another meeting in five."

"Might as well install it." She throws up her arms. "If Holly and Robert don't like it, that's their problem. I'll be out of a job by then, anyway."

Joe removes the pen stuck behind his ear and smooths the order on the countertop. "Sign *heeyah*."

Erika dashes her signature across the bottom line and returns to Holly's office, closing the door against Joe's admonitions to his employees to "mind the fuckin' *flauh*." Slipping in front of her laptop, she says, "Sorry about that."

LuAnn clears her throat in reproach. "Rewind, Xavier, and repeat for Erika what you just told me."

"So Reddit is blowing up over this car thing and I don't get it." He links and unlinks his long, ringed fingers as he flicks back excessively long black bangs to keep them from dangling over his tortoiseshell glasses. "I mean, like, so what? A Kia was found in the woods. The only crime there is that it's a Kia."

Erika refrains from pointing out he's talking about her beloved car.

Xavier is the top communications honcho, the point person who connects *TMB*'s Facebook, Twitter, and Instagram accounts along with *TMB*'s own dedicated feed with marketing, advertising, and influencers across social media. An indication of how hot the water and how deep Team H&R are in it is that never before have they needed to meet with Xavier.

"Help me out here, Erika," he says. "What's really going on with Holly and Robert, if you know?"

LuAnn says, "I'd appreciate some on-the-scene reporting, too. I spoke briefly with a Vermont state trooper yesterday. Pinard? Picard? All he wanted to know from me is when I last heard from them. I forwarded him the text Robert sent early Sunday morning. Otherwise, I'm in the dark. Is it true what they're saying online, that the car's yours, Erika?"

"The gas line is turned off, am I right?" a contractor shouts. "No. Not that gas. This gas, yah bonehead."

Erika covers an ear. "Yes. The car's mine."

"Oh, shit," Xavier interjects. "My bad."

"It's okay. I loaned it to Robert so he could take Holly to Montreal without worrying about where to charge the Tesla." She'd rather not go into Robert's visit to her apartment. "I'm sorry. I thought you knew that."

"No. You didn't make that clear," LuAnn says tightly. "Along those lines, I procured a copy of their contract. It states in black and white that the talent may not seek a leave from the show without prior written approval from the producers. That's me."

"Guys, I think you should prepare yourselves for the fact that there might be more going on than appears." Erika doesn't mean to be so forward, but these people are missing the larger issue. "I haven't been able to find a hotel in Montreal where Robert and Holly have registered, even under pseudonyms. Trooper Kashi said she'd let me know if my car was parked at the any of the stations along the Adirondack line. I checked with her this morning. No confirmation that it was, at least not in any official Amtrak lots. And there's something else . . ."

LuAnn and Xavier lean into their cameras, their faces filling most of their screens.

A text lights up her phone screen.

UNKNOWN: Can you call me? Important.

Erika doesn't recognize the contact, though it's likely not from Robert and Holly. If they were back in touch, they'd call the house or show up. They wouldn't send vague requests.

"What?" LuAnn presses.

"Robert's been getting threatening letters."

Xavier slaps his mouth.

"What kind of threatening letters?" LuAnn asks cautiously.

"I found them in the bottom locked drawer of his filing cabinet. I happened to have a key." Best not to divulge she found them two days ago, the day LuAnn threatened to ruin her career if she was holding back information. "They're handwritten. I took a photo of them spread out on the floor. I'll email it to you."

She sends the group the photo from her phone and waits for their reactions. LuAnn reads the poem out loud. " 'Arm for an arm. Eye for an eye. You steal my house. I kill your wife. Then take your life. Thieves rules.' What the hell? Who sent these?"

"I don't know for certain, but my best guess is the prior owner of this property, a mentally disturbed man named Zeke Strickland."

"Because. . . . ?" LuAnn's eyebrows are arched, lips pursed. She looks about to explode.

Erika cracks her knuckles out of nervousness. This is so unfair. Why is she the one to be yelled at by the producer when she didn't do anything wrong? Honestly, she has half a mind to get up and walk off the job right now. At twenty-two dollars an hour, she's not paid enough to deal with this kind of shit.

Inhaling deeply, she says, "Because Robert evicted him from the house in February."

LuAnn whips off her glasses. "February! He never told us the rehab was occupied when he signed the contract. He said it was his free and clear. We never would have made an offer if an eviction was involved."

Oh, this is worse than she expected. Erika takes a long sip of water from the bottle to buy herself time and slow her pulse. So this was why Robert didn't go public with the letters, because he lied to *TMB*. Big time.

"Goddammit, Erika," LuAnn snarls. "I thought I made it clear to you that I needed to be informed of everything. I knew, I just knew, you were holding out on me."

Erika bites back the temptation to cry. "I'm sorry. I just found out." A lie, but whatever.

LuAnn turns to Xavier. "Did you know about this?"

"Me? How would I know?"

She flicks her hand. "Reddit. Social media. Don't those gremlins have a way of unearthing this stuff?"

"You mean trolls? Lemme check." He retreats to his other computer. Anything to avoid the producer's wrath.

"This is a cluster." LuAnn massages her brow. "If it gets out that Robert evicted a . . . Oh, my word. Don't tell me he kicked out a family. Please, not children."

"His wife and twins had already left, I believe." Erika can't quite recall the Strickland family dynamic. Her mother will know. "Zeke was on his own. My understanding is there were allegations of domestic assault. He had a lot of guns and used to shoot at people from his front porch."

LuAnn lets out a moan. Erika texts a reply to the anonymous number.

ERIKA: In a meeting. Who is this?

The response is instant.

UNKNOWN: Colton's father, Rick. Sorry to bother you. Thought maybe you've heard from him.

Rick Whitcomb? Erika recalls a ruddy man in a peach polo shirt over a potbelly holding court at a Labor Day family reunion at the Whitcombs' camp in North Hero on Lake Champlain. By then, Colton had completed his transition from financial paraplanner at Edward Jones to spiritual woodworker, and their romance was on the rocks.

Erika shoots back a text.

ERIKA: He was supposed to drop off a farm table yesterday and didn't. I waited all evening.

"Who is LadyAntebellum62?" Xavier taps on his keyboard. "Seems like she must have an inside connection, because she is real-timing this shit. She knows about the honeymoon. Says the cops have checked with border patrol. Holly and Robert never crossed into Canada."

So much for the spare passport theory.

"Oh my *god*!" Xavier flicks his bangs. "You should see what data just sent up. LuAnn, wanna let me drive for a bit? This is *amaaaaaazing*. Look at our stats! They're off the charts!"

LuAnn is on her phone. "I'm with legal. Be my guest."

From the kitchen comes, "Geesh. What the hell? This unit's electric *and* gas and I got no two *fahty*, just a wimpy one ten for, like, a fan."

Erika braces for the summons. It comes a minute later. "Knock, knock," Joe says from the other side of the door. "Mind stepping out here for a few?"

The tone of his voice is not encouraging. Erika joins him in the kitchen. "What's up?"

"*We-ah* gonna need a *mah-stah* electrician. Stat." He wipes sweat off his broad brow, though it's not even warm. "Gotta kill the *pow-ah* and install a two *fahty*. This is a dual range and you can't run dual on one ten. We got *anoth-ah* job in Methuen and Waltham this week so we won't be able to come back until next Wednesday."

After the reveal. If there will even be one.

Vowing not to be undone by this latest land mine, Erika returns to the office and scrolls through the contacts in Holly's address book, searching for a local contractor who might be able to arrive in a flash. This is futile. No master electrician is sitting around Snowden twiddling his or her thumbs waiting for a call from the shit show on the hill. The freelancers they used in the summer are likely all booked now.

"Erika, have you left us again?" LuAnn inquires in her ear. "Xavier had to go. I've arranged for an emergency Zoom meeting with legal. In the meantime, keep me posted about everything. No more surprises, okay?"

Joe lingers in the doorway, waiting for word about an electrician.

"Okay," Erika says, glad, at least, that she hasn't been fired. Not yet.

"And may I remind you," LuAnn adds. "That you signed an NDA, too. Stay off social media and be very, very circumspect about your verbal conversations, even with family. I come from a town about the size of Snowden and I am all too familiar with how rumors spread. I don't think I need to spell out how this story could blow up for us. Evictions of fathers are antithetical to *TMB*'s mission statement."

LuAnn's lack of concern for Holly's and Robert's welfare is striking. So corporate. If Zeke has actually hurt or injured them, will she sweep it under the rug? She might. Erika could see *TMB* taking down their website and erasing their vlog as if they simply never existed.

She clicks out of Zoom, takes one more swig from her water bottle, and turns to Joe. "I'll call around, but I doubt we'll be able to get a master electrician here on such short notice."

"That's what I figured. Look, I don't want you paying for these boys to loaf around. How's about we put the range in place, but don't connect it. You don't actually need it working for Monday, do you? It's just for the viewers, right?"

Erika could kiss his stubbled cheek. "Fantastic. Yes, that'll work!"

"Just as long no one tries to use it, it'll be okay." He scratches the back of his neck, debating this. "Leaves me uncomfortable, though. Not exactly up to code."

"It'll be fine. Like you said, it's just a show, an illusion."

As the installers proceed to put the range in place, disconnected, Erika goes to the fridge and gets out a cherry yogurt. She's famished. It's almost two and the only calories she's consumed are from the cream in her coffee. There's another text from her mom that Tammy Beauregard's been calling the office about her daughter and would Holly please call her back.

If only.

Then Erika remembers the file of nondisclosure agreements the contractors were obligated to complete before working. It was Erika's job as the assistant to scan and email to *TMB*'s LA office each NDA along with the contractors' 1099s and contact forms—a treasure trove of info.

Most of the electrical wiring was done over a compact number of days in mid-August, around the fifteenth. Not an ideal season to search for skilled labor, since so many people were on vacation. She sets aside a couple of them who might be around—an electrician from New Hampshire and another from Manchester, Vermont—and scrolls through the rest until she comes to one from . . . Zeke Strickland.

Wait, what?

Erika does a double take. Is this a gag? Blowing up the image for a clearer view of the application, she zooms in for closer inspection. Sure enough, penciled in shaky lettering at the bottom of the NDA is ZEKE STRICKLAND. There's no mistake.

There's also no email or cell or mailing address. There's no attached certificate of insurance or 1099, either. How did he slip past the general contractor without a COI? How did it slip past *her*, since she's the one who scanned the NDAs into the system? Was he actually in this house while she and Holly were here?

Does that mean he has a way in?

She gets that sense of being watched again, as if he might be here, right now, spying on her through a knothole in the log wall. Maybe he's one of the technicians in the kitchen. A landscaper planting rugosas on the hillside. A painter touching up the trim on the garage. A mason's assistant grouting the outdoor entertainment area.

It occurs to her she wouldn't recognize this monster if he walked into this very room. She has absolutely no idea what he looks like. Is he short or tall? Fair or dark haired? Long or short hair? Muscular or wiry? Workers have been entering and exiting this house every day and she hasn't given them a second thought.

Any one of them could have been—*could be*—him.

All of a sudden, she's struck by a paralyzing hunch. The letters!

Going to Robert's file cabinet, she tugs the lower drawer. It should be locked. She specifically remembers turning the small key and hearing the click. But the drawer's not locked. It opens easily and, as she feared, it's empty.

Robert's laptop and the file of hate mail are gone.

TMB: LOVE AMONG THE ACTUAL RUINS

POST #66: PROPERTY IS THEFT—OWN IT!

I'm Robert Barron, husband of Holly Barron, and we're contestants on *To the Manor Build*, a super popular rehab show with millions of dollars at stake.

This is a hijack of my wife's unfiltered, no-holds-barred, honest, behind-the-scenes peek at the craziness of turning a run-down Vermont log cabin into a net-zero awesome house with ~~a hot, sexy guy I am about to~~ me!

My motto: Whatever you can do, I already did!

Follow me to see how!

Let's say you've got some spare cash—probably not much—but unlike your chump coworker who's losing his pants on Ameritrade, you've got the smarts to know there's no way to corner a market that's run by high-speed electronic traders. Problem is, all the good seats are taken, and you're left circling round and round, searching for the perfect ground-floor investment opportunity in a rigged game of musical chairs.

So what's left?

Precious metals: Just because some old WASPy dame in pearls is counting gold doubloons on a cable TV ad doesn't mean hoarding gold, silver, platinum, diamonds, what have you, will be a guaranteed return. Like any other commodity, precious metals are subject to the same market woes that affect, say, pharmaceutical stocks. Except with pharmaceutical stocks you at least have an edge in research. Not your style. Hard pass.

Bitcoin: Yeah? Really? Here's my quick-and-dirty on cryptocurrency: Figure out how much money per month you could blow in a casino and not care, and dedicate that amount to Bitcoin. Your odds are about the same and the payoff is bigger—unless you get hacked. Then all bets are off.

Real estate: I invest in real estate because it's *real* property, unlike the personal, disposable, or intellectual kind. It's here to stay. It's a limited resource—they ain't making more of it—and, yet, the population's growing. Everyone needs a place to live. They need yards for their kids and dogs. They need a place to plant their American flag.

You can survey real property and map it, record it for prosperity with your name in the corner. You can fence it off and call it yours and yours alone. You can electrify its perimeter. You can call the cops if someone steps on it. Chances are someday you'll be buried in it.

Can't say that with cryptocurrency.

I also prefer investing in real estate because that's my world. I grew up assessing distressed properties, envisioning their potential. My father made his fortune rehabbing run-down Boston-area neighborhoods, building (pun intended) on the fortune HIS father made constructing developments in Woburn, Massachusetts. Depressions and recessions boomed and busted and, still, real estate rose in value. A classic Boston triple-decker that might have sold for $140,000 the day I was born is now listed in the millions.

Which brings us back to our original question: How can you make money investing in real estate during a bloated market?

Ah, but bloated markets are exactly when you *should* be hunting for great deals. Bloated markets inevitably lead to overextended owners who end up watching their property sold out from under them. You're not going to find these properties on Zillow or even Craigslist, because they're not for sale by a Realtor or an owner.

They're for sale by the government.

Depending on your state structure, counties, and even municipalities, recoup unpaid property taxes by offering tax liens or tax deeds on delinquent properties. In some states, such as New Jersey, the government will auction off tax liens, with very generous interest-rate returns: think 18 percent. That's what the owners must pay you before they can sell their land.

Other states, like Vermont, where I found <u>my million-dollar property for $8,500</u>, are tougher. They actually put up the property for auction with the unpaid taxes as the starting bid. The properties can be sold in an hour and, if there's no redemption period, that's it. You just landed yourself an estate for the cost of a freaking Subaru—provided you don't get overexcited during the auction and bid too high. ***Not my issue, as you'll find out below.***

With any investment, there are risks. Banks can be leery of writing mortgages for properties with tax-sale deeds for fear an unknown lien holder might have a claim on the property. But in most tax sales, all liens—including mortgages—are wiped out after the redemption period. And you can pursue legal efforts to "quiet the title," if that allows you to sleep at night.

From my experience, the biggest risk to actually owning a house bought at tax sale vs. winning a tax lien is dealing with the original owner. After all, you are taking what he believes to be his property, and that can be, well, messy.

In the case of the Vermont farmhouse on eighty acres with mountain views I won at a tax sale run by the Town of Snowden, the owner was one mean, gnarly son of a bitch. He wouldn't think twice about putting a bullet through your head if he caught you turning around in his driveway and he didn't take to the idea of some slick Bostonian "stealing" what was rightfully his.

Hah! If only he'd known he was dealing with the legendary Robber Barron.

Let's just say that guy is no longer my problem. The way I see it, I've done the world a favor.

You're welcome, world.

How will I avoid taking a tax hit on that windfall? To find the answers to this along with numerous other insider tips about how you can legally steal real estate, too, subscribe to my newsletter, Thieve Like The Robber Barron. And don't forget to follow our renovation of this house on ToTheManorBuild.com for design ideas that buyers *want*.

Until next time, remember all property is theft . . . own it!

r/ToTheManorBuild: Talk about the episodes and your favorite rehab teams

Posted by vtayup26–5 min. ago

r/TMB: Rumors that Robert Barron's body just found in VT woods near the abandoned car he was driving. Male 30s-40s. Waiting for police confirmation.

(6 comments)

teambarron4thewin–2 min. ago

Where are you getting this? This is awful. AWFUL!! If it's true

Mandywiththemany675–2 min. ago

Fake news!

Absolutelyfabulouslyme!–1 min. ago

Ditto that. Reddit should suspend/ban/block.

vtayup26 (OP)–just now

Not fake news. came over the VSP scanner. Body found, Very upsetting. Sorry!

65372eldoradogold–just now

You read his blog this AM? Dick move to that guy he kicked out of that house. Had lots of enemies

vtayup26 (OP)–just now

What guy?

TWENTY

KIM

THURSDAY MORNING

"Barron took out an eight-hundred thousand mortgage." Doreen slides a set of documents into the scanner and presses Scan on her computer screen. "Cosigned by his dad, Robert Barron Junior, if you can believe it."

I've been intently drafting the BCA committee evaluation on the Rogerses' house, so it takes me a beat to switch gears to understand that Doreen's referring to the paperwork she's processing. As the person responsible for all the land recording in the office, including warranty deeds, quitclaims, mortgages, discharges, survey maps, and zoning applications, my assistant's the first to know who's moving in, who's moving out, and who's going bankrupt.

Doreen refills her delicate bone china teacup, decorated in

pink roses, from a matching pot. She's been going through a tea phase lately, having become infatuated with the ritual during a walking tour of Yorkshire she and Elliot took last month. There's something very amusing about an amateur bodybuilder and former navy sailor with a tattoo of an anchor on her forearm lifting her pinkie to sip from a cup that could easily be gracing the lips of Lady Crawley.

"Is eight hundred a lot?" I ask.

"You're asking me? I own my house straight out. Bought it for fifty-five grand twenty years ago. I'd say eight hundred's crazy." She reviews the scans to ensure all the pages have been imaged and hits Save. "Interesting that he owned the property outright and now he's up to his ears in debt. And by interesting, I mean dumb."

"Erika says that on *TMB* you have to pay for all the renovations up front. Holly and Robert got a discount on the appliances, but unless they win the contest, they'll have to eat those costs."

Doreen clips the Barron mortgage and slides it into a prepaid envelope. "He could have sat on the property for seven years to avoid land-gains taxes and made a profit of at least half a million without lifting a finger. More, if he'd subdivided it into eight, ten-acre lots. A hundred grand each. Cha-ching!"

Which would have been a disaster for our town. "The last thing anyone wants is to turn Snowden into New Jersey."

"Yeah, but his father's a developer. You'd think that's the course his son would take." Tossing the envelope onto the pile of outgoing mail, she says, "Maybe he couldn't resist the allure of internet fame."

"Who?" Dexter the Lister pops out of his hidey-hole office, hands in pockets.

"Robert Barron. The 'Robber Barron.'" Doreen finger-quotes. "Just recorded his eight-hundred-thousand-dollar mortgage to pay for that *To the Manor Build* reno."

Dex lets out a whistle. "Those monthly payments are gonna be through the roof."

"Four grand," I estimate. My monthly take-home pay.

"Forty-eight thousand a year." Dex readjusts his Red Sox ball cap. He never takes it off, not even the office. "Before property taxes."

"Who we talking about?" Morty, the other Lister, tall, white-haired, and jowly, joins his partner. "Where's he live? Have we been to his house?"

Doreen says over her teacup. "Yes, you've been to his house. It's Robert Barron."

"The Robber Barron." Morty rubs his chin. "We've got that at fifty percent completed but by April first, could be ninety." His bushy eyebrows bounce with glee. "I can't wait to get into that place. Could be over a million and a half, even ten percent shy of completion."

"I'm telling you, those two are nothing but a couple of phonies." Dex throws down his hands. "They're yuppies. They've never hammered a nail in their lives. It's all smoke and mirrors to sell fancy dishwashers."

This is why people detest Listers. First they act like they have a divine right to butt into their neighbors' bedrooms and then they automatically assume their fellow residents are up to no good. They're forever accusing some innocent homeowner of sneaking in an unpermitted addition or hiding a kitchen remodel, converting a closet to a powder room and hoping the town doesn't add in the extra fixtures to up the property's value. They're wired to suspect the worst in others.

"Classy wedding, though," Morty adds. "My wife showed me a clip on her computer. She's a sucker for anything Scottish."

"Bah." Dex slaps the air. "Those Barrons are about as Scottish as spaghetti. Any fool can rent a kilt and hire a bagpiper."

"And you know this how?" Doreen asks.

Dex hitches up his pants. "Let's just say I have my sources. Supposedly when it comes to greasing palms down there in Boston, the old man's got the butter. Ya gotta if you're in the construction business. You don't win those big bids by being Howdy Doody."

Doreen turns to me, brows furrowed. "Howdy Doody?"

"Good thing for the boy, though. Daddy will bail him out when he defaults on that ridiculous mortgage." He thumbs at the paperwork Doreen's just recorded. "*Again.*"

Morty folds his arms philosophically. "Now how does that work if the tax sale is overturned in court? Will Barron still be on the hook for the eight-hundred-thousand-dollar note?"

My jaw drops and I shoot an accusatory glare at Doreen, who puts down her teacup and swivels right around to busily process the next document in her pile. She's been talking behind my back to the Listers, that pinky-lifting, tea-sipping rat. And she doesn't even like the Listers.

"What makes you think the tax sale will be overturned in court?" Dex asks.

Doreen begins to hum a tuneless tune.

"She screwed up." Morty flings an accusatory finger in my direction. "Ask Doreen."

"No, ask me," I say, getting up and turning my back to my assistant. I'll deal with her later. "It has recently come to my attention that I failed to properly notify the original owners by regular and certified mail of the upcoming sale. I have since informed them. The ball is in their court, so to speak."

"They won't stand a chance," Dex says. "Old man Barron will bleed them dry. Developers love to drag little people through the legal system. He will eat them up and spit them out!"

That does appear to be the going consensus. However, now that the question's been raised, I'm more curious about what would happen to the mortgage if Robert loses the property. "But if the court does overturn the sale, does that mean the mortgage disappears?"

"Only if it was on the property before the original sale," says Dex, who would know, since he's a former farmer and if there's one thing farmers know, it's tax sales. "Barron took out the loan after he got the property. If the title's bad, you could argue that's the bank's fault for not doing better research. Might be able to wring cash from the title attorney's malpractice, but when it's all said and done, the promissory note buried deep in the paperwork means Barron's responsible."

"With no collateral," Morty adds. "Could be ugly for him. Could be the ruination of the, ahem, legendary 'Robber Barron.'" He chuckles low in delight.

Another reason for the Barrons to pummel the Stricklands

in court, and now I've gone and made things worse by raising Gretchen's hopes she could get her house back. She was right; I should stop interfering.

After Tweedledee and Tweedledum slither back into their office, Doreen sheepishly says, "Sorry. Morty saw the Strickland tax file in the copier and asked what it was doing out."

I'm not nearly as peeved as I was when he made that crack about me screwing up. "It's okay. Everyone's gonna find out eventually. This gave me a chance to explain it myself."

We return to our duties in resolved silence, Doreen tidying up her recording while I apply the finishing touches to the BCA report. When the office phone rings, I'm so focused calculating the view value of the Rogerses' Hedgerow mansion, it takes me a minute to recognize the panicked voice on the other end.

"So sorry to keep bugging you, Kim, but have you heard the latest?"

A lump of lead drops into my stomach as I register the panic of Tammy's tone. "No, what?"

"It's all over the internet. Apparently, they found a body near where your daughter's car was."

"A body in the Green Mountain Forest?" My mouth goes dry. "Male or female?"

"Male, thank God, but still. They're saying it's Robert! Oh, my word. I feel like a cockroach that got sprayed by Raid, running around with my head cut off. Where the hell is my daughter?"

Doreen is now out of her chair and at my side, tapping into her phone. "On it," she whispers.

I remind myself to take this minute by minute, second by second. "Let's not leap to conclusions, Tammy—"

"I can't stay here and do nothing. I booked a flight from Tampa to Burlington, leaving this afternoon."

Doreen taps me on the shoulder. *I'll pick her up*, she mouths.

We'll pick her up, I mouth back. "No problem, Tammy. My assistant and I will meet you at the airport."

"That's awful kind of you. I'm hoping Haylee will be back by then and she can fetch me. If not, I don't know how I'm gonna cope. You're so lucky to have your daughter in town where you can keep an eye on her. I'd give anything to hug my baby, just once."

Hanging up, I can't remember the last time I gave Erika a hug and decide to give her another call.

It goes straight to voicemail.

Now my worries are taking root.

TWENTY-ONE

ERIKA

"Please, please, please don't be Robert."

And what about Holly?

Erika's not one for prayers. She wasn't raised with any formal religion, aside from her grandmother taking her to the Easter sunrise service down at the United Methodist Church, and that was mainly because there was an egg hunt afterward. But this morning with the news about a dead male body found suspiciously near where her car was trashed in the forest, she is down on her knees.

"Dear God," she begins, hands clasped. "I know what's done is done, but if this really is Robert who's dead, please keep Holly safe. Don't let Zeke kill her, too."

She thinks of the empty drawer at the bottom of Robert's

filing cabinet. She hasn't been able to stop thinking about it, actually. "And please don't let Zeke Strickland come after me, either," she continues, her kneecap aching on the hard floor. "I haven't been perfect, but Holly and I don't deserve to die because some guy's pissed off about losing his house, okay? Thank you for listening, God. I trust you'll take care of this."

She exhales, feeling strangely at peace. Perhaps all those positive affirmations on Twitter about the Lord Shepherd sheltering his lambs aren't bullshit after all. We'll see, she thinks, getting up and heading to the shower. Until Holly and Robert are safe and sound, the jury's out.

Routine helps, too. Her coffee is in its pink metal travel mug. The day's schedule is printed out and secure in its plastic page protector. A cherry yogurt is in her purse and she's wearing one of her favorite outfits: a gray blouse over ankle-length black trousers patterned with barely visible stripes and a white blazer. Holly's castoffs, because Robert likes her to wear bright colors, not neutrals.

It feels like she's donning a coat of armor.

◇ ◇ ◇

The house on Holly Hill looms large and ominous under the gray sky as Erika passes the electronic gate slowly and ascends the gravel driveway with trepidation. This sense of dread is so different from her usual attitude.

During the course of the project, she approached her work with enthusiasm, especially if Robert was around to add a touch of spice. His energy was electrifying, inspiring. The way he bounded down the halls, his booming voice bouncing off the walls as he engaged in jovial banter with the carpenters. His approving smile, a reward for a job well done, was so addictive, she routinely went above and beyond just to see it, again and again.

Please, please, may the body not be Robert's.

Robert was so proud of the house. He was like a little boy when he showed off its coolest parts—the rubber roof, the instant firepits, the hidden doorway in the great room bookshelves. ("Just like Batman!" he once gushed.) His passion was contagious, too.

Erika never had a smidge of interest in real estate until she met Robert. He taught her to appreciate the nuances of different trims, the beauty of wood grain and the smell of fresh paint, how technological advances in glazing have drastically improved the thermal dynamics of windows.

If the Redditors' speculation is correct that Robert is dead, she'll never forgive herself from withholding info from the police simply because she didn't want Holly and Robert to discover she'd been going through their personal things. What does any of that matter when lives are at stake?

Erika parks the Tesla in the garage, hooks up the battery for recharging, and punches in the security code on the door leading to the mudroom. The camera overhead is an unlit useless brick. She can't restart it without the app, and only Robert and Holly have access to that.

She opens the door to disturbing silence. Normally, the place is a site of frenzied hammering and drilling. The one moment she gets to herself is in the evenings, after the laborers pack up and leave at five p.m., sharp. But aside from a furniture delivery scheduled for tomorrow, flowers on Monday morning, and, of course, Colton's farm table, the house is finished.

Forgotten.

It's over. They've lost the contest.

Not that *TMB* has made this official, but the signs are there. Hector was scheduled to shoot Holly and Robert today. But since they have yet to return, he's been reassigned to South Carolina to film the doctors, whose retreat is leading the polls in popularity. Running a close second are Sean and Joel in New Mexico, their therapeutic ranch for LGBTQ2+ teens being featured, apparently, in the upcoming Sunday *New York Times*.

Viewers don't care about the Vermont project, which has been trashed by the ruthless gods of social media as "indulgent" and "pointless." The growing consensus online is that the wedding was less a romantic must-see event and more a desperate ploy to boost ratings. The energy-efficiency hook has been slammed for being opportunistic. The owners have been slammed for being self-centered.

In short, no one likes them.

"Even H&R don't give a shit," aintmisbehavin22 posted the other day on the *TMB* subreddit. "Why should we?"

You might change your mind when you find they've been kidnapped, Erika thinks, tossing her schedule onto the daybed in Holly's office and booting up her desktop.

"WE NEED TO TALK" is the all-caps subject line of LuAnn's email sent a mere ten minutes ago.

Erika lets her mind go blank as she logs into Zoom. She takes a fortifying swallow of coffee and waits for the producer to join the meeting.

LuAnn looks like she's just rolled out of bed after a sleepless night. Her braids are pulled back into a ponytail and she's wearing her glasses, no makeup. She doesn't bother to say good morning; she gets right to it. "I'm assuming there's no word from Holly and Robert, right?"

"Not that I'm aware, unfortunately." Erika checks Holly's outbox, just in case. The last message is still the one she sent on Saturday. "In fairness, Robert did say Thursday at the latest."

"Oh, please. It's admirable you're staying positive, but let's be real. For reasons unbeknownst to us, those two decided to drop out of what has been a very expensive race. Maybe they got cold feet after getting those threats in the mail. Dunno. That's all I can reason." She brings a huge earthenware mug to her mouth. "But now we're seeing the effects of their absence. Our numbers have never been lower."

"Yesterday, Xavier said our numbers were up due to the car being found and now—

"A blip that went by the wayside once Joel and Sean announced they're having a baby." LuAnn rolls her eyes. "Did you hear about that? A baby for their reveal. You don't stand a chance against one of those."

Erika has to hide her smile. Throughout their show, Joel and Sean have been talking nonstop about how much they want to have a child of their own. They'll be older parents, sure, but loving ones, too. It's nice that at least someone will have a happy ending.

"Did you see the thing online about the body?" Erika asks, tentatively.

LuAnn lowers her heavy mug. "What body?"

Erika fills her in on what she knows so far, which isn't much. A male in his late thirties or early forties found near where her Kia was abandoned. "They don't have an ID yet, but there's a lot of chatter it might be Robert."

"Shit! Why didn't you say so?"

I just did, Erika wants to say. "I didn't want to raise unnecessary alarm. It could be anyone. A hiker who had a heart attack, for example."

"Or our talent who's been missing for going on five days." LuAnn rocks back in her chair, running her hands over her head. "This might be a game changer. Have you spoken to the police?"

"No. And they haven't called me or the house, either, which I'm taking as a good sign that it's not him."

"Nevertheless, I'd like to check. I have that trooper's number. Picard. Do you want to give him a call?"

Erika would prefer not to let the producer know that Andre and she have been enemies since high school. He's the last person she wants to hear her confession about withholding what might very well be evidence that now happens to be missing from Robert's drawer. She wouldn't put it past the cop the use that against her, to set her up as being the mastermind behind by their disappearance.

He'd profile her as a scorned woman out for revenge—*again*.

"He's probably pretty busy with this case," Erika says. "Why don't you try? Being a producer from LA, you are way more important." Flattery gets you everywhere, right?

LuAnn nods. "Okay. I'm gonna shower and shift into work

mode. If you don't hear anything by then, I'll reach out to him. It'll be a whole different show if the corpse turns out to be Robert's. We'll have to move to Investigation Discovery."

Is that the producer's version of dark humor? Erika wonders as she logs out and checks on social media for any developments. Lots of theories, but nothing concrete. She debates returning her mother's calls and texts her instead.

> I'm okay. No news about H&R. About to be unemployed. Hahahaha.

Talk about dark humor.

With nothing aside from waiting anxiously on her plate, she decides to take a trip to the post office. The mail is usually delayed on Thursdays, but it should be sorted by now. While she's there she can get a cup of coffee at the general store, which undoubtedly is aflutter with wild speculation about the dead body. That could be illuminating.

Dylan the postmaster is sitting on the steps outside the Snowden post office smoking a cigarette, cocooned in a dark green hoodie to protect himself against the faint autumn drizzle. Erika braces herself for questions about whether it's Robert's body in the forest down in Peru.

Thankfully, Dylan's never been one for gossip, a breath of fresh air in this claustrophobic village. He simply grinds out his cigarette and stands, stretching his arms. "You've got a big bundle. Want me to bring it out?"

"That would be awesome," she says, grateful for his tact.

He returns with a stack of mail secured by a thick, red rubber band. Flipping his hair, he points to a grimy envelope on top. "This one's addressed to you."

Erika's vision tunnels at the sight of her name on the envelope, in the exact same penmanship as the ones Robert received. Dark-blue ink, the pen point pressed so hard it's pierced the paper.

It's from *him*.

Sliding out the envelope, she hands the bundle to Dylan as she slices open the flap with an acrylic fingernail and removes a sheet of folded graph paper. It's smudged with dirt or ink, hard to tell. The message is short and written in block letters cut from a magazine and it makes her dizzy.

yOuR NEXT

"Wrong 'you're.'" Dylan is reading over her shoulder. "What the fuck does that mean?"

It confirms she's officially on Zeke's hit list.

TWENTY-TWO

KIM

THURSDAY NIGHT

The Burlington International Airport is awfully busy for a weekday evening in my recent, albeit limited, experience. It's been several years since I've had an occasion to travel or greet someone coming off a flight, and I'm as timid as a child making my way to the arrivals gate. Another downside of the pandemic, I suppose: becoming a hermit.

"Her flight's on time," Doreen says, reading the digital boards reporting arrivals and departures. "Another sign of the looming apocalypse." It speaks volumes that my assistant's willing to drive an hour after work to greet a stranger. Usually, she's out the door by three on the dot.

Doreen jabs me in the ribs. "Hey, I bet that's her."

A tiny figure topped by a mass of bright blond hair and engulfed in a puffy sunshine-yellow parka bobs toward us on stiletto heels dragging a Barbie-pink plastic case.

"Gotta be her. Florida colors." Doreen waves her arm like a windshield wiper. "Yo, Tammy!"

She instantly brightens and returns a friendly wave. "Hey! Y'all must be Doreen and Kim." Coming to a halt, she points a long red nail at Doreen and says, "Physically fit. Triple earrings. Tells it like it is. Doreen." To me, she says, "Sensible shoes. Sensible haircut. Can-do gal. Kim, the clerk. Mother of my daughter's assistant."

Doreen and I are speechless. Who is this tiny witch?

As if we were on the fence about that, she closes her eyes and says, "My baby's nearby and she's alive. I can feel her." Lifting her blue lids, she lets out a big sigh and smiles. "That was half the reason I wanted to be here, to get the vibe. Okay, I'm ready to find her now."

◇ ◇ ◇

"This is a highway?" Tammy peers out the windshield at the black ribbon of asphalt. It is nine thirty and we are the only cars on Vermont Route 7.

"It is and it's a dangerous one," Doreen says from the back seat. "Two lanes are the pits. If you're not swerving for a dumb deer or getting clocked by a moose, some idiot's drunk or checking his cell and crossing the center line smack into you. Got too many morons in this state crossing the center line and killing people."

Thanks for your tact, I mentally message her, gripping the wheel extra tight. Concrete pilings can be more sensitive than Doreen.

"I ain't never seen a moose," Tammy says, her face pressed to the window. "Deer we got in Florida. Monitor lizards the size of palm trees lying across the road. Reptile speed bumps, I call 'em. No moose."

"October's their mating season. Their brains are so doped on hormones they'll walk right into your car and you'll never see them 'cause they're big and black. Eyes don't reflect off the headlights and wham! Next thing you know, you're waking up in the ICU." Doreen pauses to revise her doom-and-gloom report. "If you're lucky."

"Mercy!" exclaims Tammy, flinching from the door as if a moose were on the other side, ready to charge.

"I gather you haven't been up this far north?" I ask, changing the subject.

"No ma'am. The farthest I've been is Tallahassee for Haylee's graduation from Florida State. I've been itching to visit, but she said there's so much going on with the rehab she wouldn't be able to pay me much attention. Then, when she told me she was getting married, I looked into flights. I'm her mama; it's a given I'd be at her wedding, right? But she didn't want me around for that, either, 'cause of that mean owner she was so worried about showing up and making a scene at the ceremony." Tammy goes back to looking out her window. "Or so she claimed. Deep down I know Haylee's never forgiven me for being a shitty mom, even after all these years."

Doreen and I keep quiet because how do you respond to

that kind of comment? We met the woman in person only twenty minutes ago.

"Don't get me wrong. I wasn't abusive or anything. I didn't cuss or use the paddle," Tammy clarifies, recrossing her legs. "I just wasn't around, what with working during the day and stopping by the bar in the evenings where I solicited most of my clients. Not exactly a wholesome lifestyle for a child."

Doreen slaps one of her mitts on Tammy's shoulder. "Don't be ashamed. My great-grandmother raised five kids as a widow during the Great Depression up north of Boothbay Harbor in a piss-poor town called Sumsquat. She'd leave her children for weeks on end while she went down to Portsmouth Naval Ship-yard to entertain, so to speak, the sailors on shore leave. When you're a single mom, you do what you gotta do to put bread on the table, you know what I mean?"

"Well, uhm, no. Not exactly." Tammy slides me a puzzled side-eye. I smile like a simpleton and keep my focus on the dark road, pretending as if my assistant did not just imply she was a prostitute. "I ran my own accounting firm, you see. Started it from the ground up. Beauregard and Associates. Pretty success-ful, if I do say so myself. Those clients I was picking up needed their books balanced or their taxes prepared."

"Then when were you homeless?" Doreen asks, confused.

"Homeless?" Tammy coughs a laugh. "We were never homeless. For the past twenty years, I've owned a three-bedroom house on the Homosassa River, private dock and all. What're y'all talking about?"

"I think what Doreen's referring to are your daughter's blog posts where she mentions, for example, that she never thought she'd be so fortunate to live in a house this beautiful growing up as a homeless teen," I explain, rescuing the wide-mouthed frog in the back seat.

"Oh, that? The only time Haylee was homeless was when she ran off when she was sixteen. She broke curfew and she was none too pleased when I laid down the law, grounding her for a week. She was gone for one, two, maybe three . . ."

"Months?" Doreen offers.

"Nights," Tammy answers. "Lemme tell ya, living off microwaved hot dogs at the Circle K gets real old, real fast. Say, are we pretty close to the place where the body was found? I heard it was on a remote road like this."

I've just turned off the state highway onto the main drag that leads into Snowden. "Every road from here on out is remote. I believe the body was found in the Green Mountain National Forest, about forty minutes south of here, but I have no idea exactly where."

And I'm not about to start searching at this hour. All I want to do is drop off Doreen at town hall, where her car is parked, and Tammy at the Snowden Inn, go home, take off my bra, and grab a bowl of cereal. It's been a long day with a lot of stress and driving. I'm ready to call it quits.

"Mad Tom Notch Road mile marker sixty-six, according to the state police press release." The light from Doreen's phone bounces off my rearview mirror as she hovers in the back seat Googling. I'm surprised she can get reception. Surprised and bummed, since this means I won't be in my jammies, feet up, anytime soon. "You can knock off twenty minutes, Kim, if you cut through Landgrove."

"If you don't mind going out of your way, I know it's a bother, but if this is where they killed my son-in-law, then my baby must be . . ." She can't go on. She's too upset.

"Don't think that way, Tammy," Doreen urges. "Be positive. We don't even know for sure it's Robert."

Tammy sniffs and dabs at her nose with a tissue. "Oh, you know it is. That's near where Erika's car was found, right? The car Robert and Haylee were driving. No one's been able to find them since and . . ." Her shoulders heave in a quiet sob as I turn off the main road to Snowden and take a right toward Landgrove and the Mad Tom Notch Road.

What else am I supposed to do?

"How did Haylee and Robert meet?" Doreen asks. "A Floridian like her and a Yankee like him. That's gotta be a cute story."

It sounds like she's being nice, trying to distract Tammy from her daughter's disappearance, but knowing Doreen, she's up to something.

"Whacked is what it was," Tammy says, clearing her throat. "Haylee had been bouncing around trying to make a career out of her communications degree from FSU, not having much luck. Came home broke and discouraged. Ended up subletting my girlfriend's apartment and waiting bar on the strip to pay the bills and, on my recommendation, studying to get her real estate license. I had a couple of clients who were Realtors and they were doing quite well, financially."

There are no streetlights after we leave Landgrove, which is easy to miss if you blink. Which I don't dare attempt, not with animals poised to leap into my headlights. I grip the wheel and sit forward, forcing my aging eyes to be alert in the darkness. I can barely make out the edge of the road as we inch up the mountain.

"Then she took an online course on vlogging, or whatever you call it. Making videos. Next we knew, she had seventy thousand followers on Instagram and even more on TikTok following her vlogs about properties for sale in the greater Citrus County area. Very popular with snowbirds up north looking to retire."

"You want to make a left at the intersection with Mad Tom," Doreen interrupts. "Should be one point four miles down the road. Be careful. It's definitely dropped a few degrees. Could get slippery."

I turn left and shiver against a chill. During the day, the view is spectacular, especially during foliage season with the sweeping mountain and valley swales brimming with color. In the dark, it's downright scary because at any moment my wheels might slip off the berm and we could go tumbling, crashing down the hill.

Tammy prattles on, oblivious. "Last fall, right around this time of year, she reached out to Robert."

At the mention of this timeline, Doreen drives her finger into the back my neck for me to pay attention.

"She emailed him a suggestion that he incorporate video into his Robber Barron blogs about real estate. He blew her off—or so she thought—until, out of the blue, he called her around Christmas and asked if she wanted to go to Vermont to shoot a video of this house he got for a steal."

"Had she ever been there before?" Doreen asks. "I mean here, in Vermont."

Tammy turns slightly in her seat, thinking. "I don't believe so. We weren't living together then, so I guess I may not have been aware of her comings and goings. Uhm, no. I remember her distinctly asking me what to wear when she came here in December because she'd never been this far above the Mason-Dixon Line before. Why?"

"Just curious," Doreen says, giving my neck another poke.

To me Tammy's response doesn't prove squat. Holly could have sneaked up to Vermont weeks before without her mother's knowledge. Or, possibly, it was a mere coincidence that the person who came to research our records last fall had the same name. Surely there had to be many, many Haylees in this world.

"Slow down," Doreen commands. "Pull over. This is the spot."

I park in a turnoff and kill the engine. The silence is deafening, broken only by the *whsssh* of wind blowing through the pine trees. The woods loom, tall and mysterious, engulfing us.

"Oh, my." Tammy rapidly pats her chest. "It's so deserted. Not a soul for miles."

"That's why people like it," Doreen says, opening the rear door and getting out. "Oh, smell that!" she exclaims, stretching. "This is why people come to the woods."

We get out and breathe the clean mountain air. Tammy clutches her coat. "It's freezing."

Suddenly, we're blinded by a beam of light so bright we have to shield our eyes. I grab Tammy's arm as footsteps crunch across the gravel toward us. Doreen, I don't have to worry about. She's got one hand on her pistol.

"You ladies in need of assistance?"

His voice is gruff, official. I don't have to see a badge to know it's a cop keeping watch on a crime scene, perhaps to protect its integrity. Perhaps to see if the murderer will return.

"Looking for my daughter," pipes up Tammy, lowering her hand and extending it for a shake. "Tammy Beauregard. I'm the mother of Haylee Beauregard. Or, as y'all call her up here, Holly. Holly Barron now."

"ID?" asks the cop.

As Tammy fumbles through her purse for her wallet, I make a mental note of his brass nameplate. V. Drury. Vermont State Police. Does not ring a bell.

"Here," she says, handing him her license. "Please, if you have any information on the body they found, I'm worried sick it's my son-in-law, Robert Barron. I flew all the way up from Florida 'cause I can't take the not knowing. My daughter's been missing since Sunday."

He returns her license. "Thank you. I'm sorry I can't help you, ma'am. If you have any questions, I suggest you contact the state police barracks in Westminster tomorrow. Meanwhile, we're trying to keep this area clear. So, if you—"

"Would move along?" I finish for him. "Gladly. Come on, Tammy." I tug her jacket, but she doesn't budge.

"This is my daughter, officer," she says firmly. "Be a human being and ease a mother's heart. Tell me what you know."

He lowers the flashlight. "What I know is that I'm not authorized to answer any questions." In a kinder tone, he adds, "And everything's better in the morning, ma'am. Trust me. Now, drive safe and be careful. It's a jungle out there."

TWENTY-THREE

ERIKA

FRIDAY MORNING

Shortly after eight a.m., Erika rolls the Tesla as quietly as possible down the driveway past her mother's house to her apartment. She's showered and clean, but she'll need a fresh change of clothes for work, having spent the night before in the cheapest hotel she could find, a Days Inn outside Rutland.

No way was she willing to spend the night alone in her apartment, or Holly and Robert's house, not after getting the "YOUR NEXT" note. The Snowden Inn was too rich for her blood and, besides, it was packed to the gills with leaf peepers. No vacancies.

So the Days Inn with its noisy buses and idling tractor trailers in the parking lot had to fit the bill. A quarter pounder with cheese and an order of extra-large fries in her belly, she crashed on the hard bed, awaking with the realization she hasn't been sleeping much these past few days, the constant stress fraying her nerves. Once this show is over, once Robert and Holly have returned, Erika promises to treat herself to a well-deserved vacation, a beach retreat.

It's not as though she'll have to punch a clock. In five days she will be officially, blessedly, on unemployment.

For now, though, all she wants to do is get through the unpleasantness ahead, which might include the sobering news that the body found near her car's last location belongs to Robert. That'll be a biggie; she'd better prepare.

The quick trip up the stairs of the carriage house to her small studio is a harrowing experience. She enters with 911 on her phone's keypad, opening the door cautiously and then scanning the room on high alert. There aren't many places Zeke Strickland could hide, so that's a bonus to living in a sardine can. The closet is empty and the space under her daybed is populated by only dust bunnies. No one's lurking behind the shower curtain. All is clear and she can finally let out the breath she's been holding.

No lingering, though. Teeth brushed. Makeup refreshed. She's suited up in black trousers, a simple white cotton top, and a flowing beige cardigan with a scarf to tie the look together. Subdued and professional, she thinks, taking stock of herself in the mirror. An ideal outfit for going to the cops, as she plans, to tell them about the now-missing letters, the disarray of her employers' private quarters, their forgotten passports, and the latest threat she received yesterday in the mail. She looks like a person to be taken seriously.

She hopes she doesn't look like a suspect, though when it comes to Andre Picard, there's no telling how he'll react when she reveals she's withheld this info for days. Considering her history and his hatred, she fully expects him to target her as a person of interest. If she had the money, she'd get herself a lawyer—though, on second thought, wouldn't that make her appear guiltier?

In the interim between arriving home to change and now, the Tesla's been parked in by her mother's Subaru. Not uncommon. Her mother often pulls this move when she wants to have a talk. No doubt Kim is itching to know where she was all night.

The door to her mother's kitchen opens on the first knock. The woman answering is small with a halo of blond, curly hair, and she is dressed in a fuchsia velour tracksuit.

"You must be Erika. So glad to finally meet you. I'm Tammy, Haylee's mom. We've spoken once or twice. I hope you have news because I am going crazy over these internet rumors about the body being found by the car. Absolutely crazy."

That entire line was delivered without the woman taking a single breath. It was dizzying.

"Nice to meet you," Erika says, mentally matching the strange person to the familiar voice, "but I have no information about the body. I'm sorry. Fingers crossed it's not anyone we know." Except Zeke Strickland. That would be okay.

Erika barely has a moment to process that Holly's mother, the alleged neglectful party girl, has arrived from Florida and is in her own mother's house before she catches sight of something odd on the kitchen table, where newspapers have been spread out underneath a small pink bundle.

Following her gaze, Tammy says, "Yeah. Those are the bloody PJs your mama found the other day in your garbage. Maybe you should come in and set a spell. We got a few queries."

◇ ◇ ◇

"I have never seen those before." Erika pries at the thawing bundle with her index finger until her mother slaps it away.

"Don't. You'll get your DNA all over it," Kim says, shaking her head at Tammy, who shakes her head back as if to say, *Kids.*

"Where'd you find it?"

"Like Tammy said. In our garbage." Kim pours coffee into a mug on the counter, where Tammy's sitting with a pack of menthol Kools and a lighter in a tidy stack.

The sight of the two of them in the same room is jarring. Tammy is Holly's mother and, therefore, allocated to Erika's work life. Her mother is *her* mother. How did they connect? Why is it that Tammy's here and not, say, in a hotel? Are they friends?

Erika would inquire but with Tammy front and center, that would be rude. "When did you find that in my garbage?" she asks, slipping onto the other stool, keeping Tammy in her periphery.

"Let's see." Kim takes a sip and stares at the ceiling. She's in jeans and a paint-spattered Wheaton College sweatshirt as if she's ready for a day of yard work instead of going to the office. Maybe Tammy's being a bad influence. "Whatever night that was when Robert came to your apartment to switch cars. Saturday? No, Sunday morning, early."

"What were you doing riffling through my garbage?"

Tammy's head rotates to Kim, a riveted spectator in a mother-daughter volley.

"It's *my* garbage, too," Kim says, putting down her cup and bracing herself against the kitchen counter. "You happen to use it at no charge, I might add. That's okay. Robert dumping his stuff is not. Hauling fees have skyrocketed this year."

Tammy shoots up her hand. "Excuse me. As a CPA, I know household budgets are important, but as Haylee's mama I have a few concerns about these PJs your mother's been storing in her downstairs Frigidaire. She was kind enough to bring them out, but now I want them taken to the police because I suspect they could be evidence."

"Agreed," Kim says. "If Holly had returned the next day, that'd be one thing. But she hasn't been heard from since the wedding."

Erika rubs her forehead; her mind is swimming. The PJs are monumental, not because they're spattered with blood—that could have been from Holly's period or a paper cut—but because Robert obviously thought it was important to hide them not in his own trash, but in hers.

Why?

"We are going on day six," Tammy says angrily. "The police need to take it up a notch. This ain't a lovey-dovey couple on a romantic escape. They're goddamn missing!"

"If it's not Robert in that woods, then where are they? Did they cross the border to Canada or not? From all accounts, it appears not. Clearly something has gone awry if they've walked off this big, important show. And what about this former owner who was so scary Haylee wouldn't let me come to—"

"Wait," Erika interrupts. "Are you talking about Zeke Strickland? Did you just say your daughter called him scary?"

"Who's Zeke Strickland?" Tammy asks.

Kim fills her in about the tax sale and how Robert had Zeke forcibly removed from the house. Erika's listening as patiently as she can when her phone buzzes with a message from LuAnn asking if there's been any word from Holly and Robert.

Erika types back a curt No and returns to the conversation.

"I was just telling your mama that we got Stricklands in Homosassa," Tammy says. "Decent, churchgoing folk. Wonder if they're any relation."

"Doubt it. Zeke is . . ." Erika hesitates in her description, not wanting to add to Tammy's angst. She needs to dial down how disturbed he is. "Let's just say he's had issues."

"What kind of issues?" Tammy presses.

"Issues involving Robert, mostly. He hasn't forgiven him for getting the house. That's why I think he's the one who's been sending him hate mail. Don't worry. It's nothing graphic, more like 'get out of my house.'" No purpose would be served by telling Tammy the letters outright threatened to murder her daughter. "Robert hid them in a bottom drawer. I came across them by accident, but yesterday I got one in the mail addressed to me."

"Oh, geesh!" Kim explodes. "What did it say?"

Erika removes the envelope from her purse. "As you can see, it was mailed Wednesday from Snowden. Dylan, the postmaster, said it was probably dropped off in the stamped mail slot in the lobby. Which means Zeke's in town. The ones addressed to Robert came from Burlington or Manchester, New Hampshire. So, he's closing in."

Pinching the envelope by one corner, an ashen Kim says, "I can't remember if they have cameras in the post office."

"Dylan told me that until now our little Snowden PO hasn't needed them. Let me remove the letter. My fingerprints are already all over it."

The two women peer at the graph paper with its cutout lettering.

"Y-o-u-r." Kim runs her finger under the letters, careful not to leave any of her DNA on the paper. "Using the wrong 'you're' is so obvious it borders on intentional, don't you think? As if someone wants the sender to come off as uneducated."

Was her own mother doubting her? "That's the kind of grammatical mistake a guy like Zeke would make," Erika retorts.

"You don't know that."

"Yes, I do. There are stories all over town about him shooting at innocent hikers crossing his property. He put bullet holes in some guy's backpack!"

Tammy gasps.

"Just because he's violent doesn't mean he'll be violent to everyone." Her mother surreptitiously nods to Tammy, who's stock still in shock, a message to lower the volume. "It also doesn't mean he can't spell."

Erika snatches up the letter, refolds it, and replaces it in the envelope, peeved. "Whatever. I'm going to take this to the police. I'm sure they'll consider evidence, even if you don't."

"Hold up." Kim moves to the door, blocking her exit. "Come with me down to the firepit. I wanna show you something."

"I'm already late," Erika protests, trying to inch past her.

Kim puts out a hand. "What I found in the firepit has to do with that kind of letter. It'll take only a minute. Let's go."

"Amen. I need a smoke." Tammy grabs her cigarettes, tagging after Kim, who's already out the door.

The two women follow, Tammy in her Keds trying not to slip on the fallen leaves, and Erika, clutching her bag, cursing and muttering under her breath. She can't get over how Kim's not instantly taking her side. A normal mother would. A normal mother would wrap her in a hug and stroke her hair and assure her she's safe from the monster.

Not ol' Kim.

They arrive at the ring of rocks around the charred remains of earlier fires and pieces of cardboard Kim's been meaning to burn. Tammy lights her cigarette as they watch Kim gingerly pick up a soggy, tattered copy of *Us* lying under a crushed Amazon box.

"Is this yours?" Kim asks.

Erika looks it over, curling her lip at the trash. "No. What would I do with an old magazine?"

"Exactly." Holding it open, Kim flips through the wrinkled pages. "See? Put the letter next to this ad for Old Spice cologne that has a section cut out. Do a comparison."

Begrudgingly, Erika unfolds the letter again and places it against the magazine. "Not exactly the same . . ."

"Same vintage, at least." Kim tosses the magazine back

onto the heap. "Who dumped these cut-up magazines here if you didn't?"

"That Zeke Strickland." Tammy blows a blue plume. "He must have been here. Could it be he's stalking y'all?"

As soon as she asks the question, Erika knows with a gut punch Tammy's right. Zeke's been lurking in the woods monitoring her comings and goings, committing her schedule to memory. He's been watching her because . . .

. . . he's already taken care of Robert and Holly.

"Oh," she moans as her mother finally slides an arm around her shoulder.

"It's okay," Kim murmurs. "You're fine. Nothing's happened to you and nothing will happen. I won't let it."

"What about my daughter, though?" Tammy asks, the cigarette shaking as she studies the ripped magazines. "If he's been here spying on Erika, what does that mean for Haylee?"

A car door slams and the skittish women jump in unison as two state troopers shuffle through the leaves down the slight hill to the firepit.

"Cops." Tammy reaches for Kim. "Oh, dear Lord have mercy. Please may they not be here to deliver bad news."

Kim puts her other arm around Tammy. "Stay strong. We're here for you."

It's done. It's over, Erika thinks. They're here to inform them the body belongs to Robert. There will be questions, an interrogation. The edges of her vision darken as Trooper Kashi approaches, papers in her hand.

"Erika Turnbull," she says, handing her the papers. "This is a bench warrant granted from the criminal division of the

Vermont Superior Court allowing the Vermont State Police permission to conduct an unsupervised search of your dwelling, vehicle, and perimeter."

The blood drains to her feet. What? Why would they be searching her? And then it hits her: Andre's been building a case against her all along.

"What about my daughter?" Tammy cries as Erika and Kim nervously scan the affidavit supporting the warrant.

Kashi says, "And you are, ma'am?"

Tammy flicks her butt into the burn pile. "Tammy Beauregard of Homosassa, Florida, mother of Haylee Dawn Beauregard, otherwise known as Holly Simmons Barron, missing for six days now."

"Nice to meet you, Ms. Beauregard." Kashi nods. "I'm afraid I don't have any information on the whereabouts of your daughter."

"How about her husband?" Tammy asks. "Was it his body in the woods?"

"No, ma'am," Kashi says.

Kim and Erika both look up from the affidavit. "Then whose body was it?" Kim asks.

"According to identification found at the scene and confirmation by his parents, the individual appears to be one Colton Whitcomb."

TWENTY-FOUR

ERIKA

EARLY FRIDAY AFTERNOON

The Vermont State Police barracks is a low building with a tidy brick facade and the classic green metal roof. It's clean and eco-friendly with low-flow toilets, wood trim, and a cheerful vibe identical to that of the welcome center down the interstate—aside from the prison cells.

Erika might be mildly interested in the photo history of the Vermont State Police displayed on the lobby wall if she weren't completely numb.

Colton. Dead.

This still doesn't compute. If they told her how he died, that would at least provide a frame of reference. But all she can glean in this petrifying span of endless waiting is that this man with whom she had a brief, albeit intense, fling exists no more.

The once warm body that melded with hers, flesh on flesh, is now ice cold on a slab in some morgue.

Colton will never deliver that ridiculous table. He will never again commune with tree spirits, and just when he'd found his life's calling, too. It's so sad, the grief physically hurts.

His father. With a pang of guilt, she remembers Rick's inquiry about whether she'd heard from his son. She assumed he was following up about the table, but probably he was worried sick that he hadn't heard from Colton. She should have called him instead of whipping off a pissy text complaining about having to wait around for his son, but she'd been too busy with meaningless worries like the wrong color of the French range.

And now she's in the barracks while the state police mysteriously rummage through her apartment and the Tesla searching for anything linking her to Colton's death. Or maybe Holly and Robert's disappearance. She doesn't know which. The search warrant was vague and alarming, especially the line about seeking "material relating to an ongoing criminal investigation." How could she be under investigation when she hasn't done anything wrong?

The scenario is all too disturbingly familiar, unearthing hurtful memories, long suppressed, of the trauma she endured in high school after Amber's death, when overnight she went from normal teenager to local pariah. All because of an invisible patch of ice on a frosty October morning while she was rushing to class at age seventeen.

She can still feel the terrifying sensation of her tires losing contact with the road, her steering wheel spinning helplessly, her frantic stomping on the brake right as an oncoming car crested the blind hill. She can recall with crystal clarity the horrified expression on the face of the oncoming driver, Amber Allen, a girl she not only knew, but who was once her closest friend before Jake Waskow entered the picture and Amber became her rival.

Sitting on the bench in the barracks a decade later, Erika fights the urge to cover her ears to mute the deafening crunch of metal on metal and metal on wood as Amber's car crashed through the trees, down the embankment, rolling over and over until it landed in the river with a death-knell splash. The gut punch of the airbag, the crack of her ribs, the searing pain of the safety belt cutting across her chest, are as palpable as if they're happening in real time.

And then the aftermath, more brutal in many respects than the accident itself. The suffocating knowledge that she'd caused Amber's death. The rumors and whispers so cruel as to be beyond belief that she'd intentionally run Amber off the road because Jake, a summer boy whose parents had built one of the big houses on Hedgerow, liked her better than he liked Erika. As if she were capable of committing murder over a crush!

That's what the police theorized, grilling her up and down, inside and out. Their forensics team was out there taking measurements, calculating speed and conditions, while, at the barracks, troopers scrutinized her postings on social media for indications of homicidal intent. Amber's parents refused to allow her to attend the funeral, even after the state's attorney concluded that both drivers were guilty of negligent operation, at most, and declined to file charges.

The official absolution didn't matter; the damage had been

done. In the court of public opinion, Amber was an innocent and Erika was a criminal, case closed. Since then, she's done her best to keep her head down and go about her business, trying not to mind the cold shoulders and sneers, such as when her former third-grade teacher hurriedly left the general store the other day, refusing to acknowledge Erika with so much as a nod.

They say time heals all wounds. Not when it comes to law enforcement. If she's a suspect in Colton's murder or Holly and Robert's disappearance, it's because vengeful cops like Andre Picard have been itching to make her pay for an offense she committed ten years ago. Now here she is at last, under his authority. The situation makes her ill with grief and worry and relentless regret.

The electronic door buzzes and tall Freddie Crenshaw with his skewed tie and bushy mustache emerges from the bowels of the barracks. "Here's this," he says, handing over her cell phone. "They had no right to take it. They're grasping at straws."

Freddie's the Snowden town attorney, the only lawyer her mother knows besides the real estate lawyers who research land records. At least Freddie has some experience in litigation, albeit in lawsuits involving rights of way and violations of local animal ordinances. He's a genius at resolving disputes over dog bites that occur on public roads, often going the extra mile by locating no-kill shelters to avoid putting down the misbehaving pets.

A police inquiry involving bodies discovered in the Green Mountain National Forest is not technically in his area of expertise. But Erika's trying to be hopeful.

He slides on the bench next to her, reeking of spearmint gum. "You holding up okay?"

She's touched by his concern. "Not really. I can't believe Colton's dead. He left a message on my voicemail just the other day saying he was going to deliver the table. He sounded fine."

"That was Tuesday, according to my notes."

"Monday at six p.m., actually," she corrects. "He said he'd be bringing the table the next day, but he never showed."

"Which gives us a timeline." He rests a leather briefcase on his lap and removes a yellow legal pad. "The police are going to ask where you were between the hours of six p.m. Monday when he left that message and yesterday morning."

A ridiculous question. Jogging her memory, she tries to separate her days and nights from the blur that's been this week. The only person who can confirm she was home on Monday, Tuesday, and Wednesday nights is her mother, unfortunately. "Is that why they're searching my apartment, because of Colton?"

"Partly." Freddie clicks his ballpoint. "Also, the police have officially opened a missing persons' case regarding your employers and seem to be extraordinarily interested in your relationship with Robert Barron."

A lump forms in Erika's throat. "He was—is—my boss."

"Yes, obviously. They question whether it might have been more than that." A patch of red forms above Freddie's Adam's apple, as if he's embarrassed by the insinuation. "Sorry. I have to ask. Was there more to . . . ?"

"No!" she says firmly, insulted and furious. Again, this is all Andre's doing. "We were strictly professional."

Freddie writes this down. "Might be a wise idea for you to lower your voice. When was the last time you saw Mr. Barron?"

"Around one a.m. Sunday morning. In my apartment."

"Alone?"

She shifts on the hard bench, uneased by this line of questioning. "Yes, alone. He wanted to switch cars so he could take Holly on a spur-of-the-moment honeymoon to Montreal."

"What about his own car? Or his wife's?"

"Holly's Range Rover's in the shop and he was worried there might not be enough charging stations along the way for his Tesla."

"Uh-huh." Freddie looks up. "Can't they go for three hundred, four hundred miles? Montreal's only a hundred and eighty away at the most. And there are charging stations there."

Erika shrugs. She could care less about a Tesla battery's capability. She just wants to get out of this awful place and mourn Colton in peace.

"Is there anything else you think I should know before we go in there?" He thumbs to the locked door leading to the barracks' inner sanctum. "Anything you've come across that—"

"Yes!" The letter. She pulls out the envelope from her purse and, pinching the corner as her mother did, holds it up to show Freddie. "This came to me in the mail yesterday. It's postmarked Wednesday in Snowden. And it looks a lot like the other letters I found in Robert's locked filing cabinet." She unfolds it on the bench.

"Your next," Freddie reads aloud, frowning. Then, examining the envelope, he adds, "There's no return address."

"There wasn't on the ones sent to Robert, either. Here they are. I laid them out on the floor and took a photo." That was so smart of her to have done that, considering they ended up being stolen.

Freddie squints at her phone. " 'Arm for an arm. Eye for an eye. You steal my house. I kill your wife. Then take your life. Thieves rules.' What the hell? You have any idea who sent these?"

"I can't prove it, but the obvious guess is the prior owner— Zeke Strickland. I mean, Robert had to have him evicted after he got Zeke's property at a tax sale."

"Really? Huh." Freddie clicks his pen. "Have you shown these to the police?"

"Until today, there wasn't a reason. I didn't know Holly and Robert were officially missing persons. I will now, though."

"It's probably wise for you to let the police confiscate them, instead of you."

She sighs, imagining how Andre's going to react to what she's about to tell her lawyer. "That's the sticky part; the letters are gone."

"Gone from where?" Freddie asks, clicking his ballpoint again.

"Robert's locked filing cabinet back at the house."

Another pen click. "How did you get them if they were in a locked filing cabinet?"

"I happen to have a key. Robert gave it to me so I could hide Cuban cigars he bought illegally for the wedding and didn't want Holly to see."

"Anyone else have a key?"

Erika can feel her cheeks flush. "Just me. Is that bad?"

"Might take some explaining, which we're not going to do. Listen to me, Erika, when the police ask you a question, answer only that question. Do not go off on a tangent offering them unsolicited information, got it? No mention of the letters or your theories about the prior owner unless they ask, okay? And even then, look for my approval."

She nods. This is going to be tough. She's scared.

Freddie grins reassuringly. "Why don't I pop in and tell them we're ready? I'm sure it won't take long." He gets up and readjusts his tie. "One other thing: What car are you driving if yours has been totaled?"

"Robert's Tesla."

"He traded a fifty-thousand-dollar car for a Kia?"

"Actually, it's an S model so, um, more like a hundred thousand dollars."

Freddie's grin slumps into a frown.

TWENTY-FIVE

ERIKA

EARLY FRIDAY AFTERNOON

The interrogation room bears no resemblance to the harshly lit concrete spaces on TV. There's no one-way mirror or glass wall, only overhead cameras in each of the four corners. Freddie and Erika sit on one side of the table, while Andre and Kashi sit opposite.

Right off, Erika observes they're distracted, whispering in one another's ears and leaving the room repeatedly for hallway conferences before the interrogation starts. Andre, freshly returned from the search of her premises, does not even say hello, which she finds disconcerting.

Perhaps this is a technique to get her to break, though Freddie dismisses her theory. "You're not the only case on the books," he says, flipping to a fresh page on his legal tablet. "The VSP is stretched way too thin. Trust me."

At last, the two troopers return to the room and settle down. "This is purely a discussion," Kashi says, more to Freddie than to Erika. "No charges have been filed. We are simply looking for information." Turning to Erika, she says, "Please tell us about the last time you saw Robert Barron."

Again? She feels like she keeps answering this same question over and over. Exasperated, Erika turns to Freddie for a cue, but he says only, "Go ahead. I'll stop you if necessary."

"Like I told you on Tuesday when we went to look at my car, shortly after midnight early Sunday morning."

"It's our understanding you left the wedding approximately eight hours earlier in somewhat of a huff," Andre says, twirling his pencil.

A huff? "I didn't leave in a huff. My mother was getting on my nerves, I was tired after a lot of wedding planning and wasn't in the mood for dancing."

"Because you were so upset Robert Barron married the rival for your affections?"

Erika's jaw drops. This is so beyond the pale she's speechless.

"This questioning is out of line," Freddie jumps in. "If you're here to settle old scores, Trooper Picard, you should step off the case."

Thank you, Freddie, Erika thinks, though she's curious as to how he's aware of Andre's ax to grind. Perhaps her mother put a bug in his ear when she called to ask him to provide legal representation after Kashi insisted Erika come with her back to the barracks.

Andre sinks slightly lower in his chair while Kashi picks up the ball. "To recap, the last contact you had with Robert Barron was Sunday morning?"

Oh, my god. Again? But, since Freddie doesn't object, Erika answers, "That's right."

"And what about Holly?" Kashi asks.

"Saturday at the wedding. Briefly. To congratulate her."

"And what about Colton Whitcomb?" Kashi asks. "When did you last have contact with him?"

Freddie nods to indicate she can answer.

"About three weeks ago. He came by the house to take measurements for the farm table Holly commissioned. But I didn't really see him that day. By then, he and Holly were working closely on a design. All I did was introduce them at the farmers' market. Holly was blown away by his smaller pieces and his whole philosophy, so to speak, of woodworking. So she asked him to build her a farmer's table with a breadboard. Having a table featured on *To the Manor Build* is a big deal, as you can imagine. A career maker. He was pretty psyched." She glances at Freddie, hoping that wasn't too much information.

"Were you and Colton still in a romantic relationship when you introduced him to Holly Barron?" Andre's back with his annoying suggestions.

Freddie holds up a hand, but Erika needs to set the record straight, especially in light of Andre's grudge against her. "No. Long over. Colton and I dated for six weeks last year, from July Fourth to Labor Day or thereabouts. Classic summer romance."

Andre smirks. "Who ended the relationship?"

She looks to Freddie, who shrugs. "Go ahead, if you want, Erika."

"It was mutual. Colton quit his job as a stockbroker and started smoking a lot of dope and living in the woods. Not exactly my idea of Mr. Right."

Kashi snorts and quickly tries to hide her smile with her coffee cup.

"But you continued to have contact with him," Andre says.

"Like I just said, only professionally. Actually, Holly had more contact with him than I did. She apparently went to his workshop last week to check on the table's progress, according to a few emails I found in her outbox."

Kashi says to Andre, "Have we secured that computer, yet?"

"We've included it in the affidavit," he says. "The judge should have approved the warrant by now so I assume that'll be part of the search."

Which means they'll find the passports, Erika thinks. That's far better than her admitting she riffled through Holly and Robert's personal belongings without their permission. She's beginning to understand why Freddie told her to limit her answers to their specific questions.

Kashi flips to a new page in her notebook and Erika senses a shift in the atmosphere when she asks, "What can you tell us about a man named Zeke Strickland?"

Finally! Erika relaxes slightly when Freddie doesn't object. Stick to the question, she reminds herself before answering. "I know he's the prior owner of the property Robert bought."

"When did you last have contact with him?" Andre asks.

What's he implying now, that they're colluding? Erika turns to Freddie, who says, "C'mon, Trooper Picard. You know better than that. Rephrase."

Andre smirks. *Can't help a guy for trying*, he seems to be saying. "Have you ever had contact with Zeke Strickland?"

Erika thinks of the NDA with his name on it. She doesn't want to the cops to accuse her of lying if they come across it in their search of the house, which they're bound to do. "Not that I know of."

"Interesting." Andre arches a brow. "Not that you know of? Could you expound on that?"

Freddie studies her like a hawk regarding a field mouse, ready to pounce if she speaks out of turn. "I mean to my knowledge we've never met. For all I know he could have been one of the contractors in and out of the house for the past few weeks. I don't know for sure because I don't know what he looks like, though I've tried Googling him. He's not on the internet."

"Why were you Googling him?" Andre's eyes gleam.

She doesn't want to tell him about the letters, since that will lead them down a whole other rabbit hole. "I've heard stories about how pissed he was after Robert had him evicted. I just wanted to know what he looked like, in case he came around the house and started causing trouble."

"Where'd you hear these stories?" Andre asks.

Erika cocks her head. "Are you kidding? Didn't you grow up here, too? Everyone talks about everyone." And then, because she can't resist, she adds, "You know how harmful that is, right?"

Andre meets her gaze, but says nothing. Kashi seizes the opportunity to jump back in. "Did your employers ever mention Mr. Strickland? Did they warn you that he was dangerous, that he might have a weapon and that you shouldn't let him into the building, that kind of thing?"

Erika thinks back. Oddly, she realizes, they hadn't. They routinely referred to him as "the prior owner" and never as someone to avoid, which is weird considering she is almost totally convinced Zeke has done them harm. "No. Not that I can recall. We never discussed Zeke by name in any context."

"And, yet, you were so concerned about Mr. Strickland," Andre says, leaning close, "that you went hunting for his image online. I'm curious. Why would you go to all that effort for no reason?"

"That's it. We're done." Freddie pushes back his chair. "This line of questioning is getting ridiculous. Come on, Erika."

Startled by the abrupt end of the interrogation, Kashi says, "We will likely have more questions. So we would advise your client not to leave the jurisdiction."

"My client has no intention of going anywhere," Freddie says, shrugging on his suit coat. "Though since she's not under arrest, I want to make it clear she's under no obligation to stay. Erika?"

She follows him to the door and then pauses, turning to the troopers with one last question of her own. "I have to know. How did Colton die?"

"Just like your father, Erika." Andre gives her a knowing grin. "Interesting. That looked like an accident, too."

TWENTY-SIX

KIM

"How *did* your husband die, Kim?"

When Freddie Crenshaw knocks on my door after dropping off my daughter, this is the last thing I expect to hear out of his mouth. "Is that important to Erika's case?"

"Could be. Do you mind?" He waves his briefcase inside, where Tammy and I are finishing up a late lunch.

The lawyer looks as if he's been in a windstorm, brown curly hair mussed and tie half undone. His disheveled appearance and grumpy demeanor might be part and parcel of the job of being an overworked attorney, but I have a sinking feeling it didn't go well at the barracks. If it had, surely Erika would have stopped by for an update instead of zipping off in the Tesla, freshly searched by the Vermont State Police.

Tammy and I watched the search from the bedroom window as the police officers carried my daughter's personal belongings to their cruisers—a banker's box of stuff, a blanket, several items of clothing in a plastic ziplock bag and a dark green coat similar to the Barbour my husband, Craig, wore the day he died.

The scene boiled me with maternal outrage. A ziplock bag of Erika's soiled underthings—was that really necessary? Did they really have to go through our trash? I was coming around to Erika's point of view that a certain segment in town has it out for her. Never gave that much credence, until this charade.

She's not a drug dealer, for heaven's sake. This isn't a meth house. What judge in their right mind granted the cops' request to search the studio apartment of a twenty-seven-year-old executive assistant with no criminal record? An imbecile, that's who. Or maybe someone on the take.

Supposedly, the police would have had to produce concrete proof that a crime had been committed in order to get a warrant but, like Tammy said, crooked cops have sneaky ways of cooking up evidence. When this circus is over, I plan to file a howler of a lawsuit against the VSP. How dare they allow a trooper with a vendetta to abuse his power like this.

In light of the circumstances, I wanted to ask Freddie about whether or not to turn over the PJs I've returned to the basement freezer. Instead, he's asking me about a tragic event nearly a quarter-century old.

"Have a seat," Tammy says to the lawyer, carrying a plate with the remains of my sandwich to the sink. "I'll make some coffee and clean up, Kim. That is, unless you'd like some privacy."

"Are you kidding? Everyone the greater Snowden area knows this story. I'm surprised you don't, Freddie."

Freddie helps himself to a potato chip spilling out of the open bag. "I've heard bits and pieces. I'd like to hear it from you, if you don't mind."

I retell the story that's become Snowden legend. How it was my twenty-sixth birthday, March 15, the Ides of March, and I was making myself a cake. Banana with chocolate ganache. My mother, the town clerk at the time, was in Florida recovering from a town meeting with her sister, Aunt Julie, who'd recently retired there. My father had died the year before from a sudden heart attack and Julie was pulling out all the stops to convince Mom to live with her.

I was alone with Erika, who was also alone. She'd turned four in December and was already reading to her dolls between frequent scolds and remonstrations. We used to joke that unless she had a younger brother or sister to boss around, she was going to boss us around. As if she wasn't doing that already. That pixie with her bouncy brown pigtails had Craig wrapped around her little finger.

March fifteenth was also the height of sugaring season. The sap was flowing that year and Craig and his two friends from high school had built a sugar shack amid a stand of maples—a "sugar bush"—in the back land. Boiling was nonstop and required constant supervision, lest the syrup burn. Craig and his buddies had to take turns stoking the wood fire and stirring the evaporating sap, carefully adding more until it reached the "boiling off" stage. A steady supply of hop-based beverages helped fuel their stamina.

Some mornings, I would step outside and inhale the smell of maple wafting from the sugar shack's chimney and feel a craving for waffles swimming in melted butter and warm syrup. Craig would bring home a quart and reduce it to the hardball stage on the stove, pouring a spoonful or two over snow Erika gathered into her plastic bowl.

"Sugar on snow. As yummy as you are, chipmunk," he'd say, pinching her chubby cheeks.

"It's all gone." Erika would pout at her empty bowl, tears brimming in her big eyes.

And Craig, who couldn't resist our daughter's charms, often sneaked her another helping behind my back. Now that I think of it, maybe that's how she learned to sweet-talk men.

He'd forgotten my birthday, though. He always did. Wedding anniversaries, too. No big whoop. We all have our strengths and mine was not expecting others to make me happy. So I baked myself a birthday cake, letting Erika lick the spoon as a treat. A light snow was falling and it was cozy in the post-and-beam house. The woodstove on the brick hearth glowed brightly and Erika's new kitten, Sammy, was playing with a ball of scrap yarn on our wide-planked wooden kitchen floor.

I reminded myself how fortunate I was to have a husband with a solid job at the post office, a healthy daughter, a helpful mother, and free housing on forty acres in Vermont. True, I hadn't lived out my childhood dream of becoming a working girl in a bustling city, but I was better off than most.

And then the dogs barked.

I have never heard dogs make hair-raising sounds quite like

that before or since. To this day, I have no idea whose dogs they were or if they even existed. All I remember is how, from a distance, there came a howling that flayed my soul. The kitten leaped and scampered down the hall, its fur on end. I dropped the knife I'd been using to spread the frosting. Erika instinctively burst into tears.

The back door flew open. Tim, Craig's best friend, rushed in shouting, "Call 911! There's been an accident!" I turned to see Wilson, the other member of the threesome, filling up the door with his bulk. The only one not calling for help was my husband.

I put Erika in our bedroom, turned on the TV full volume, and shrugged on my coat and slipped into my farm boots, following the boys and the dogs down the path to the sugar bush. My mind was a blank. My peripheral vision was gone as I focused, step by step, on my boots crunching through the wet snow. I tugged my coat tighter. I blinked up at the blue sky peeking through the clouds.

I tried not to scream.

Craig was in the new Barbour, my Christmas gift, spread eagle on the snow, the top of his head—or what was left of it—bathed in a halo of red. Off to the side was the tree limb that had crushed his skull. A widow-maker, they call it. Checking the buckets of sap had disturbed the equilibrium of the forest, causing the massive log to dislodge from where it'd been hanging by a thread to clobber my husband.

I got as close to him as I could stomach, peering down at his ashen face, searching for signs of life, praying there were none. If he lived, he'd be a vegetable, and my husband was a strong, self-sufficient man for whom 24/7 care in a nursing home would be excruciating.

The EMTs came with stretchers and oxygen and crackling radios. We gave them wide berth. Tim and Wilson made themselves useful by clearing brush so they could haul Craig to the ambulance. He was already dead by the time they closed the doors.

"The police did just a cursory investigation, since neither Tim nor Wilson was within sight of Craig when the limb fell," I tell Freddie, who's devoured all the potato chips. "There was scuttlebutt in town that the accident hadn't been random, but the rumors didn't go anywhere. Craig wasn't in debt to anyone. He had no enemies. You know how small towns are; everyone's got a theory."

"And gossips," Freddie says with a shake of his head. "Some things never change."

"I'm sorry, Kim," Tammy says from the kitchen sink, a hand across her fuchsia velour bosom. "That breaks my heart. It really does."

Freddie isn't exactly tearing up, which tells me that the "bits and pieces" he's heard are the nasty rumors. "I assume Erika knows all this," he says.

"Yes." I push my cup to Tammy, who's pouring coffee. "Why?"

"In speaking to the troopers, I get the impression they're profiling Erika as a femme fatale, if you will, who's so obsessed with men, she's willing to commit foul play."

"Because she allegedly drove her car into a girl Jake Was-

kow liked better than her back in high school?" Disgusting.
"Honestly, after all my hard work for this community, you'd
think people would treat us more decently. I'm half tempted to
pack up and move tomorrow."

"You can come live with me in Florida," Tammy pipes up.

"I hear you, Kim, and I concur," Freddie says. "However,
if I may play devil's advocate, let's say Erika does suffer from
some sort of obsessive disorder." He lifts a hand to block me
from objecting. "If she's been formally diagnosed with a mental illness, that could be helpful in our defense."

"Defense?" I'm gobsmacked. This ridiculous thread needs
to be snipped at the source before Erika finds herself entangled
in a web of lies. "For what? She's done nothing wrong."

"Manslaughter," Freddie says flatly. "That's the most likely
charge the state will file against her in the death of Colton
Whitcomb, who was killed by a fallen tree limb, much like
your husband."

That's it. Sliding out of my seat, I get close enough to Freddie to count the hairs over the bridge of his nose. "You tell
those lazy-ass cops to leave Erika alone. They need to roll up
their sleeves and put their shoulders to the wheel instead of
picking on an innocent woman with a big heart who might be
a little lonely, *capisce?*"

"Maybe that way, they'll find my daughter, too," Tammy
adds, arms folded. "Instead of throwing shit on the wall to see
what sticks."

r/ToTheManorBuild: Talk about the episodes and your favorite rehab teams

Posted by vtayup26–20 min. ago

| r/TMB: Body found in VT forest is ex-boyfriend of H&R's assistant. NOT Robert! Asst questioned by police. H&R still missing.

(8 comments)

teambarron4thewin–18 min. ago

| Thank GOD (about it not being Robert). Wish there was better news about H&R.

8lifegrand–17 min. ago

| Prayers to the family of ex-boyfriend. So sad. Cause of death?

grape2grain–15 min. ago

| R the police investigating H&R disappearance?

vtayup26 (OP)–13 min. ago

| Asst's house + car was searched. Affidavit says she was last to see R alive. Removed clothes/papers this morning. Person of interest, I'd say. Houston, we have a suspect!

teambarron4thewin–11 min. ago

| This is HORRIBLE. I'm so scared for them. Is she a nutter or what?

vtayup26 (OP)–8 min. ago

| Fatal attraction case most likely. Holly's only bridesmaid. 'Memba her? Dressed exactly like her. Same hair . . .

grape2grain–6 min. ago

Yes!!! So creepy. Just Googled her. Erika Turnbull. 27. Snowden. OMG, she could be sooooo dangerous. Definitely stalker material. Team, you know what to do. . . . #doxxing.

Byebyebooboo77–2 min. ago

On it. Uploading the map of assailant's. She gonna regret ever being born . . .

TWENTY-SEVEN

ERIKA

"Good afternoon, West Coast team." LuAnn's expression can be described only as grim. "Good evening, Erika. Thank you for staying after hours on a Friday to attend this important meeting. I hope to have your undivided attention."

Erika taps up the volume on her spare laptop and adjusts the lighting in an unsuccessful attempt to improve her appearance. Though it's only seven p.m., after this long and brutal day it might as well be midnight, and the last place she wants to be is in this big, cold house, the source of all her distress and fear.

Just get through the next twenty minutes or so and then you'll be done, she tells herself, forever. She'll never have to return here. She has few illusions about LuAnn's hastily called assembly. She can read the writing on the wall. Or, to be completely accurate, the posts on Reddit.

She's about to be kicked to *TMB*'s manicured curb.

Pasting on a smile, she nods in agreement with whatever LuAnn is saying. It doesn't matter. Pretty soon she can pack up her stuff, what's left of it. The cops have ransacked the office, taking Holly's desktop computer and cleaning out the contents from all their filing cabinets. Erika peeked upstairs and found the primary suite in similar condition—drawers open, clothes in heaps. The passports, she assumes, are long gone.

Holly and Robert will be livid at the invasion of their privacy. The only consolation is that the search team appeared to be mindful of LuAnn's concerns they treat the rest of the house with kid gloves just in case *TMB* goes through with the reveal on Monday. And that decision's still up in the air.

LuAnn highlights a screen in the lower left. "I'd like to welcome Don A'Bair from legal."

A middle-aged man with a combover and french collar nods. No one has to tell anyone he was from legal. He shares Freddie's same clinical expression. No judgment. Just facts. Sheesh. She's had her fill of lawyers for a while, that's for sure.

"And everyone here knows Xavier, I trust."

Social-media guru Xavier is focused on one of his three screens. He waves once and goes back to typing. Apparently, he gets a dispensation from LuAnn's demand for undivided attention.

"If you read the memo I sent out, we have, shall we say, an irregular situation regarding our Team H&R." LuAnn folds her arms and sits back. "However, since that email went out around noon LA time, I've had several very productive—if sobering—conversations with Trooper Andre Picard of the Vermont State Police. He's been extremely helpful."

That fink. He couldn't resist calling the powers that be at *TMB* to ensure they were fully aware there's a suspected killer on their payroll—*her.*

Erika would exit Zoom and peace out, if it weren't for her burning curiosity. Just what has he told LuAnn? How far has he gone to smear her name?

"The conversations mainly concerned the police investigation into the whereabouts of our talent. It is my grim duty to report that they are now officially considered by local authorities to be missing persons and an active and vigorous investigation has been launched."

Xavier gasps and says, "Oh, dear."

Don the lawyer activates the digital hand. "I would like to clarify that the issue of whether they breached their contract remains until the investigation concludes and the police issue a written report."

No one cares about the contract, Don, Erika wants to say. Human beings are missing.

"In addition, Trooper Picard confirmed that the former owner, a mentally ill homeless individual by the name Zeke Strickland, is a person of interest. He is also, unfortunately, at large and may be considered dangerous."

Nice of Andre to let her know, Erika thinks, barely able to contain her fury. LuAnn's on the West Coast, far, far from harm's way. She, however, is right here. *In the very house Zeke wants to reclaim.*

And she's alone!

Couldn't he or Kashi have called her to let her know this is the turn their investigation has taken? Better yet, couldn't they have offered protection, an escort to safety, a freaking dog whistle?

Nope. They let her find out from LuAnn, Andre's new best friend. No doubt he's hoping LuAnn will pitch his story as a three-part series to Netflix when this is over.

"According to Trooper Picard," LuAnn continues, "Mr. Strickland may be seeking retribution against the Barrons for his eviction. It goes without saying that *TMB* sides with the Barrons, but it also means we'll have a very challenging public relations tightrope to walk when viewers learn Robert evicted a father who lost his property for failure to pay municipal taxes. Sympathies could shift drastically from them, to him. What are your thoughts on getting ahead of this with a statement, Xavier?"

"Not overtly," Xavier says, playing with a pen. "Covertly, yes."

LuAnn nods vigorously. "I'm leaning in that direction, too. My concern is that, considering the prior owner apparently has two small children, we might find ourselves in the position of defending a wealthy real estate investor who kicked a family onto the street. I don't have to tell you there'll be blowback and it will be ruinous."

"Look, he who controls the medium, controls the message," Xavier says. "Lazy, drug-addicted deadbeat who rightfully lost his house because he didn't pay his mortgage or taxes—unlike every other law-abiding American who follows *TMB*—takes his vengeance on a hardworking newlywed couple. You tell me who's sympathetic in that narrative."

LuAnn rolls her hand. "Go on."

"Anyone who's ever purchased a previously occupied house will be asking themselves what they really know about the previous owners," he continues. "Unless they're dead or in a nursing home, isn't there always a looming threat some psycho might return to reclaim what was once his? Are you really ever safe unless you're in a new build? Frankly, in my opinion, what we have here is fresh angle and I say go with it. Do the reveal."

LuAnn is nodding and tapping her chin, which means her producer wheels are cranking. "Agreed. Now that an official police investigation's underway, I can see the morning shows going nuts over this. It's beginning to gel. Give me a script."

"On it!" Xavier says.

Don the lawyer clears his throat. "Before we wrap this up, we should address the reason you brought me here, LuAnn."

LuAnn sighs and says, "Xavier, you've got your marching orders. I don't see any reason why—"

"Over and out!" He clicks off without even saying goodbye.

Erika's left alone with the producer and the lawyer. Her last chance to state her case. Honestly, she has no emotions. She is beyond numb. She is hardened concrete.

"I think I know what you guys are going to say," she jumps in. "I don't know what Andre—uhm, Trooper Picard—told you, but I swear I did not have anything to do with Colton Whitcomb's death."

Don over there is rapidly taking notes. What do these lawyers do with all these notes?

"Thank you for that, Erika." LuAnn's lips twitch in a half smile. "You're correct in your assumption. Trooper Picard did relay to me that you are, indeed, a person of interest in the untimely death of a woodworker who's had a tangential involvement with this project. Extremely unfortunate."

That's all he had to say, Erika thinks, biting the inside of her cheeks to maintain her composure while the walls around her come crumbling down. "I don't see how I can be a suspect in what apparently was an accident, though."

"From our perspective, *To the Manor Build* cannot afford so much as the taint of a scandal," chimes in heartless Don. "Whether or not this tragic death was an accident is actually immaterial. It's a matter of public perception."

"Which is why we have to ask you to tender your resignation as the Barrons' assistant immediately, Erika," LuAnn says gently. "I'm so sorry. You were very efficient and capable and often creative. One of the best assistants I've had the pleasure of working with. However, we simply can't take any chances."

That's it. Exactly what she expected. It's done.

"I'm going to ask you to leave the premises immediately. We've hired a security guard to escort you out as soon as this conversation concludes. This is standard *TMB* practice to ensure terminated employees don't take anything with them that could jeopardize the reveal. I'm sure you understand."

A security guard? No, she does not understand at all. Erika feels like she's stepped through a portal into a dystopian nightmare. Earlier this week, LuAnn dubbed her a genius. Now she's a danger to the organization who has to be physically removed forthwith!

"Goodbye, Erika," LuAnn says, leaning toward the screen. "And good luck."

Meeting ended.

Erika stares at the words on the white screen, her thoughts equally as blank. She could step on a tack or slice her finger on a shard of glass and she wouldn't feel a thing. At least it's over, she thinks, too depressed to move as her dreams vanish like dust.

Earlier, Kim left a message inviting her to dinner: pot roast and mashed potatoes with an apple pie to follow. "Tammy's never seen apples grow on trees. Then again, I've never seen a lemon on a tree!" her mother chirped, trying so very hard to boost her spirits.

That's what she will do. Go home. Take a shower. Down a glass of wine (or two) eat her mother's pot roast, and curl up under the pink covers of her childhood bed. At least she'll be warm and safe and there'll be no reason for Zeke to come after her. She is no longer part of Holly and Robert's world.

Bert was right when he cautioned her against working for them. This project does, indeed, have bad karma.

Her senses are so dulled, she doesn't hear the office door open and a security officer enter. Unlike the ones at the wedding, he's in all black. Black leather jacket over a black T-shirt. Even a black knitted cap.

"Come with me," he says, waving toward the hallway.

"I have to pack my laptop." She unzips her case. "It doesn't belong to *TMB*, it's borrowed."

"No, now. You're coming with me."

She unplugs the cord. "You'll have to wait, okay? My coffee cup and—"

"Now! I'm not fucking around."

Glancing up, she finds herself eyeing the barrel of a gun, and it hits her he's not here to escort her out per *TMB* protocol.

She's pretty sure she's meeting Zeke Strickland—at last.

TWENTY-EIGHT

ERIKA

FRIDAY NIGHT

A pressure that's been building inside her all day pushes up through her diaphragm and forces out what little food and coffee remained in her stomach onto the lovely white rug in Holly's office. If Zeke didn't clutch her upper arm, it's likely she would have passed out, too.

"Beautiful," he says in a faint southern accent. "That's gonna have to be professionally cleaned."

Her eyes water from vomiting and she has bend over to wipe her mouth. "I need to call my mother," she says for some reason, as if this is a request a guy with a gun would be cool with. "She's expecting me for dinner."

"I don't think so. We're gonna take a long drive before we call Mama. Come on, I got your boss's fancy Tesla all charged up."

She holds on to those words about calling her mother like it's a lifeline, proof she'll get through this okay. Not that she has any clue of what's going on, as Zeke leads her down the hallway to the garage. Why is he doing this to her? She didn't steal his house. She's only the assistant! *Ex*-assistant.

"No hero moves," he says, opening the car with his phone. Leading her to the passenger side, he keeps the barrel of the gun trained on her as she steps in. "Scoot on over. You're driving."

How does he expect her to drive when she can't even think? *You don't have to think*, an inner voice tells her. *All you have to do is survive. Do what he says.*

"Back up, pull around, go."

She does as he instructs, robotically backing up, closing the garage door, exiting the driveway onto the road, going below the speed limit to give passersby more time to peer into the car. It's not a night for a stroll, however, or a bike ride. The wind is biting cold and it's pitch black. Anyone on the road will be too focused on their own driving to be interested in anyone else.

Zeke slinks down as they pass the lights of the Snowden Inn. "It's not worth it, Erika," he murmurs, intuiting her temptation to step on the gas and send the car flying into the wraparound porch. "You'll be dead before you turn the wheel. We'll both be dead and, you know, I don't give a fuck about living."

Is he right? No. He's not, she thinks, but that's not why she doesn't take her last chance. Someone on the porch could be injured or killed, though she suspects that's not an issue for him.

"Take this left onto 100 North. You're going to the Ludlow Park and Ride. Twenty miles. Thirty minutes. I don't want to hear a peep."

She clenches and unclenches the wheel, closing her nose against the acrid stench of her own vomit as she concentrates on the white fog line. If a deer leaps out, will he shoot her? Don't think that way, she tells herself. Keep going. You have thirty minutes to figure out how you're going to get out of this.

"Can I lower the window, it smells—"

Zeke presses the gun into her ribs, painfully. "Shut. Up. Drive."

The thought of her mother making up a plate of pot roast and mashed potatoes, eager to hear about her day with the police, to offer her consolation about losing her job and giving her a reassuring hug, chokes her throat. Her nose goes hot and her eyes hurt. She can barely see what's beyond the windshield, her vision's so blurry with unshed tears.

"Don't fuck up. You'll be okay if you don't fuck up," he says.

She's dying to ask him what he did with Holly and Robert. At the same time, she's too afraid to learn the truth. So she does as she's told. She drives.

There's a buzz from her phone in her laptop case. He reaches in and holds it up. "It's Mama. What's your password?"

Erika can barely spit it out. "1–5–3–9."

He inputs it with his right thumb, keeping the gun on her. She should grab it while he's distracted. That's what they'd do in the movies. But Zeke's out of his mind, not thinking straight. She wouldn't stand a chance.

"Mama wants to know when you're coming home." His upper lip curls. "How about N-E-V-E-R?"

"Please, don't," she whispers. "It'll be hard enough as it is.

Just tell her something like, I'm staying over at the house. Too much work. I'll see her tomorrow."

He thinks about this. "Not bad. Buys us time." He inputs it. Erika figures they're about ten minutes from the park and ride.

"She wrote back. This is it: 'OK. Want me to save you some pistachio ice cream?' "

It is all Erika can do not to burst out cheering at her mother's mention of their special code phrase. Amazing. How did she figure out she might be in trouble? "Tell her, sure."

"Done." Then, lowering the window, he chucks her phone, where it lands onto the pavement and bounces into the woods. "Been quite a while since I had spumoni."

Erika keeps her eyes on the dark road. "Me, too."

◇ ◇ ◇

They reach the Ludlow Park and Ride a little after eight thirty, Erika scanning the lot for a Good Samaritan who might be able to save her. There's a bus depot nearby, so surely people will be milling around—a random maintenance worker or an attendant, a strong, brave person who will see her tearful face and suspect she's in danger, who will act on instinct.

But that doesn't happen in real life, and when Erika sees the vast lot is largely empty, she whimpers in despair. It's a Friday night. The commuters have come and gone. No one's around. Naturally, Zeke would have thought this through. He would have cased out the area beforehand, planned every step with contingencies. He wouldn't have taken her to a populated location.

"Hook a left and go over there, to the corner," he directs, waving his pistol. "Stick to the edge. No cameras."

Maybe he won't kill her; maybe he'll put her on the bus. The Greyhound to New York City. "Go get lost and don't come back," he'll say. "This never happened, got it?"

Then she remembers whom she's dealing with: a madman who vowed to kill Holly and then Robert and followed through on his threats. A deeply disturbed individual who illogically blames her for his misfortune. She won't be going to New York City. She won't be going anywhere. Her fleeting chance of staying alive rests entirely on her mother persuading the state police to act fast.

"There. Over there." He gestures to a large black SUV so perfectly camouflaged, she sees the orange New York license plate before she sees the vehicle. "Park. Don't get out until I say so. Otherwise this is the end."

Killing the engine, she does as she's told. In her mind, she hears her psychologist, Jill, urging her to breathe. *Breathing is literally the essence of existence*, her therapist used to say. *As long as you're breathing, you exist.*

A figure in black appears on her left, the door flings open, and a gloved hand presses against her mouth. Another hand digs painfully into her armpit as he pulls her out and pushes her into the back seat of the SUV. Facedown in the leather, she feels the steely barrel of the pistol press into her vertebrae, hard.

"Don't move," he hisses. "Gimme your wrists."

The kiss of death. Once confined, she's a goner, but what option does she have? Complying, she clasps her arms behind her. He yanks them hard as he binds them in the sharp plastic, which is burning her skin, the ominous sound of the zip tie sealing her fate.

"Her phone's about five miles down the road, in the woods," Zeke says. "Sent her mother a text that she'll be staying the night in the house and tossed it. That'll give you time."

"Not much. You should have taken it from her and left it at the house. You fucked up."

"Yeah, well, fuck you. I'm outta here."

She hears an engine rev and a car squeal out of the lot on two wheels, like he can't leave fast enough. This makes no sense. She's totally confused. Why would Zeke be leaving? He couldn't be working with someone else. He's a loner with his own agenda and vendetta.

The door of the SUV slams shut. The driver gets into the front seat and adjusts the rearview for a full view of her in the back. A slow grin spreads across his handsome face. He's enjoying, actually relishing, her shock as she recognizes that the man who's ordered her kidnapping at gunpoint is none other than the real Robber Barron doing what he does best:

Stealing lives.

TWENTY-NINE

ERIKA

FRIDAY NIGHT

Questions. So many questions, starting with *Is this actually happening?*

Erika inches to the side, leaning against the back seat for a better view of Robert. She can't gauge his mindset from here. Is this a prank he's pulling for the show? Is he really going to harm her or will he dump her off at a hotel with instructions for her to lie low until further notice?

"Robert?"

"Don't talk," he snaps, checking his mirrors, which he's been doing repeatedly since they started driving. "You're only going to make things worse for yourself if you talk."

"But—"

"Shhh!" He shoots her a dark glance, his once manly brow

furrowed angrily. He hardly resembles the man she knew—she *thought* she knew. He's not a charismatic, energetic entrepreneur. He's an alien. A monster.

A Plexiglas screen rises from the seat between them, a power divider. Usually, those are activated by the passengers in a limo, not the driver. But this SUV has been tricked out for the reverse, a serial killer's fantasy vehicle, she realizes with a nauseating chill.

Craning her neck to see out the window, she tries to spot any street signs and buildings for points of reference. All she can see is the night sky and trees. So many trees. Pine. Beech. Maple. White Birch. Majestic sentinels, reminders that she's not alone. They are with her. Witnessing.

They drive until the SUV bounces so hard, Erika feels as if her neck is about to snap. Clearly, they're off a class three road. This is rougher than even a class four. It might be a logging trail. Robert is struggling to maintain equilibrium. Branches scratch against metal and glass. Twigs snap.

And then they stop.

He gets out and opens the rear door. Or he tries. Due to the thick underbrush, it opens only a few inches. "Come on," he says, hauling her from the back seat, her calves scraping across the car's edge.

Her foot lands in a divot, her ankle wobbling under her weight until it twists so painfully, she automatically lets out a cry.

"Shut. Up!" Reaching down, he slides off her shoes and snaps off the heels, replacing them on her feet like a disturbed Prince Charming. "Go!" He gives her a push into the brambles.

Stinging thorns scrape her cheek. Unable to protect her

face with her hands, she keeps her eyes closed as he pushes her stumbling over roots and brush. She has to curl her toes to keep going. The smells of must and loam rise from the damp earth. Prickers attach themselves to her trousers. Branches recoil painfully with a *thwack*.

Her heart is pounding so hard, she can't hear her own churning thoughts. She tells herself to think like an animal, to act if she sees an opportunity to run. At last the brush clears out. Erika feels a breeze and opens her eyes. They are at a field's edge. She follows the tree line, up the hill to a house. Huge glass windows glow golden in the night. She's disoriented, confused and, now, slightly hopeful.

"We're circled back," she whispers, dizzy. "We're at the house." He's not going to harm her, after all. He's brought her home!

"Not for you," he says, leaning down and removing a plank from the ground. "You're here."

That's when she notices the hole.

Reaching into the underbrush, Robert removes a makeshift ladder no more than six feet in length and lowers it down.

"NO!" Erika shouts, backing off, instantly falling sideways into a bush. She tries getting up again only to tip backward. She's helpless with her wrists tied.

"Get in," he says.

"I, I, can't with my wrists like this. I'll fall."

"So?"

"I could hurt myself. Undo the ties and then . . ." And then I'll run, she thinks. If I can just make it to the field.

He pulls out a knife, gets behind her, and cuts off the ties.

Snip. Snip. Then he brings out a gun from his back pocket. "Get in," he orders. "Or I'll shoot you in the head and throw your body down. Your choice."

What little bile's left in her stomach rises up her esophagus. She can't. She'd rather be dead than buried alive. No. That's not true. As long as she's breathing, she still has a chance—even if it's in a grave.

The ladder's rickety as she takes each rung in her broken shoes. The earthen smells of rot and damp and soil and mold greet her when she reaches the rocky bottom. She looks up and sees Robert above, peering down.

A light goes on and she turns to see a cavern illuminated behind her. The ceiling's high enough for her to stand straight. The walls are hard-packed dirt, the stone floor covered here and there with old carpet remnants. This isn't any old hole; it's an old New England root cellar that's been tricked out with a small woodstove and a heap of blankets.

"Holly!" Erika cries, simultaneously horrified by what this monster's done to his own wife and grateful she won't be alone in this awful crypt. "Are you okay?"

Holly sits up slowly, adjusting the flame in the Coleman she must have lit. Her cheeks are hollow, her eyes sunken, and her beautiful hair is matted.

"Holly, speak to me. It's Erika. I'm here with you."

Blinking, Holly squints and murmurs, "Erika?"

"Yes, yes, I'm here." She assesses their surroundings. The room is no more than twelve feet wide. There's an empty bottle of water and a plastic bucket that even a slight distance away smells vile. What her grandmother used to ironically call a honey bucket because it wasn't filled with anything close to honey.

Judging from her condition, Holly must have been here all week. She needs medical care for dehydration and probably the cut under the bandage on her arm, Erika thinks. He can't let her die. They've got to get her out of here.

There's a commotion by the entrance and the two women scoot back as Robert enters the cellar, head bent. His gun is pointed at Holly. He says nothing, only flicks it toward the ladder.

Holly runs her fingers through her greasy hair and slowly rises.

"Hurry!" Robert commands. "Every second counts. You," he says, swiveling the barrel to Erika. "Get away from her. Sit!"

Erika does as he orders, plunking herself down on a heap of old, rank blankets. The last thing she wants is to make any trouble for Holly, who is crawling on her hands and knees toward Robert. "Water," she whispers hoarsely.

He tosses his wife a small bottle. She grabs it, barely able to twist off the top, she's so weak. Finally, it's open and she gulps its contents.

"Not so fast. You'll make yourself sick," he says, snatching it out of her hands and throwing it to Erika. "That's all you get," he says, assisting his wife to her feet.

Erika gapes at the half-empty bottle. It can't hold more than four ounces. It's not nearly enough to sustain her for . . . *how long?*

That's when it hits her. Robert doesn't care if she dies of thirst; he has no intention of letting her live.

Robert gives his wife a boost up the ladder, following closely behind. Erika rushes after them, panicked, grabbing the ladder and holding it fast. They can't leave her down here, not for a day, an hour, a minute. "Let me up. I won't say anything, I promise. Just don't leave me here!"

The ladder slips from her hands so fast, splinters dig into her palms and she lets go, staring up helplessly as the plywood falls over the hole with a loud, terrifying *thunk!*

Then she hears the rocks, one by one, and she thinks, crying, This is what it must sound like when the gravedigger shovels dirt over your coffin.

TMB: LOVE AMONG THE ACTUAL RUINS

POST #67: A GIRL CAVE OF ONE'S OWN

Hi, I'm Holly Barron, a contestant on *To the Manor Build*, a super-popular rehab show.

This is my unfiltered, no-holds-barred, honest, behind-the-scenes peek at the craziness of turning a run-down Vermont log cabin into a net-zero awesome house with a hot, sexy guy I ~~am about to~~ just married.

My motto: Whatever I can do, YOU totally can do better!

Follow me to see how!

Hey, Fellow Manor Builders!

Less than three days until the Big Reveal! The excitement is absolutely killing me, y'all. I am totally, rip-roaring convinced you're going to be inspired by our beautiful house that's so energy-efficient you can heat all 2,000 square feet with a candle. And if you're under the misimpression that this kind of square footage won't provide the grandeur you demand in a luxury home, let me disabuse you of that notion right now.

By installing window walls, a welcoming front porch, a secluded upper deck, and a generous entertainment area in the back, we have expanded the house's footprint, so to speak, through illusion and by taking advantage of the outdoor spaces. Yes, even in Vermont you can live outside all four seasons, relaxing by the fires on the heated entertainment area, warming up in our Swedish sauna, even swimming in our geothermally heated pool. There's no reason to be inside. Ever.

Except when you need to be alone—am I right?

Ladies, let's talk. Guys, you go watch a game or shoot a deer or something.

Now, we hear a lot on property rehab programs about "man caves." I don't have to tell you what they are—big, ugly spaces, usually in converted garages or attics or basements—featuring these must-haves: huge TV with the state-of-the-art technology, reclining chairs with beverage holders, a gaming system ("to blow off steam"), and a door to shut out the family.

Occasionally, they're personalized depending on the man. A billiard table and a classy bar instead of Barcaloungers and an Xbox, for example. Motorcycles. Tools. Fishing rods. Guns. Those boys do love their toys.

I think we ladies can agree that our needs for girl caves are far more complex and we must pay them heed.

Here are my three must-haves:

Two doors to your girl cave, locked. Why? Because one door does not prevent a child or husband from knocking and asking what's for dinner or where so-and-so's shirt is and whether it's ironed, or what to do about the meowing cat that needs to be fed as you're trying to steal a few minutes of privacy in the tub.

When I designed our suite, I insisted on actually three doors: one from the hallway to the bedroom, one from the bedroom to the walk-in closet, and one from the closet to the bathroom, because that, you see, is *my* girl cave. I get it. Some of y'all might have craft rooms or workout rooms. Either way, you're gonna need those extra doors to keep out the barbarians.

Soundproofing and/or distance. If you dream of a craft area, put it in the attic, way, way, way from the house activity. You cannot get the rest and relaxation you need if you have one ear cocked for the glass that's been dropped or the kids squabbling. You want to be in the zone at your sewing machine zipping through those colorful quilt squares. You do not want to be worrying if that scraping in the kitchen means the dog has—once again—gotten into the open jar of peanut butter left by the squabbling kids.

Pamper yourself. We give so much to our children and husbands, your girl cave is not a place to scrimp. For instance, y'all know that I'm a water baby by nature. So we installed a triple steam shower with a rain head built into the ceiling. Girlfriends, it is like taking a shower and a bath at the same time. All your troubles simply melt away. I also use this Parisian body wash that smells like lilies of the valley and leaves my skin silky soft. Is it more expensive than Calgon? Yup. Am I worth it? Yup. Yup.

Is sewing your therapy? Then consider splurging on this divine Bernina sewing machine. Your husband may ask why a person needs a $7,000–$17,000 machine to mend his pants and I give you permission to reply that if he has the nerve to ask that again, he can find another woman to mend them. *Mm-hmm.*

If you've committed to an exercise regime, good for you! That is a gift you've given to yourself and your loved ones. They should bend over backward (like you) to support this endeavor. So go ahead and buy that stationary bike or treadmill or StairMaster. Heck, get all three! And while you're at it, I'm sure no one will dare object to you hiring Eduardo, the tanned, fit, hunky personal trainer who comes to your girl cave three times a week to, you know, *keep you in shape.*

See above: Two doors. *Locked.*

Welp, this is the last blog before the Big Reveal Monday. Too bad, so sad. Until then, please log on to ToTheManorBuild.com to chat more about girl caves. Cannot wait to see you live!

–Holly

This post may contain affiliate links, which means I earn a small commission when you make a purchase through those links, at no additional cost to you.

THIRTY

KIM

The past fourteen hours have been brutal. My phone has become part of my hand, a magic portal with all the hopeful answers—and agonizing questions. I don't dare drag my gaze from it. Any minute now, surely, Erika will call or text, I tell myself, anticipating the cool flush of relief when I see her *Sorry, had my phone off.* But to my utter frustration and mounting anxiety, the frantic messages to my daughter remain unanswered, the calls disappearing into voicemail.

Where is she?

I would have contacted the VSP right away after I sent her our code phrase and she responded with "Sure!" if it hadn't been for that damned Apple Watch. It's constantly spitting back automatic replies, sometimes when she hasn't read the original message. Erika would be mortified if I jumped the gun and begged the police to put out an APB when she was just having a glass of wine at the Snowden Inn or simply taking a few minutes to herself, mulling over what certainly has been a traumatic day. She'd never forgive me.

Besides, it's not as though she has a stellar track record when it comes to responding in a timely fashion. There've been plenty of occasions where she's failed to get back to me despite my pestering. Usually, the lame excuse is her phone ran out of power and she couldn't find a charger or she was in a place with no service, though I've suspected she's simply tired of being virtually tethered to her mother. And who could blame her? We live right on top of each other. She's an adult woman, and yet I'm always in her business.

Except this time it's different. Erika hasn't been under this much stress—or police scrutiny—since the accident in high school. The VSP clearly have her in their crosshairs now that her former boyfriend, Colton Whitcomb, is dead under mysterious circumstances, and a male employer with whom she's infatuated has been missing for days. Andre, especially, seems out for blood. I can't help but feel she's being bullied by a man with baggage and a badge. I mean, searching her apartment? Totally over the top.

Tammy and I went by the apartment to tidy up and were appalled. The place was a mess, in chaotic disarray. Drawers hung opened, couch cushions upended, trash cans overturned. A tornado could have landed here and it would've been neater. We put it back together before she could see it. And now I wonder if she ever will.

"You might feel better if you drove around and looked for her," Tammy finally said after hours of watching me pull my hair out. "That's what was killing me in Florida, the endless waiting, the inability to do anything. You gotta take action."

Shit. In my self-centered obsession about my own daughter I'd forgotten the reason Tammy was in Snowden, to search for hers. How could I be so insensitive?

"*Psssh.* Stop," she said when I apologized for my thoughtlessness. "Look. Let's finish the dishes. If she's not back by the time we punch the button on the dishwasher, then why don't we see what we can find?"

We went from clutter to clean in a flash. I spooned pot roast, gravy, and mashed potatoes onto a plate, covered it with Saran Wrap, and put it into the fridge for when Erika got home. As if she were working late.

"Atta girl," Tammy said with a wink. Grabbing her sunshine-yellow parka, she said, "One smoke and then we'll go."

Tammy took the wheel of my Subaru, squinting at the night road ahead and grimacing whenever we hit a pothole or a rock. Clutching my phone, always, I stared out the window searching for the Tesla or a break in the trees where a car might have plowed through. Once, I thought I saw a person standing with her thumb out, but it was only a white birch.

We headed to the Barrons' house and had to park the car at the gate and walk up the driveway. The automatic outdoor lights flicked on, but clearly no one was home. The windows were dark. I rang the bell and even tried the doors, in case one had been left open. But they were locked tight.

Then we drove to the Snowden Inn, where the bartender was closing down for the evening. He knew Erika but told us she hadn't stopped by for weeks.

"How about her friends?" Tammy asked me next.

I shrugged. "If she had any."

This is a huge part of Erika's problem, in my opinion, lack of companionship. She's always been a bit of a loner, a daydreamer who's happier in her room scrolling through social media than actually engaging in human interaction. Or maybe that's my distorted view.

Running out of options, we ended up driving aimlessly around Snowden as I mentally fended off the scenarios maliciously creeping into my thoughts: Erika dead in the woods like Colton. Erika injured, captive, trapped . . . *drowned*.

Finally, I bit the bullet and called the VSP. Seeming less than interested in a twenty-seven-year-old woman who hadn't responded to her mother for three hours despite the exchange of their mutual code words, a dispatcher nevertheless promised a trooper would stop by the house. Tammy and I went home and waited. No trooper.

There was nothing left to do but hit up the local cop— Andre Picard. I had problems with him, but at least he'd approach Erika's disappearance seriously, if skeptically. After all, according to Freddie, Andre and Trooper Kashi had instructed her not to leave the area and here she was, disobeying.

"She's gone!" I said, when he answered the door in his flannel pants, half asleep and blinking. "You have to search for her now! Put out an APB. We've already wasted too much time."

Andre made us a pot of coffee and called the barracks, issuing a missing-person alert. He took my statement, calmly asking important questions that, in my turmoil, I hadn't thought to ask. Who last saw her? She was supposed to go to work for a meeting. Did she have that meeting? Who was at the meeting? Did I have contact info?

He, of all people, had the telephone number for LuAnn Cowles, the *To the Manor Build* producer in LA, with whom he'd apparently spoken early in the day. Or the day before. Or the day before that. I have no idea. Details flit in and out of my brain like butterflies through a field. Nothing sticks.

Andre managed to track down LuAnn, even putting her on speakerphone for my benefit. She came across as a genuinely nice person, though I got the sense from the way she hesitated when she answered a few of his tougher questions that she had another agenda, besides my daughter's safety. To her, Erika was an assistant she'd met once at a wedding and subsequently via Zoom. She was peanuts compared with the all-important success of *To the Manor Build*.

And then she dropped the bomb: Erika had been fired.

When LuAnn said the word *terminated*, I tried not to curse. Erika must have been devastated. Becoming the Barrons' assistant had been life changing for her, proving to the community of haters that not only was she valued, but she was valued by Important People. For her to lose this beloved job, and all because of some wild, unsubstantiated allegations involving an ex-boyfriend and a vengeful cop, could send anyone over the bend.

It was Amber Allen all over again. An unfortunate accident,

a small-town rumor mill painting her as a woman scorned, followed by harsh judgment and merciless repercussions.

"I hope she hasn't done something drastic," I said, under my breath.

"She's okay," Tammy whispered. "She's not gonna harm herself over a stupid job. Anyway, she wouldn't have used her code word, right?"

"I was so sorry to let her go," LuAnn said. "Kim, I want you to know that our decision had nothing to do with your daughter's abilities. Like I told her, I have never worked with such a capable assistant and capable assistants are worth their weight in gold. I will gladly write her a glowing recommendation once this is all cleared up."

Too little, too late, I thought.

Andre asked LuAnn for details of the meeting. When it began, when it ended. It had begun at seven p.m. our time and ended about fifty-five minutes later. By then only LuAnn, a *TMB* lawyer, and Erika were in the meeting.

"This is going to come across as severe, but remember *TMB* must ensure one-hundred-percent confidentiality among our talent, staff, and vendors," LuAnn prefaced defensively. "Whenever you terminate an employee, you run the risk of sabotage. Therefore, in situations such as this where there is no supervisor on the premises to oversee the terminated employee, per *TMB* policy we follow a process where as soon as the employee is informed of her termination, security is on hand to immediately escort said employee from the work site."

My jaw dropped in horror. What kind of operation was this?

Tammy went, "You can't be for real."

"We've had bad experiences," LuAnn said. "Terminated employees have stolen pricey staging pieces or downloaded confidential internal emails in an attempt to embarrass *TMB*. Dented fridge doors. Smashed windows. Even, once, defecation on an antique hand-knotted Persian carpet. That case set our security policy in stone forever."

"Erika Turnbull is not the type of girl to take a piss on your fancy rug," Tammy said, outraged on my behalf. "Y'all should be ashamed for treating a loyal employee with such a lack of dignity."

"No shit," I agreed.

Andre stayed on task. "Do you have the contact information for that security officer?"

"HR does, I'm sure," said LuAnn, seeming less authoritative after Tammy's dressing-down. "They've gone for the weekend, unfortunately. They won't be back until Monday. I do know that when we were setting this up earlier, they were looking for suggestions in the area. I mentioned the security firm Robert Barron hired for the wedding. They were out of Boston, as I recall."

The beefy men in suits ringing the perimeter of the ceremony with their white earbuds and impenetrable sunglasses. Tammy was right. Calling in professional bouncers to remove an assistant who'd busted her ass to ensure this ridiculous reality show contest ran without a hitch was not only overkill, it was insulting.

Andre thanked LuAnn and hung up the phone just as

an alert from a dispatcher crackled across his portable radio. "Missing person located. Code 452. TH 117 at mile marker—"

My heart leapt. Erika!

He turned down the radio, got up, and went to the other room, shutting the door behind him and leaving me in a cold sweat. Had they found her and, if so, in what condition? The way Andre silenced the radio had me worried as I rapidly Googled "Code 452" on my phone, along with "Town Highway 117."

"That's her. I just know it," Tammy said, brightly. "All that fretting for nothing, Kim. Bet her car broke down and she had no cell service. You know how that is."

I showed her my Google results. "Town Highway 117 is the Mad Tom Notch Road in Peru."

Tammy frowned. "Isn't that where you took me the night I got in? It's where Colton Whitcomb's body was found and . . . Erika's car."

"You're right. Good memory."

Just then, the door opened and Andre appeared, phone to his chest. He looked to me, then to Tammy, and then to me again.

"We found her."

r/ToTheManorBuild: Talk about the episodes and your favorite rehab teams

Posted by vtayup26–30 min. ago
> r/TMB: Robert and Holly Barron found!
> Hey–guys this just came over the Vermont State Police blog. It's all over the local media here. Reprinting for your benefit.

STATE OF VERMONT
DEPARTMENT OF PUBLIC SAFETY
VERMONT STATE POLICE
NEWS RELEASE
CASE#: 35801564

RANK/TROOPER FULL NAME: Trooper Andre Picard
STATION: VSP Westminster
DATE/TIME: 10/21/22 @ 0445 hours
INCIDENT LOCATION: Peru, VT
UPDATE: Missing persons located safe

Holly Simmons Barron
AGE: 36
CITY, STATE OF RESIDENCE: Snowden, VT

Robert Barron III
AGE: 40
CITY, STATE OF RESIDENCE: Snowden, VT

SUMMARY OF INCIDENT: On 10/21/22, @ 0230 hours, Troopers from the Vermont State Police were dispatched to reports of two missing persons having been located by the side of the TH 117 in Peru, VT, at mile marker 66. Upon arrival, the man identified himself as Robert Barron of Snowden and the woman as his wife, Holly Barron. They were transported to UVM Medical Center in Burlington for treatment of dehydration and lacerations. This incident is still under investigation and anyone with any information is asked to call the Westminster Barracks.

(12 comments)

dramamama78–22 min. ago
| OMG Is this real?

pennypinch2345–20 min. ago
| Yes! Confirmed. They're safe.

Awwwsnap90–18 min. ago
| So, so happy. But . . . what happened?

pennypinch2345–16 min. ago
| Where u getting this? Reddit? (Hahahahaha)

Awwwsnap90–15 min. ago
| Source in VSP say they were majorly f'd up. Like near death. Tied up and got out after kidnapper dude didn't come back.

dramamama78–12 min. ago
| What dude? u/Awwwsnap90.

Awwwsnap90–10 min. ago
| Former owner of the house. Name's Zeke Strickland. Payback for Robert taking

his property. Turns out, he had a leeeetle help from our obsessed assistant. She gave him keys to in the house. Let him use her car . . . the one found trashed in the woods.

Agirlandherdog82–7 min. ago

You mean, the fatal attraction bridesmaid???

Awwwsnap90–5 min. ago

That's the girl! Erika Turnbull. Now that her ass is in hot water, she's on the run. Missing since H&R were found.

Braindoesnotcomput119–3 min. ago.

With the kidnapper?

Awwwsnap90–1 min. ago

¯_(ツ)_/¯

THIRTY-ONE

LUANN

SUNDAY MORNING

"Come on, people. Let's stop chatting and focus." LuAnn hunts for the right button on her MacBook so she can mute everyone in the Zoom meeting. Normally she's a whiz with computers, but she's not firing on all cylinders today. Her head feels like it's stuffed with feathers.

She touched down in Burlington last night to find that the rental car company was unmanned in the ghost town of an empty airport. That was a hassle. Then she had to drive more than an hour down strange, dark country roads to reach the Snowden Inn. When she got there, she was informed at check-in that the bar and the kitchen were both closed and the closest place where she might find food at that hour would be Rutland, fifty miles way.

As if she'd even consider getting back in that car.

The manager on duty took pity on her, went to his own home, and fixed a sandwich. Turkey and swiss. It was the best thing she's ever eaten.

Anyway, now she's here, on the scene, along with passel of news media who are descending like a plague of locusts.

Holly and Robert Barron have been found. CNN, NBC, CBS, and Fox are clobbering one another for their story. But there's only one outlet that's going to get it and that's hers: *TMB*.

She is salivating with glee. They are going to win this contest. It's practically in the bag, provided there are no slip-ups or leaks. All they have to do is manage the next thirty-six hours until the reveal at eight p.m. tomorrow night. They need to ensure Robert and Holly talk only to the police and that the police are airtight about keeping details confidential so that all eyes will be on ToTheManorBuild.com at when they livestream the reveal.

Thermador, Kohler, GE, LG, have rushed to purchase more advertising. Lacanche is scrambling to see if they can get a six-burner blue range installed by tomorrow. The bucks are rolling in.

After the reveal, let come what may. Holly and Robert have already signed agents who've lined up the Tuesday-morning shows, adhering to the strict talking points being crafted by legal. *People* wants them for next week's cover story, and Investigation Discovery is bandying about a six-week series. While she was boarding in LAX, LuAnn got a call from Paula Zahn herself. *The* Paula Zahn.

Spin-offs, book deals, brands at Target and Home Depot. There's no telling how far this can go. LuAnn takes a sip of bad coffee from the local general store and reminds herself not to count her chickens before they hatch.

She gets back on Zoom and clicks on Jasper, the college intern she sent on gopher duty. "Let's start with you, Jasper," she begins. "For those joining us who may be unfamiliar with the events that have transpired in the past twenty-four hours, our intern Jasper has been scrolling through the news sites to bring us a report. Go ahead, Jasper. Make it snappy."

"Right." Jasper wipes perspiration off his top lip, his purple bow tie tilted. "Um, as I'm sure you guys have heard, our talent, Holly and Robert Barron, were discovered early yesterday morning near the entrance to the Long Trail on the Mad Tom Notch Road in Peru, Vermont."

Xavier asks in the chat space:

XAVIER: Mad Tom Notch Road?
XAVIER: Is that like for real?

LuAnn ignores this.

"I did some research," Jasper says. "And it turns out the Long Trail is a two-hundred-and-seventy-mile hiking trail that runs the length of Vermont and connects to the Appalachian Trail, so there are lots of hikers this time of year making their way south from Maine."

LuAnn rolls her hand. "If you could speed things along, Jasper, that'd be great."

"I mention it because that's how Holly and Robert were found, by hikers getting an early start. They were huddled together leaning up against a trail sign. The hikers thought at first they were sleeping, but then one of them had the good sense to realize something wasn't right. They called 911, covered them with those thin thermal blankets that look like foil? Anyway they gave them sips of hot tea from a thermos until the EMTs came. They were in pretty bad shape, shivering, but conscious, possibly suffering from mild hypothermia. Dehydrated."

Vanessa the interior designer writes in the chat

VANESSA: OMG, that's so awful!

"My understanding is they've been released from the hospital," LuAnn says. "We've booked them an entire floor of a Marriott in nearby Burlington. They'll recover there until tomorrow."

Xavier asks to be unmuted. LuAnn complies.

"The Burlington hotel is brilliant because it serves two purposes," he gushes. "Lets them get the rest they need, but also keeps the press away from the house in Snowden. The premises must be secure to intruders. A leak would be deadly."

"Excellent, Xavier. We'll up the security here. What else?"

"We've been inundated with interview requests. *Good Morning America* wants to lead with them in the nine a.m. East Coast slot tomorrow." He breaks out into applause.

"As a teaser, I hope," LuAnn says, reining him in. "Because no way are we giving up the candy on this."

"Oh, totally. We'll get that in writing so viewers tune in

later for the reveal. In the meantime, social media is on fire. *TMB* is trending on Twitter—a first!"

"Fabulous." LuAnn can barely stand the way the pieces are falling into place. "Let's make sure we keep it trending. Negative or positive, I don't care."

"Does anyone know what happened?" Vanessa asks, after LuAnn unmutes her. "There are loony rumors flying around. Hard to tell what's true and what isn't."

Xavier laughs. "Truth? Who needs truth? We just need people to log on. All Robert and Holly have to say was that it was a 'nightmare' "—he makes finger quotes—"And a 'blessing' they were found. Leave it at that."

"That was going to be my advice," chimes in Don A'Bair, the *TMB* lawyer. "We don't know what the fact pattern is in this case and the contracted talent needs to be extremely careful about slandering any third parties with unsubstantiated allegations while a formal police investigation is pending. We do not want to invite litigation from an unfairly-accused party making a claim of libel or slander because, I can guarantee, *TMB* will be named as a defendant. We are the deep pockets here."

"As far as I know from my discussion with Trooper Picard, the police already have publicly named a person of interest, the former property owner, Zeke Strickland," LuAnn says. "Apparently, he's the one who's been sending those threatening letters to Robert Barron. He kidnapped them out of revenge and then went AWOL himself. That's how Robert and Holly got away. When he didn't return, they freed themselves."

"Um, that's not the chatter online," Xavier says. "Word is your little assistant there, the local girl, was the one who let this Strickland person into the house while they were sleeping. I heard—and, again, this is only internet gossip so it's about as reliable as the rhythm method—that that's why *her* car was found near the camp where they were held hostage, because she loaned it to Strickland and then took Robert's. Now that Robert and Holly have been found, she's in hiding."

Damn these state police, LuAnn thinks. They'll never make it to the reveal without the juiciest tidbits getting out so soon.

"This is how I envision tomorrow playing out," she says, returning to the business at hand. "We tease the reveal with strategically placed clips online of our talent at their wedding. Edit ruthlessly. I want adoring looks, clasping hands, tears of joy as they begin their new married life together, oblivious that in hours they'll be attacked in their own marital bed."

"Ooooh," coos Vanessa approvingly.

"Xavier, have your people put out a statement expressing *TMB*'s best wishes for the recovering couple and asking for privacy at this time, but also mentioning that they will be streaming and airing live as scheduled."

Xavier jots notes. "Totally."

"Legal, I think you'd better arrange a consult with our contracted talent sooner rather than later so they fully grasp the legalities at stake. We don't want them going off script."

"Already done," Don says.

"Meanwhile, Jasper, please keep me apprised about the assistant. Any word on her whereabouts?"

Jasper's mouth moves, but no sound comes out.

"You're muted, Jasper," LuAnn says. "You can take yourself off mute."

He succeeds. "Sorry. None."

LuAnn says, "Pardon?"

"I mean there's no word on the whereabouts of Erika Turnbull. Allegedly, the car she's been driving, Robert's Tesla, was located yesterday morning in a commuter parking lot in Vermont where there's a bus station. The cops say she might have left the area. But her mother posted on Facebook that her daughter went missing immediately after she was fired and she has reason to believe she's in danger. She disputes the rumors that Erika is in partnership with Zeke Strickland. What do you think, LuAnn? You and Don were the last to speak to her."

"I think I'm seriously jet lagged. Text me if you have any updates, guys. If not, let's check in tonight. Okay, team?"

LuAnn backs out of Zoom and lies on Holly's daybed, staring up at the beamed ceiling, thinking about Erika Turnbull. How did it come to pass that a nice young woman like her ended up helping a madman like Zeke Strickland kidnap and hold hostage Robert and Holly Barron?

There's only one answer.

THIRTY-TWO

KIM

SUNDAY MORNING

It's been, let's see, forty-one hours and thirty two minutes since I've heard from Erika. The only development in her case, for lack of a better description, is that the car she was last seen driving—Robert's Tesla—was found in the far corner of the Ludlow Park and Ride lot. I nearly lost it when Trooper Kashi called earlier to confirm the sighting.

"I'd like to update you in person, if you don't mind," Kashi said quietly, when she called to arrange a meeting. "Is there a neutral spot where we can talk in private? A conference room in town hall, perhaps? I assume you're not open on a Sunday."

We can't meet at my house, because reporters are camped out on my driveway, unable to resist the juicy saga of a scorned assistant conspiring with an evicted to homeowner to wreak revenge on the Boston yuppies who stole his property.

"Local Vermonters versus Massholes," is how someone put it on social media.

"Gives 'Take Back Vermont,' a whole new meaning," was another comment.

There's no such thing as bad publicity, goes the old saying. After being glued to my computer turning the whites of my eyes red from scanning posts for possible clues to my daughter's whereabouts, I am here to testify that this saying is a lie.

When did people become so mean?

To be honest, I'm petrified of my one-on-one with Kashi. I dread that the reason she won't give me the updates over the phone is because police protocol advises that loved ones be informed of horrific details in person. Though I have steeled myself for the worst, I feel as fragile as a dandelion past its prime. One gust of bad news and I'll disappear.

"I want you to know we've contacted all the nearby buses and train stations," Kashi says, hands clasped on the conference table outside the town clerk's office. "The only sighting we have was taken by a dashcam on a parked vehicle. It shows a blond woman driving a Tesla entering the lot at approximately eight thirty-five p.m. After that, nothing."

I drop a mental pin on the Ludlow Park and Ride, my daughter's last known location. "Then where did she go?"

"That's what we've been investigating. She could have walked out of the lot and three miles to the interstate, but, again, there are no reports of a woman along I-91 or nearby roads at that hour or since."

Erika would not hitchhike. "That's not even a remote possibility," I tell her. "She wouldn't do that, trust me. She's watched too much Investigation Discovery to take that stupid a risk."

Kashi does not appear swayed by this. "Alternatively, she could have left in a different vehicle. The lot doesn't have security cameras, unfortunately. We got lucky with the dashcam."

She and I understand the implications of that statement. Either Erika left willingly with Zeke or, as I fear, he took her against her will. I am 100 percent certain it's the latter.

"Erika wouldn't have gone off with him. That's why she used our code word," I tell Kashi. "He's got her and you know it and I'm worried sick."

Kashi nods once, which I interpret as agreement. "Trust me, Kim, we're doing all we can to find her."

Are they? I twist Craig's thin gold wedding band on my right ring finger, urging myself to stay strong. Kashi is all too familiar with my stand on the absurd theories circulating on the internet that Erika conspired with Zeke Strickland to harm Robert and Holly. There's no proof of their collusion and, besides, I know my daughter. Never in a million years would she have given this stranger the key to their house and, for heaven's sake, loaned him her car.

I've told the police about what I saw that night when Robert showed up at Erika's apartment. I've even given them the bag of bloodied PJs he tried to stash. For some reason, they weren't impressed by that. They seemed to think, if anything, Robert was being sweetly protective of his wife. Maybe he didn't want strangers pawing through his garbage and posting the soiled PJs online. Anyway, it was a moot point, they argued, now that Robert and Holly have been located.

The police have been far more interested in the timeline involving Erika's car. I've told them again and again that Robert took it that night, yet they don't appear to believe my eyewitness account.

"But did you actually see him drive it away?" Kashi has asked me repeatedly.

And, always, I have to regretfully answer no.

"There is a bit of good news," Kashi says. "You should know that no charges will be filed in the death of Colton Whitcomb. The medical examiner ruled this morning that he was killed when a thirty-foot branch of an ash tree infested with borer beetles broke off and fell fifty feet and landed on the back his neck, breaking it on contact. At least he didn't suffer."

I am relieved Erika is cleared, not that I ever doubted her innocence, and still furious she was ever implicated. Mostly, I'm devastated for Colton's parents. The loss of a child at any age is a horror impossible to overcome.

Kashi's phone buzzes. She pulls it out of her pocket and checks, arching an eyebrow. "Okay, then. It appears they've found a white pickup truck with tags matching Zeke Strickland's registration."

My heart stops. I clasp my chest, unable to breathe. "Where?"

"On the access road off the town gravel pit." She glances up, her gaze pointed. "There's a deceased individual in the front seat." She exhales. "Male."

Blood drains from my body, my extremities going cold. I reach for her hand, grasping at it as if she's my lifeline. "Not Erika."

Kashi gives me a reassuring squeeze. "Not Erika."

Thank God. "Zeke?"

She shakes her head. "Don't know. Undetermined at this point."

If he took her, then she must be nearby. "I have to go there. I have to find her!" My legs are like rubber as I slide out of the chair, leaning on the table for support. Where are my keys? My purse? I, I don't know. I can't think.

"Kim, it's best—" Kashi starts to object, and then stops. "All right. But you're in no condition to drive. I'll take you."

◇ ◇ ◇

The gravel pit is a gash of exposed rock on the side of Braxton Hill, far from our picturesque village. It's remote, accessed only by the highway department when the crew is digging out winter sand. No one goes there at night or on the weekends except for teenagers, the smashed beer bottles and bullet-ridden targets being evidence of that.

The white pickup is half hidden by brush in the access road to the far left. The police have marked off the scene with orange cones and yellow tape. On our way, Kashi and I pass an ambulance headed in the opposite direction, lights off and in no rush.

"DOA," she says, having already learned from the responders that the deceased was found with a needle in his arm and, in case that didn't do the trick, his throat slit. "The scene's pretty bloody. You need to stay here," she says when we pull into the pit.

I get out of the cruiser and lean against the car, shielding my eyes against the waning sun as Kashi goes to meet her fellow troopers. Hope against hope he left a note in the car admitting his crimes and telling the police where to find Erika. Maybe he untied her and she's finding her way back to civilization.

A message from Doreen pops up on my phone.

DOREEN: Any news?

KIM: Not yet. You?

DOREEN: SVFD told E it's Zeke. No?

E stands for Elliot, Doreen's husband, a former member of the Snowden Volunteer Fire Department. If they've confirmed it's Zeke, then it's Zeke. Now the haunting question is, what did he do with Erika?

My sick hope is that he killed himself out of guilt instead of killing her and then himself. I know that's not the pattern of these psychopaths. They don't do themselves in until they've slaughtered their innocent victims. But if what Gretchen said is true, that he's a loner who's not inclined to hurt others, then maybe, just maybe, he saw the light before he committed suicide.

If he didn't leave a note, then my daughter's whereabouts are a secret that died with him.

There's a loud crunch of gravel behind me as a small blue car bounces into the pit. Gretchen Strickland's behind the wheel, dressed in her pink scrubs. She parks the car and gets out, slamming her door. As soon as she catches sight of the truck, she lets out a howl and covers her face with her hands.

Trooper Kashi and I reach her at the same time, Kashi gently moving me aside as she takes Gretchen by the shoulders. "Mrs. Strickland," she says, giving her a slight shake. "Mrs. Strickland. I need to ask you a few questions."

Now? Obviously, this is a shock and Gretchen is distressed. Can't they give her a minute?

"I can't believe he did it!" She lowers her hands, revealing wet cheeks streaked with rivulets of black mascara. "He promised he wouldn't, for the children. He swore!"

Kashi takes out her notebook. "When did you last talk to your husband, Mrs. Strickland?"

"Uhm, I think it was maybe Friday night." She sniffs, wiping her nose on her hands. "He was rambling about going to meet someone. They had a plan to get back the property, but that was nothing new. He always has a plan. That's all he talks about." She pauses. "*Did* talk about."

"Did he happen to mention who that someone was?" Kashi poises her pencil over her tablet.

"I, I, I don't remember. There wasn't a name. He said . . . it was a guy. 'I'm meeting a guy,' he said."

Kashi and I exchange looks. *A guy.* Meaning, not my daughter. I'm only slightly relieved, since this still doesn't get me any closer to finding Erika.

"Oh, my god. I can't get over that he's actually dead!" Gretchen explodes into a fresh round of sobs. "How am I gonna tell the kids?"

Fishing tissues out of my purse, I hand her one. Gretchen snatches it and dabs her eyes, only then recognizing me . . .

. . . *and I her.*

With her contacts in and salt-and-pepper exposed—unlike when we met at her apartment, when her hair was wrapped in a towel—I realize why she seemed familiar that night when I visited her apartment to tell her about the tax sale. She was the waitress catering Holly and Robert's wedding, the one who criticized me for not recognizing her.

Shame on you, she practically spit.

Now I understand, because I was the collector of delinquent taxes who auctioned away her family home. At the very least, I should have known who she was. I'm embarrassed by my callousness, but also, suspicious.

Why was Gretchen Strickland working that particular wedding?

And why has she been in contact with the man who kidnapped my daughter?

THIRTY-THREE

ERIKA

There is no way to keep track of the passing hours in a root cellar. There is no light, only thirst. And cold and sleep.

The water bottle Robert left Erika is empty, but she's found one of Holly's that was caught in the blankets. A full thirty-two ounces. She is as abstemious with it as a monk. When her guts cramp, she takes a sip. When the headache pressing against her temples begins to inch across her forehead, she takes a sip.

Sip. Sip. Sip.

She will never take water for granted ever again if she gets out.

When, she makes herself say. *When.*

She cannot give up. She refuses. Her only goal is to reduce her body's requirements to bare subsistence. Therefore, she doesn't move unless she has to, curling into a ball under the covers, taking only shallow breaths. *Hibernation.* This is how bears survive and how she will, too.

She imagines being above in the light, running through fields of yellow goldenrod, sinking her nose into her mother's pink rugosas. She swears she can smell the rose perfume and then, once, bergamot. Robert's signature scent, so powerful, it's like he's right there.

Footsteps pierce her mental fog and, blinking against the bright white glare of an LED light, she shades her eyes as she gets her bearings. A man is standing over her. It's him, is it? No. She's hallucinating.

She tries to sit up, but he says, "Don't." He kneels and hands her another water bottle. On reflex, she snatches it, tucking it under the covers so he won't steal it away—like he does everything else.

"There's more." He places another bottle on the floor along with an orange and a granola bar.

He wants her to live, she thinks in a flush of hope. This isn't the end after all. He's put her in cold storage to keep her out of the way. "When are you getting me out of here?"

There is no reply.

"Now?" she whispers, trying again to sit up.

He pushes her down. "No. Not now. I only stopped by to give you these." He holds out a baggie of pills. In the phone's light, they're a light blue. "Sleeping pills." He smiles and strokes her hair back from her forehead. "I can't stand to see you suffer."

She is to kill herself. That's what he wants.

The realization produces a dull ache in her chest. She's

confused the way mistreated dogs must be confused after being caged and cruelly treated by the masters they only want to serve. "Why?" she whispers. "Why won't you let me live?"

He's silent for a while and then says, "You've been written out of *TMB*'s script. I'm sorry. You were valuable once, but now you're not. I'm afraid I've got too much invested to risk you ruining the story line. Does that make sense?"

Of course it doesn't. It's the talk of a lunatic. Reasoning doesn't stand a chance.

She falls back and closes her eyes. She hears him get up, his footsteps crossing the stone floor, ascending the wooden ladder, replacing the plywood, dropping the rocks. And then the dirt.

Her crypt is sealed.

She slides under the ratty blankets, pulling up the zipper. Then she opens the baggie and shakes out the blue pills into the palm of her hand.

There's just enough water left to get them down.

THIRTY-FOUR

KIM

MONDAY MORNING

"Mrs. Turnbull, I'm going to have to ask you to calm down and speak more slowly," Kashi says on the other line. "What's this about Gretchen Strickland?"

"She was at the wedding. Holly and Robert's. I saw her. She was waitressing." I couldn't sleep last night, thinking about this. At first, I passed off her appearance as a coincidence. Lots of people work catering jobs on the side to pick up extra money, which Gretchen obviously needs. Then, the more I tossed and turned, the more it occurred to me that she would have mentioned this at our meeting.

Unless she's hiding something, which I'm beginning to think she is.

"What does her waitressing have to do with anything?" Kashi asks.

"Maybe she was the one who let Zeke into the house."

I can hear Kashi take a sip of something. "Okay. That's plausible."

"Which means it wasn't Erika. But it also means, more importantly, that if she was conspiring with her husband, she might know where Erika is."

Kashi takes a deep breath. "Mrs. Strickland advises that contact with her husband was limited to telephone conversations about the children. She has a restraining order against him and affirms they have not met in person. Judging from her affidavit attached to that restraining order, I take her statement as credible. There is no evidence Zeke and Gretchen Strickland were physically in the same space at the Barron event, either. MMD Security confirmed that, too."

This is exasperating. "At least check it out. We're going on hour sixty of Erika's disappearance. From everything I've read on Google, you can't last more than three days without water. If Zeke has her tied up like he did Robert and Holly, then her window of survival is closing fast!"

"Like I said, we've got all our resources on this case." Kashi sighs. "When was the last time you slept, Kim? Or ate? Insomnia and calorie deprivation can totally mess with your head. I see it all the time."

I have to pinch the bridge of my nose to keep the focus on my daughter and not on how much I resent the inefficiency of the police. "All I want for you to do is shake some info out of Gretchen Strickland. *Please!*"

"I'll reach out and ask her about the wedding, if that sets your mind at ease," Kashi says. "Meanwhile, why don't you call your doctor and get him to prescribe some medication for your nerves. It'll help."

Click. That's it. There goes my last chance. I place my head on the kitchen table, defeated.

"She's not wrong about food." Doreen waves a bowl under my nose. "Yum. Yum. Instant oatmeal with apples and cinnamon. Just like grandma used to make, right out of the microwave."

I push it way gently. "Please, I can't."

Doreen places the bowl on my kitchen table and pulls up a chair, leaning in close. "It's Monday, Kim. You haven't had anything to eat since Friday night."

"And I won't until I find her." I fold my arms and bury my head in them, exhausted and drained. *Text me, Erika,* I will my phone that's always on, always powered up, and always in reach. *Call me.*

I mentally recite my mantra: *Erika is tough. Erika is smart. Erika is a survivor. As long as her body hasn't been found, there is hope. This is out of my control. Erika is tough. Erika is smart. Erika is a survivor. As long as her body hasn't been found, there is hope. This is out of my control.*

The kitchen door opens and I snap my head up. *Erika?* But it's only Tammy, back from the Burlington Marriott. She kicks off her shoes and shrugs off her coat, going directly to the woodstove to warm her hands. She doesn't say hello.

She didn't come home last night, having stayed in Burlington in case Holly changed her mind about meeting. Judging from her subdued demeanor, my guess is she didn't. I'm glad she feels comfortable enough around us to feel welcomed here. I need every ounce of support I can get.

"Car hold up okay?" Doreen asks.

Tammy, lost in thought, takes a beat. "Um yeah. Great. I can see why y'all drive Subarus up here. This funny white stuff came out of the sky and it handled it like a champ." Her tone is flat. Definitely not her usual upbeat southern lilt. "The press outside are playing games on their phones, which I'm taking to mean there's nothing new about Erika."

"Unfortunately, not," I say. "The cops aren't taking my concerns about Gretchen seriously."

"Been there, done that," Tammy says. "Unholy aggravating."

"Fresh pot of coffee," Doreen says, holding up a pot. "Want a cup?"

"Nah, I'm good. Thanks. I've had so much coffee, I've burned a hole in my stomach." Tammy sits on the hassock in front of the stove, keeping her back to us, her hands outstretched. "I was sure Haylee was gonna see me, but the producers said no way. Not until the show airs tonight."

At least you know where she is, I think.

"I'm sorry, Kim." Tammy turns from the stove appearing as wan and drawn as I feel. "I have been in your situation and it stinks. I wish I had a magic mirror that'd show us where Zeke's got your daughter hidden. Wouldn't that be wonderful?"

"From your lips to God's ears," I answer, the clock forever ticking my head. *Where are you?*

"Hey, Tammy, there's something I've been meaning to

ask." Doreen brings her own cup of coffee to the couch and takes a seat next to me. "Last fall, was Haylee hanging with a guy with a blond ponytail, stocky, who might have had an affinity for marijuana?"

"Sounds like Kyle. They dated off and on for a couple years. He's a cook at this barbecue place called the Blind Pig down in Homosassa where Haylee used to bartend. I didn't care much for the man, what with him being such a pothead. They broke up last winter, before she came up here. Why?"

Doreen and I exchange looks. Doreen winks, signaling for me to let her hit this ball. "I'd like to ask Kyle a question. You don't have his number, do you?"

"Not on my phone. But he's probably at the Pig. They do a pretty decent lunch service. He might be working days. If he is, this would be a good time to reach him. Not too busy. I can call him, if you want, since he knows me."

"Worth a shot." Doreen Googles the bar on her phone and hands it to Tammy. She doesn't put it on speaker until Kyle gets on, whereupon she introduces us and explains our situation.

"Saw that on Twitter," he says. "Been following Haylee pretty regular. Glad to hear she's okay."

"Amen to that," Tammy singsongs. "I wish Kim here has the same good fortune. Her daughter's been missing since Friday and we're worried awful sick that the same dude who took the Barrons took her."

"Whoa. For real?"

"Afraid so. Look, I'm gonna put on my friend, Doreen. She has something to ask you." She turns it over to Doreen.

"Hi, Kyle. Listen, I work in the town clerk's office up here in Snowden, Vermont. This might be a long shot, but I wondered if you ever accompanied Haylee to our town when the two of you were dating."

Tammy widens her eyes. "New one on me."

Kyle groans. "Uhmm, I'm not sure."

"You're not sure?" Doreen makes a face. "Like, you don't remember?"

"Oh, I remember. Just that Haylee made me promise to keep it between us. I hate to go back on my word."

If my arms could extend down to Homosassa, I would wrap my hands around his throat and make him sing like a canary. Instead, I snatch the phone out of Doreen's hand. "Excuse me, Kyle, this is Kim Turnbull. I'm the mother of the missing woman and any information, no matter how insignificant, might save her life. This is not the time to be keeping secrets."

"Why don't you just ask Haylee?"

"Because the producers of the show she's on cut off all contact, okay?" Tammy interjects. "Now, I had no idea Haylee came up here last fall. Can you recall why she would have made such a long trip?"

He hesitates and sighs. "There was a guy who came into the bar. He had some connection to where y'all are up there, I forget what. Anyway, he was going on and on about he had this million-dollar property in this Vermont ski town that was stolen from him. He just needed to hire a lawyer or whatever to get it back. Claimed he was gonna sue."

Holy shit. "Was his name Zeke Strickland?" I blurt.

"I don't know. Haylee talked to him way more than I did. She came up with this cockamamie scheme to fly up to where you live and personally check out the situation to see if it was true. I guess you guys refused to email records or whatever."

"That's right," pipes up Doreen. "That's our policy."

"So what happened?" I ask, on the edge my seat. This feels significant.

"She found what she was looking for. I don't know what. But I do know it ended our relationship because she called that guy, the one on the show, the one she ended up marrying, you know? Anyway, she told him about the records. He was quite interested. The next I knew, I was history and she was off with him. End of story."

I'm stunned.

And energized. Holly lied, which, now that I think about, makes sense.

She lies about her name, about how she and Robert met, and I suspect she's the one spreading lies about Erika online. She's no innocent victim. At the very least, she's an accomplice.

Maybe more.

"Well, I'll be," Tammy says, shaking her head. "You got an inkling of what scam she was pulling?"

"Yeah, but I ain't gonna say. Haylee would kill me."

"Aw, c'mon, Kyle," Tammy coos. "She dropped you like a cold fish. You don't owe her doodley-squat. She probably has forgotten all about you by now, seeing as how she's so rich and famous."

He thinks about this. "If I had to say, and it's only a guess: blackmail."

Tammy clicks off and turns to me, lips pursed so tight, they're purple. "I'm gonna step outside and have a smoke. Maybe two. And after I get my fix of nicotine, I'm gonna come back in here, Kim, and you, me, and Doreen are gonna hatch a plan. What time is that stupid property rehab show live-streaming?"

"Eight p.m.," Doreen answers. "Erika sent Kim and me e-vites before she disappeared."

"Make that three. Haylee may not want to face up to her mother, but I'm her mama and I'm telling you right now, I am so mad at my only child, I could chew nails and spit out tacks."

THIRTY-FIVE

HECTOR

MONDAY NIGHT

"Cut!"

TMB's premier director, Hector Aldridge, squeezes his hands in frustration, silently praying for serenity. You'd think a professional camera operator, even a Neanderthal from a cable news show, would have more sense than to enter the frame.

He's been tolerant of the producer's insistence that designated cameras from the news pool be allowed on set. Or house. Or whatever you called these blasted home reality show settings. He's been adamant that they not be permitted inside due to space restrictions and is of the opinion that allowing one or two operators to shoot the talent from the sidelines is an extremely generous compromise on his part.

But if you give these brutes an inch, they take a mile, rushing in for close-ups, shouting the talent's names as if they're walking into the Academy Awards. He cares not one wit that LuAnn promised a certain prime-time cable news show an exclusive simulcast. He's had it up to here. Enough!

"Break?" His assistant slips a vape into his hand and just the sensation of the warming metal device in his palm unwinds the tension crippling his shoulders.

"Bless you, my son," he murmurs, shielding himself from the lights and cameras as he inhales a medicinal dose of purple kush. Much better.

He smiles at the talent, a starkly photogenic couple despite their recent, newsworthy trauma. The man, this Robert, tall and moodily handsome, faintly Byronic with his aquiline nose and cascading dark locks, is a fascinating creature. Hector envisions him in an oil painting, elbow resting on a windowsill, quill in hand, his throat encased in a white cravat, gazing wistfully at the heath beyond.

The woman, however, is pure low-country trash, and Hector is here for it. He enjoys meeting people who aspire above their birth stations, admires their gumption, their embrace of the American dream. This Holly has obviously employed every available beauty enhancement on the market to upscale her appearance—the eyelashes, the nose job (maybe even cheekbone implants, too), the de rigueur bee-stung lips—brava for her! But she's been savvy, this one. She's darkened her roots and enhanced the shadows under her eyes in fitting with the publicity stunt she and her husband pulled.

Of course, it was a stunt, this business about being kidnapped by an assistant who *conveniently* cannot be located and a troubled former property owner who *conveniently* slit his own throat. Eventually, the threads in this web of lies will unravel, as history dictates, and the talent's fraud will be exposed as a cheap, tawdry sham. For now the country is riveted and he, Hector Aldridge, a director snubbed by the industry for a teeny-tiny mishap on a movie set years and years ago, is back in . . .

"Action!" He squints over his camera operator's shoulder, hoping the talent has taken to heart his prior lecture about emotive authenticity. No fake gasps. No, "Oh my gosh!" No clasping hands to hearts. He wants genuine tears, screams of amazement, even—if she can manage it—fainting in her husband's arms upon stepping across the threshold.

They perform better than one would expect from a couple of amateurs, the man swooping up his delicate bride, fragile from her "ordeal," kicking open the front door and carrying her inside. In his ear, LuAnn gushes, "Gold. Solid fucking gold. Trending on Twitter."

Twitter. He snorts. Maroons.

Inside, without fear of a news crew ruining the scene, the talent shifts into domestic bliss, a guaranteed crowd pleaser. Holly runs her hands over the rented couch and gawps in wonder at the vaulted ceilings, his camera operator maneuvering to avoid the mirrored glare cast by the humongous windows.

"Are you telling me a huge space like this is energy efficient?" she inquires, as if she hasn't designed every centimeter.

The man rattles off statistics. He seems to be the brains behind the engineering. She's the designer, boldly approving of her own color scheme and complimenting an insipid watercolor by a local artist she's purchased at a community craft fair. Then again, sexist tropes are standard on these shows. Hector will not allow her to compare the size of her closet to her husband's, however. He has his standards.

Holly *oooh*s and *aaah*s at the kitchen with its fancy French stove, its pricey marble counters and its bump-out window complete with window boxes springing with light green shoots of fresh herbs. She blinks at the chandelier twinkling over the authentic Vermont farm table (handcrafted by a newly deceased artisan!) and lightly strokes the pyramid of waxy lemons in their wire basket.

"Can't you picture the family dinners we'll make here?" she asks, opening a drawer and marveling that it is actually refrigerated.

"I can't wait." Robert spouts his scripted line. He gives her a scripted kiss.

"Cut!" Hector shouts.

Lucrative advertisements featuring refrigerators that can text your mother and robotic vacuums ridden by cats follow for those who don't subscribe to *TMB* and, therefore, must suffer the torture of commercial breaks. The cameras are repositioned while makeup teases Holly's hair and dabs at Robert's nose.

Upon return, the talent slowly climb the floating staircase, keeping up a constant chatter of more awe. The steel railings are *sleek*. The stairs are *grand*. The up lighting is *brilliant*. The atrium to the floor below is *unreal*. "I like how you can call down to the kitchen from the top floor," she says. "Just imagine the parties."

"Wench, fetch my flagon of wine!" Robert jokes.

Hector takes another hit of his vape.

They pause so the crew can enter the rooms on the second floor to catch their reactions, the only shots they'd need, since the rooms themselves are cued up and ready to go. Holly shakes her head at the Murphy bed in the guest room/office. "We could convert it to a nursery, too." She utters her scripted line with an appropriate blush.

Robert responds by placing a suggestive hand over her belly and leaning down for another kiss. "Linger on that shot. We're Tweeting that as a very suggestive hint," LuAnn prompts. "Hashtag Barronbaby here we come!"

"Ah, my favorite room—where the magic happens," Robert says, winking at his wife, who is doing an impressive job of keeping her face flushed in modesty as they view the king-size bed. While the canned shots roll, the couple changes into their swimsuits.

Commercial break featuring bedding from Wayfair and high-end bathroom fixtures.

The crew reconnoiters on the outdoor entertainment area. Miracle of miracles, the night sky is clear in this godforsaken state, despite flurries the day before. It's unseasonably warm, which makes the talent's display of the geothermal swimming pool's properties a bit easier to handle.

Wineglasses have been set out, along with skewers of mushrooms, tomatoes, and zucchini in the exact same order as the canned shots. Hector thinks of the local assistant who did all that last week. Hard worker. That he was side by side with a suspected cokidnapper leaves him tingly.

When they return, Robert is glistening wet from the pool. Market testing has showed a high female approval for him bare chested and slick, though not so sexy that viewers would be staring at his treasure trail instead of the five-figure outdoor kitchen that is generating six-figure advertising dollars per minute.

"Take your positions," Hector commands to the small group of actors playing friends. "Are the firepits lit?"

Out of the corner of his eye, he notices movement. Someone is frantically waving. *What the . . . ?* There's no time for this. They're back live in three.

"There appears to be an incident brewing," LuAnn says in his ear. "We're cutting to another commercial while we figure out what's going on. This is why I hate live-streaming, *people!*"

Incident? What kind of incident?

He glances over at LuAnn, who is directing security to where three middle-aged women stand in the shadows, arms folded—except for a short blond overdressed in a huge bright parka the color of Gatorade, smoking a cigarette.

They don't look like trouble; they look like the local bowling league.

"What do they want?" he hears LuAnn ask.

The blond with the cigarette hollers, "I need to talk to my daughter, Haylee."

"Not now," LuAnn says. "We're live-streaming a show. And we're almost back on. Hector, get everyone in position."

"Positions!" Hector shouts. Holly and Robert stand by the pool, poised to dive in for the cameras. Holly in her tiny black bikini is hopping up and down to keep warm. Does she not know her mother is right there? How could she not have heard that bobcat yell?

"That kidnapping story is a damn lie!" the mother in the parka persists. "What have you done with Erika Turnbull? Haylee Dawn Beauregard, answer me! I am your mama!"

LuAnn goes, "What the hell is happening?"

"Five, four, three, two . . ." Hector counts down. "One!"

The cameras capture Robert's athletic dive while Holly, still apparently unaware of the ruckus her mother's causing, lowers herself into the water, the "friends" applauding.

"You guys are crazy," one of them chortles, taking a swig of nonalcoholic beer.

"It's super warm and *sooooo* lovely." Holly is careful to keep her head above water as she kicks her shapely legs.

Robert tosses his long, wet hair with the grace of a champion stallion. "Plus, the pool's heating our house!"

"When's dinner?" the "friend" asks. "I'm starving."

"Coming right up!" Robert pulls himself out and offers his bride a helping hand as she ascends the underlit steps and slips her arms into a fluffy terry cloth robe that will be available for order straight off the *TMB* site.

She's patting her face with a corner of the robe just as the fireplug blond has somehow managed to storm onto the bluestone patio.

"Haylee Dawn Beauregard!" she calls out, parting the friends. "You come over here right now. I am so sick of your bullshit, I could tan your hide!"

Holly freezes midpat. "Mama?"

"Shit," Hector says. "We need to cut to a commercial."

"No fucking way," says LuAnn. "This is dynamite. Close in!"

The fireplug marches up to her daughter, hands on hips. "You tell me right now, right this minute, what you've done with Erika Turnbull."

"Um, little help here." Robert, suddenly not so masculine in his fancy robe, is drawing a hand across his throat with a pair of rustproof titanium tongs. Unfortunate imagery in light of current events.

"I'd cut except we've got cable news here and they are all over this," LuAnn says. "If we fade to black, they get the eyeballs, we won't. Keep going. This is gonna rule the water-coolers tomorrow."

The fireplug taps her finger against Holly's chest. "I. Am. Your. Mother!"

"You need to get out of here," Holly hisses and then, as if just remembering this is being live-streamed, quickly adds, "You silly prankster!"

Hector directs the camera to catch a better angle of Robert as he moves to intervene. Big mistake, Hector thinks. Break up a cat fight, you're gonna get scratched.

"Excuse me," Robert says, affecting a patrician drawl, "but this is not the appropriate—"

"Appropriate my sweet buns." The fireplug turns on him, snarling. "You! You know what happened to that girl, the assistant. I am your mother-in-law. You tell me now."

"You need to leave my house," he says firmly.

"It ain't your house. It never was your house. Haylee knows that!" She turns back to her daughter. "Don't you, honey-bunch?"

"That is a complete lie!" he declares.

She rotates back to Robert. "Oh, please. That's how my darling daughter blackmailed you into this chicanery. If you didn't do what she wanted you to do, she'd expose you for being the buffoon you are and so much for the famous Robber Barron. Turns out the legendary real estate investor ain't nothing but a lazy-ass fool who got suckered like his sucker followers." She takes a wheezy breath. "In your case, property really was theft."

"Okay, I'm totally lost," LuAnn says. "I can't look away, but I need a playbill to keep score. This isn't their house?"

"Mama." Holly extends a steadying hand. "We'll talk later."

"Hell we will!" Tammy shouts. "You're gonna tell the whole world watching that Zeke Strickland and Erika Turnbull took you captive? You know that's a lie. Just think of the effect that will have on his children. I am ashamed to admit you are the fruit of my womb."

"That's enough," Robert thunders, storming toward the tiny, enraged blond. "I will not stand by while you insult my wife!"

"No, Robert. Stay back!" And with what seems to Hector like an unnecessary amount of force, the female talent lunges at her husband, both of her hands landing hard on his chest. His bare heels slip on the wet bluestone as he crashes backward into the electric-powered grill connected to 240-volt wiring.

The word *electrocution* is the combination of *electric* and *execution*. Not everyone who suffers a shock from a 240-volt outlet dies or is even severely injured, though most regret the pain and the burns afterward. However, in this situation, a perfect storm of factors combine to inflict a lethal dose. The flooring is stone. Robert is wet. The tongs in his hands are metal and the freelance master electrician no one noticed had ulterior motives.

The camera instantly pans away. Hector shouts for people to keep clear and for someone to call 911. The mother, aghast, clutches the hand of her daughter, the two of them frozen in place as the husband falls to the ground, his body twitching.

"Turn off that goddamn current!" LuAnn hollers. "And call 911!"

Pushing aside her daughter, the bobcat rushes to her son-in-law, parts his robe, makes a fist, covers it with her other hand, and proceeds to pound on his sternum to the rhythm of "Stayin' Alive" by the Bee Gees, actually belting the "ah-ah-ah" of the chorus with each thrust.

Too late, the twitching remains of Robert Barron's beautiful body have stilled.

A hired actor covers Robert's body with a beach towel that's not long enough to hide his pedicured toes.

"You killed him!" Holly screams. "You killed Robert, Mama!"

"At least I tried to save his life, which is more than I can say for you," the mother spits back. Squeezing her daughter's face, she says, "This is your last chance, Haylee. Where. Is. Erika? Tell me before it's too late. Tell me while there's still a chance she's alive so you won't burn in hell for eternity."

From the way Holly hesitates, it's not clear she knows or, if she does, will answer. But then her pretty pink mouth opens and she says, "Robert said he put her in a cellar hole. I don't know where, though."

"I know!" shouts one of the trio in a North Face jacket and hiking boots." I saw a root cellar on the Barrons' survey map I recorded last week."

Immediately, she takes off toward the field, everyone following while the blond bobcat with the frizzled hair hugs her daughter, the two of them rocking back and forth on the patio, weeping.

THIRTY-SIX

KIM

MONDAY NIGHT

Doreen leads the way down the dark hill and through the field, relying on her memory of the map. I am right on her heels, though keeping up with my assistant's not easy even with a rush of adrenaline. This is a woman who runs up Mount Washington, the highest mountain in New England, for shits and giggles.

The news crews hop in their cars and go around to a logging road, which is where the ambulances, initially called to respond to Robert, are headed, too.

A chainsaw starts in the distance. Lights are shining through the trees. When we reach the others, my heart flies into my throat. Firefighters with headlamps are tossing aside rocks and removing thick layers of plywood over a small entrance. Holly wasn't wrong when she said it was a hole.

Having done her part, Doreen joins my side for support. "The hole leads to a passageway to the larger cellar to get it under the frost line. That's good. She won't have frozen."

My daughter is in a hole, a literal hole. I can't even. I don't care if Gretchen and Zeke spent a winter in that cellar. That was their choice. This was not Erika's. Alone for three days in the dark. She must have been scared out of her wits. That is, if they put her in their alive.

I think of what happened to Zeke and clutch Doreen.

There's a loud crack followed by a splintering sound. It's then that I realize the chainsaw has been brought to clear a path for the EMTs who are arriving with a stretcher. Because she'll need it if she's alive—or dead.

"Erika!" I cry.

"A stretcher is standard protocol." Doreen rubs my arm. "Remember, Elliot used to be a volunteer on the Snowden Fire Department so I know all about it." Though she tells me that every time she mentions the SFVD, I find it strangely comforting.

A ladder is lowered and a firefighter climbs down and then an EMT carrying a bag of gear follows. You could have heard a pin drop as we wait, all of us not daring to utter a peep. I close my eyes and pray hard to a god I haven't spoken to in a while. Doreen does, too, her lips moving silently.

I desperately wish we were alone without the camera crews crowding us, their intrusive lenses and blinding LEDs fixed on my face, which I know will be plastered all over the news, no matter the outcome. Here I am, the anxious mother facing a parent's worst nightmare. What will be my reaction when they find my daughter? Will they zoom in for a close-up when I burst into tears of joy—or when I rend my clothes in grief? Nothing is sacred in this brutal business.

The silence, the moments that pass, are interminable. My devious mind torments me with a string of what-ifs.

And then, from the hole, a single, beautiful universal gesture of success.

A white-gloved thumbs-up.

Whoops of joy ring out from all of us. Doreen and I hug. The director and the producer hug. The cameramen slap high fives. We give wide berth to the first responders who are working their magic. An EMT reaches down to lift her from the capable arms of a colleague. They lay my beloved child on the stretcher and apply oxygen, her body so limp, I burst into a spasm of sobs.

"They've got her. She's fine," Doreen says, holding me tight. "It's over, Kim. It's over."

No. I have to see for myself, I think, worming my way to the front.

"Ma'am, please move back," says an EMT, holding up a hand.

"I'm her *mother!*" That's when I catch sight of my baby's pale face under the plastic mask, the IV drips in her hand. The only part of her I can reach is her foot and suddenly I have a vision of her as a tiny baby, her precious feet kicking in the air with joy. "Is she okay?"

"She tells us she didn't take the pills they gave her," the EMT says. "She's probably just dehydrated."

"What kind of pills?" I demand.

But the responder only shrugs.

I'm so proud of her for staying strong, for trusting that we'd find her despite sinister moments when she likely wanted to end the fear and pain. I have never been prouder of my daughter, ever. "You're okay, honey. You're safe now. I love you!"

Erika raises her head slightly and nods. I take her fingers in mine before the medics make me step aside so they can carry her to the ambulance.

"I'll drive you to Burlington," Doreen says. "That's where she's going."

We climb the hill to the *TMB* house, the flashing blue police lights reflecting on the steep rubber roof's solar panels, the latest in cutting-edge technology.

EPILOGUE

KIM

"I'm telling you, this is pure cork!" Dex, our cynical Lister, jumps up and down on the flooring in the guest bedroom of the *TMB* house. "Feel the bounce? No way is it composite."

Morty, his partner, gleams as he inputs the flooring's value into the property assessment software on his iPad. "Oooh. That takes it up to a grade eight." He chuckles in glee. "Brazilian cherry. Marble. Mahogany. This place is gonna end up being a million one, maybe a million two."

"Try a million five. Look at these windows." Dex raps his knuckles against the thermal pane glass. "From Lithuania. Custom made!"

I have never seen these two happier.

The Listers have finally wormed their way into this house, so eager to get inside that they're here on April Fool's Day, the absolute beginning of Vermont's assessment year. They were actually on the doorstep at eight a.m., clucking their tongues over the French range while Gretchen was packing her children's lunches and bundling off her kids for school.

I offered to stick around, to make sure Dex and Morty didn't pilfer a few "souvenirs" while she was out of the house.

"She'll never be able to afford the taxes once we're done," Dex says, though I can't tell if he's sad or glad about that.

"Her income's low enough that she'll qualify for the discount on her property taxes and, besides, she plans to rent it out over Christmas for an Airbnb. That'll cover the bill."

"Let's see what's down here." Morty wanders off to check the basement while Dex and I go upstairs.

"She could always take out a mortgage," Dex says. "Seeing as how she's got complete equity."

"Yeah, I don't think Gretchen has any interest in racking up interest." We pause at the railing that overlooks the great room and, with the floor-to-ceiling windows, the mountains beyond.

"That's some view. I'm rating it a ten out of ten." Dex inputs this. "Can't say I blame her about the mortgage, seeing as how that's how the Robber Barron got in over his head."

I was raised not to speak ill of the dead, but in this case, I'll make an exception. Robert Barron was already in hock for half a million in his other failed real estate ventures, according to Holly's affidavit, when she called him out of the blue to let him know the house he acquired wasn't really his due to my technical error and that if he wanted to keep this a secret until the statute of limitations expired, she had a plan.

Which she was willing to share if he promised to make her famous and give her a cut.

Which he did.

Initially, they cooked up a scheme to stage an increasingly common false police report. Holly would disappear while jogging on one of our safe roads in Snowden. There would be enough planted evidence to accuse Zeke, the former owner, of stalking and harming her because he wanted to get back at Robert for stealing the house. The public would be riveted. Donations to a GoFundMe account would pour in until Zeke Strickland was found slain by his own hand and Holly would reappear, claiming to have been his captive.

TV appearances, book deals, and a series based on the book would follow, and then Holly and Robert, their relationship never able to quite recover from the stress of her kidnapping, would split ways.

Only, something extraordinary happened. On a whim, Holly entered the Vermont house into the annual *To the Manor Build* contest and, miracles of miracles, the rehab project was chosen as one of three vying for the prize.

Robert rushed out and borrowed more money to make sure they won, certain they would and, therefore, all his debts would be paid. One little problem: they were losing and losing bad. So, they decided to get married, live-streaming the ceremony in an effort to gain valuable viewers.

When that also failed, they resorted to their backup plan—a

kidnapping. In this incarnation, they set up my daughter as well as Zeke, planting bloodied PJs in (my!) trash, Robert's blood-spattered Barbour in her coat closet, using her car, and, finally, writing and mailing themselves threats.

If Holly hadn't brought her then-boyfriend, Kyle, to check out the office records that fall, she might have succeeded. They would have won the contest, Robert's debts would be cleared and my lovely, talented, only child would be . . .

No. I can't say it.

With Erika's eyewitness testimony, Holly struck a deal with the prosecution to admit her crime in exchange for a reduced sentence of ten years in prison for kidnapping and conspiracy to commit murder. There's no proof she had anything to do with Zeke's staged suicide; that was all Robert's doing, she claimed, though, of course, she knew when he committed it on Friday night, shortly after sticking Erika in the root cellar.

Holly also agreed to quitclaim the entire property back to Gretchen Strickland. *TMB* paid off the mortgage. Having shattered viewer records with the live-streamed reveal, it was the least they could do.

Drs. Sam Chidubem and Concita Jimenez, the South Carolina doctors building the retreat for healthcare workers, split first place with Joel and Sean McVeigh, who are running the therapeutic ranch for LGBTQ2+ teens in New Mexico. The *TMB* series was not renewed for another season, having gone out with a bang.

Erika also attested to the fact that Zeke, most likely, had sneaked into the house as a contractor and faultily wired the outdoor grill, noting she'd had trouble getting it to light during one of the shoots. This gave me the chills. Had the cameraman not lit the grill with his lighter, she could have ended up like Robert Barron.

"Sadly, no sex dungeon," Morty says, coming up from the basement to meet us in the great room. "Nice man cave, though. Bar. Pool table. Eighty-inch TV. Fancy surround-sound system and leather couches. That is, if you're into caves. Me, not so much. I need natural light."

I suck in a breath.

"Geesh, Mort. Have some sensitivity." Dex thumbs in my direction. "Think before you speak."

As if tactfulness would ever occur to a Lister.

◇ ◇ ◇

"What time's the Zoom again?" Doreen asks, bringing me a glass of sauvignon blanc vinted from grapes grown in her own yard and placing it next to a wheel of brie, aged in a nearby cave. This is her new hobby, English tea ceremonies having been replaced by wine and cheese. I personally think she should go back to her home-brewed craft beer and moose jerky. Those are more her style.

"Ten minutes. But you know how Erika is, always late these days."

"Busy, busy." Doreen crunches a cracker.

Zoom is how I keep in contact with my daughter, who's living the high life in LA. After recovering from her own kidnapping—all medical expenses and therapy comped by *To the Manor Build*—LuAnn tried to hire her as her own assistant; that is, after professing she never wanted to fire her in the first place.

But Erika had other offers. Lots of other offers. She was picked up by a talent agency in Los Angeles that hired her not as talent, but as an agent. Well, that's not entirely true. She did start off in the mail room and moved her way up to the assistant desk where she is now. However, it does mean she gets to hobnob with A-list celebrities and actors who are just as fascinated by her story as she is by their glittering lives.

California suits her. She's blossomed under the endless sun and delights in blending in among all the other creative types who've successfully rewritten the backstories of their own pockmarked pasts. Snowden, Vermont, with its cold winters and hard hearts, is the rocky foundation on which she is building her castle in the clouds. I am thrilled for her.

We have one more minute until our Zoom meeting. I'm so excited because I have big news for Erika. She is going to flip!

"Tammy's home." Doreen nods to the window where the Subaru Doreen sold her is passing by.

Tammy lives in Erika's apartment now so she can be close to her daughter as she serves time in the Southeast Correctional Center. Haylee has been very needy of her mother, of late. Funny how an eight-by-eight cell rearranges one's priorities.

As for me, I will never, ever forgive her.

Ever.

"Hi, guys!" The screen expands with Erika's sunny visage. She's blonder than ever, dressed in an open-neck white blouse revealing delicate layered gold necklaces bought with her own hard-earned cash. "How's the weather over there?"

I don't have to check outside to see it's gray and rainy, typical for April. "Beautiful. Seventy-five degrees with a light breeze."

Doreen shakes her head. "It's shit. Mud up to your knees. Sky the color of clay."

Erika laughs and chats about her week, which celebrity she met and a party she went to, how she's thinking about getting into script writing. She's been sitting in on some online courses and has found them to be pretty challenging, in a good way.

"I like the concept of taking my fantasies out of my head and putting them on a screen. It's kind of . . . therapeutic," she says.

This is my cue to drop the bomb. "By the way, apparently, you're a local hero."

Erika takes a sip of water. "Never. That town hates my guts."

"*Au contraire*. The mayor informs me they're holding a day in your honor. October twenty-second is now officially Erika Turnbull Day to mark your escape from the cellar."

Duly unimpressed, she says, "That's nice, but I didn't escape, Mom. I was saved. By you and Doreen and Tammy. If you hadn't tried everything you could . . ." She bows her head.

Tears press against my eyes and I put my hand to the screen, wishing for all the world we could touch in real life. But we can't and that's okay.

Because not only has my baby bird learned how to fly, she has left the nest and built her own. All by herself.

ACKNOWLEDGMENTS

By the time a book is printed and shelved, allegedly thirty-two people have been involved in its production, or so I've been told. I am deeply grateful for every single one, beginning with my insightful agent, Zoe Sandler, who is not only support-ive, but also fun, and ending with the booksellers who delight in introducing authors to readers and, occasionally, vice versa. Thank you, thank you.

Deepest appreciation goes to my editor Emily Griffin whose thorough notes (seven pages single spaced!) could be the basis of a master class in editorial direction. Without her vision and intelligence, I am fairly certain assembly instruc-tions for flat-pack furniture would be clearer than my drafts. Micaela Carr, assistant editor at HarperCollins, as well as the whole team over there who came up with the brilliant cover and somehow transformed a Word document into a beautifully finished product are the absolute best.

Closer to home, super-sharp Liz Scharf patiently answered all my very bizarre questions about how Teslas operate in Ver-mont's less-than-ideal conditions. I'm so sorry so much ended up on the cutting-room floor.

While former Crack Assistant Town Clerk Maryke Gillis

may have served as the inspiration for Doreen, she is far nicer, kinder, smarter, and, most likely, more beloved. Also, her smile does not make babies cry. I miss her smart presence in the Town Clerk's office every day. The Listers bear no resemblance to the team who keep the town afloat. At least, not this current group!

Writing is a solitary business, which meant my husband, Charlie, spent most of the summer wondering what this crazy wife was doing in the attic. Anna, our daughter and my best friend, provided invaluable editorial feedback, while her own husband, our dear son-in-law, Tom, tackled similar publishing challenges, though far more academic. Our son, Sam, kept me laughing and positive. Thank you, my cherished family, for deciding against having me involuntarily committed.

Finally, I believe it's worth noting that the idea for this book came from our experience in purchasing a house at a tax sale. Every house has its own—not to pun—stories and this rustic cabin with its eight tons of trash, leaking roof and abandoned vehicles, has been no exception. A grandmother took her final breath here. A baby crawled on its floors. Gardens were planted. Dreams bloomed and withered under the merciless beating of life's hard knocks. Longfellow's right: all houses are haunted.

I'll explain more on my website—sarahstrohmeyer.com—and I hope you'll visit me there. In the meantime, thank you so very much for reading.

ABOUT THE AUTHOR

SARAH STROHMEYER is the award-winning, nationally bestselling author of nineteen novels for adults and young adults, most recently *Do I Know You?* Her first mystery, *Bubbles Unbound*, won the Agatha Award for Best First Novel. Her novel *The Cinderella Pact*, became the *Lifetime* movie, *Lying to be Perfect*. A former newspaper reporter, she is currently the elected town clerk of Middlesex, Vermont.